# What the critics are saying:

"The sex is beyond intense and totally graphic. This book gives new meaning to wet panties so keep several pair on hand." *~Angel Brewer, Just Erotic Romance Reviews*

"[A] suspenseful plot that has twists and turns coming from everywhere...will pull the reader in and not let them go...touching, passionate, and scorching HOT!" *~Susan Holly, Just Erotic Romance Reviews*

"Five stars are simply not enough to give this book... Action that will literally have your heart pounding... The sex in this book is quite simply outstanding...one of the most enjoyable books I've read this year." *~Adrienne Kama, The Romance Studio*

"Hold on to your hats. You are in for a thrilling, titillating adventure...chock full of intriguing characters, alien worlds, and red-hot sex. INITIATION floods readers' senses, awakens buried feelings, and all in all just heats the blood to a slow burn..." *~Sinclair Reid, Romance Reviews Today*

"The tapestry of characters introduced and developed in this book showcases a richly layered world and culture just waiting to be explored and managing to do it all in one novel without losing sight of the primary story is a talent that few can master." *~MeriBeth McCombs, The Road to Romance*

Discover for yourself why readers can't get enough of the multiple award-winning publisher Ellora's Cave. Whether you prefer e-books or paperbacks, be sure to visit EC on the web at www.ellorascave.com for an erotic reading experience that will leave you breathless.

www.ellorascave.com

XYLON WARRIORS: INITIATION

An Ellora's Cave Publication, October 2004

Ellora's Cave Publishing, Inc.
PO Box 787
Hudson, OH 44236-0787

ISBN #1-4199-5001-0

ISBN MS Reader (LIT) ISBN #1-84360-816-2
Other available formats (no ISBNs are assigned):
Adobe (PDF), Rocketbook (RB), Mobipocket (PRC) & HTML

Edited by: *Pamela Campbell*
Cover art by: *Syneca*

# INITIATION:
## *XYLON WARRIORS*


Ruth D. Kerce

# Prologue
## *City of Black Marble*
## *Northern California*

Heart hammering, pulse pounding, he had to have her. With a low groan, he eased into her from behind. Pure, hot sin.

She made that sexy little sound he loved so much—half moan, half purr. And all his.

His fingers curled around her hips.

He pulled his cock almost completely out of her, then slowly buried himself deep. He clenched his teeth, controlling his body, not wanting the ecstasy to end.

"Faster," she begged, her plea followed by a small whimper.

The needy sound in her voice made him crazy. He brushed the blonde hair from the back of her neck. So smooth. So beautiful. Soon she'd wear the mark of a mated breeder—his mark. All would know she belonged to him. He leaned over and licked the back of her neck, letting his tongue linger.

She shuddered and pushed against him. "I need...all of you."

His heart expanded. With this woman, their joining was more than physical. She was his life, his soul. He pushed deep inside her, all the way in.

"Yes. Now. Start thrusting. Hurry."

His cock throbbed painfully, and he groaned. The time had come. She wanted it, and so did he. The urge to fuck her was so strong that he couldn't hold back any longer. Nor did he intend to, for she was right. They needed to hurry.

The air beside them shimmered. "Damn," he muttered. A man in a full facemask materialized, hands on hips, and ready for battle.

"Stop the ceremony."

She stiffened and tried to pull away to cover herself against the intruder.

He held her tightly around the waist and kept them intimately joined. Nothing was stopping him from making her his.

"I've come for the woman."

Panic hit him, though he had expected this. He pushed her down to her stomach, covering her with his body. Protecting her.

The intruder tugged his pants open. "Pull out of her. I'm going to fix it so the bitch won't ever be able to breed."

No way. No one was going to stop him, or take her from him. He held her arms pinned to the mattress, so she couldn't move, then surged into her, over and over, demonstrating his possession.

"This...woman...belongs...to...me!"

She squirmed beneath him, called out his name.

He ignored her. He had no choice. He had to Brand and Breed her, before it was too late.

"She doesn't belong to you, Warrior. Not anymore. She is *my* whore now."

* * * * *

Braden Koll jerked awake. Shit!

The night air wafted over him, gradually cooling his temperature to an almost bearable level. At this time of year, on his home planet of Xylon, the temperatures were much colder. He hadn't quite adjusted to the change yet. The long coat he wore to conceal his advanced weaponry and instruments only added to the discomfort.

Earth and Xylon could have been sister planets in another age. Xylon, though more technologically developed now, had evolved from a past very much like Earth's present.

He quickly scanned the deserted surroundings. Light posts. Benches. Trees. A large, center fountain that had shut off hours ago. No danger.

Tonight was not the time to nod off. He'd exhausted himself tracking the woman. Now he was even dreaming about her...and about fucking her.

He shifted uncomfortably on the hard, cold bench. His cock, like the bench, was also hard, but not cold. No man could feel cold after dreaming about that woman. He could still feel her wet pussy wrapped around his stiff shaft, as if the dream were reality. Damn, he needed to come. Bad.

He lifted the locator from his coat pocket and punched it on. She was close. He had to get into position. He'd wanted to stop her from coming tonight but was convinced otherwise.

*Let her see the reality of her fate if she refuses to return to Xylon with us,* Laszlo had said. Maybe it would ease the path.

Braden had to convince her to breed. Xylon had so little hope left. Their planet couldn't survive without her...and other women like her.

# Chapter One
## *Midnight*
## *Black Marble Cemetery*

Shrouded in ghostly mist...

Alexa Sandor automatically reached for the camera around her neck, then remembered she had left it locked in the car. Her freelance photography business had not been going well. She could use some unusual settings to spur her clients' interest.

Unfortunately, she didn't have time to retrieve the equipment. She had a meeting — one she hoped would finally ease a lifetime of worry and confusion.

Her gaze searched the darkness.

Throughout the graveyard, specter-like mist meandered, obscuring the carved stones, swallowing the names of the dead. A perfect setting for evil creatures to roam free.

The disturbing thought caused warm breath to escape her in a rush, forming a brief ghost-like appearance before dissipating into the night. She shuddered at the sight.

Slowly, she headed toward her target.

Beneath weatherworn boots, the ground squished and oozed as she made her way through the dank and decay-ridden cemetery. Trying to keep warm, she crossed her arms under her breasts and continued toward the path she needed to follow.

Moonlight reflected off the marble tombstones, casting eerie shadows, as she moved deeper into the resting place of the dead. "Definitely not a Sunday stroll in the park, Alexa," she mumbled to herself.

Obscure images crawled along the pebbled walkway that stretched the length of the graveyard's ancient-looking crypts. The structures loomed in the night, imposing and moss-covered.

A midnight breeze stirred loose leaves and branches from the sparse foliage that grew around the tombs. The rustling conjured up visions of monsters, dead and undead, shifting between this world and the next.

When she heard a twig snap, she glanced over her shoulder. "This was probably not a good idea," she murmured, her apprehension growing with each step. Though she didn't feel she'd had much choice.

Aching cold seeped into her bones and wrapped around her stiff muscles. Alexa rubbed her arms, trying to increase her blood's circulation. Even long sleeves and a heavy trench coat failed to comfort her. She wasn't sure if it was the chill of the night or the chill of the location that affected her more.

She breathed in the musty air and looked up at the black clouds that partially concealed the moon. More winter storms were on the way. Not what she wanted. She wanted to get home. To feel safe. Unfortunately, she couldn't leave. Not until she found what she came for.

The need to recover her mother's missing journal overruled everything else. If the stranger who'd written her the note now possessed it, as stated, she'd finally have the answers she desperately needed. "Please let it be so."

When she had arrived at her mother's house to settle her affairs after a sudden fatal heart attack, she'd found several hidden documents. In one of the documents, her mother had noted that the journal was of utmost importance. It explained everything. The strange otherworldly dreams Alexa had been having since puberty. The compulsion to do as bidden in the nightly visions. The reason she always pushed away men, unsatisfied with every suitor who came along, and the secrets to a future her mother had kept hidden from her all her life. Alexa needed those answers, so she could find peace.

The note she received indicated, from the signature, that the person who had the journal was a woman. A phone call following receipt of the letter, giving her further instructions, confirmed the fact. Alexa would not have considered coming here in the middle of the night otherwise. Probably.

She chewed on her lower lip and glanced over her shoulder. Never in her life had she felt so nervous, so watched. Warily, she noticed shadows form and disappear like evil spirits creeping from grave to grave.

The woman had probably insisted on this location to intimidate her. To put her off balance, so she could get a larger reward for returning the journal. If so, it worked.

Something...

The hair on Alexa's nape twitched, and her heart slammed against her ribs. She held her breath and stood deathly still.

A whimper. An animal? Certainly not some displaced spook, she hoped with a shiver, then made a strangled chuckle at the absurd thought. She strained to locate the direction the sound had come from.

Stepping off the path, she headed toward one of the crypts. She listened at the opening. No. The sound seemed to be coming from behind the structure. A woman's whimper. Maybe the woman she was supposed to meet.

She quietly made her way around to the back. Her boots slipped on the dead leaves beneath her feet, and she sucked back the cry that almost leapt from her throat. She reached for the crypt wall and caught herself before pitching headfirst to the ground.

Movement along the rear of the crypt caught her eye, and she paused.

A cloud passed over the moon, then drifted further across the night sky, away from the globe's light to reveal four figures. Alexa covered her mouth. She stood frozen in place—this time from the sight before her instead of the chill in the air.

A woman lay sprawled on a slab of gray stone. Her pale, naked body gleamed in the moonlight. A light source Alexa couldn't identify set nearby. Its low flame illuminated the area slightly more than the moon, enough for her to make out what was happening.

Three men, with shaved heads and dressed in black, were on their knees, surrounding the supine female. One seemed to be holding her head or maybe caressing her hair, Alexa couldn't tell, since he was the furthest from her.

Another man eagerly sucked on one of the woman's nipples. He captured the fleshy bud between his teeth and tugged hard, pulling it away from her body. He let it snap back, then suckled it again. His eagerness was palpable. *Feeding on the woman*, was Alexa's immediate thought. She absently rubbed her breast, then snatched her hand away when she realized what she was doing.

The third man probed the woman's navel with one finger, and his other hand pumped something between her labia. Some sort of dildo?

Alexa shifted uncomfortably. They'd obviously ambushed the poor woman. She needed to help her, get her away from there.

The man with the dildo turned his head toward Alexa, and her heart skipped a beat. His eyes glowed yellow! A trick of the light, certainly. Nothing more. It had to be.

*Go! Run back to the car and phone the police.* She tried to turn away, but couldn't move. Panic hit her. She began to feel strange—her limbs heavy and not under her own control.

The dildo man stilled his hand and swiveled his head back to study the naked woman. He stiffened, and anger rolled off him in waves. He started pumping her again, harder this time.

Alexa pressed her thighs together in response. When he made an unearthly sound, a shudder wracked her body. The response was instinctual and fear-driven. She couldn't pull her eyes away.

His tongue slithered out. Long and red. Too long, her mind reasoned. Too thin. She gasped at the sight.

It didn't even look...human.

He moved down the woman's body, and that lizard-like feeler swiped through the curls surrounding her slit.

Alexa's breath came out harsh and fast.

The man licked furiously at what she assumed was the woman's clit, while he continued to work the dildo in and out of her.

The woman on the slab thrashed and whimpered.

With a grunt, the man pushed the object fisted in his hand deep, until it virtually disappeared. He rotated the base in repetitive circles.

The woman shrieked, her voice keening into the night.

Alexa's nails dug into her palms. *Help her! Help me!*

Okay. She wasn't totally paralyzed. She'd just moved her fingers. She needed to get her feet to move.

The woman's body twisted and arched, and moans ripped from her throat, as she climaxed hard.

The man yanked the orgasm-inducer out of the woman's quim, eliciting a long groan from her, which sounded like disappointment at the withdrawal. She collapsed against the slab of stone.

Alexa studied the scene more closely and paused in her thinking. Had the woman wanted that invasion of her body?

Lizard-man held up the object for the men to see. Long, thick, and almost blood red. The dildo gleamed. Wet from the woman's juices.

Alexa gulped. The object was actually pulsing. Her own engorged clitoris pulsed in tandem, much to her horror.

The three men nodded and growled their approval. They rolled the limp female over, and she flopped onto her stomach.

The slab must be freezing. Alexa didn't see how the woman could submissively lie there with her breasts pressed against the rough-looking, bare stone. She hadn't muttered even one word of protest so far.

Alexa's need to protest was enough for an entire fleet of women. Except she couldn't function properly to let it out. All the energy seemed to be draining from her body, and it prevented her from doing anything, other than watching the sight before her.

Lizard-man almost reverently set the dripping dildo into some sort of case and turned back to the woman. He squeezed the flesh of her butt, then spread her ass-cheeks and probed her anus with that long, thin tongue of his.

Alexa's legs felt rubbery. Her mind began to fuzz over as if drugged.

The woman on the slab visibly shivered and roused from her lethargic state. She jerked her hips, forcing the man's repulsive tongue deeper. Immediately, the lizard-tongued man pulled out and smacked her ass. The sharp sound echoed against the stones of the surrounding crypts. The woman yelped, but otherwise didn't protest.

Alexa moaned. The skin on her bottom tingled. How could that be? She hadn't even been the one spanked!

Three sets of fingers clawed at the female's flesh, scraping and scratching the pale skin. Alexa could especially feel Lizard-man's excitement as they sexually worked over the woman. He again spread her cheeks and probed the opening of her ass.

Despite her fear, moisture gathered inside Alexa's lace panties. A guttural sound escaped her, and heat shot through her limbs. She didn't know what was happening to her. *Please, someone help me.*

The man furthest away, now winding the subjugated woman's blonde tresses around one hand, raised his head and peered into the dark. Alexa's gaze flew to his. She bit the inside of her cheek to stop any further involuntary noises. His eyes glowed yellow, too! Could he see her in the shadows?

With his free hand, he popped the buttons on his pants and pushed aside the scratchy-looking material. His cock, almost as large, thick, and like-colored as the reddish dildo, sprang out.

The woman rose up on her knees. No punishment followed this time. Lizard-man simply rubbed her ass and continued his deep anal licking.

With a small cry, she eagerly took the offered cock into her mouth, sucking and bobbing until she swallowed more than half of the man's turgid dick. His hand tightened in her hair, urging her to take even more of the shaft down her throat, but his eerie stare never wavered from Alexa's eyes. A small smile crossed his lips.

Alexa stood transfixed by the intensity of his stare. He knew she was there!

Was this encounter consensual? It must be. The woman seemed...ravenous. Alexa vaguely registered Lizard-man pull out his tongue and position himself directly behind the female as if he intended to penetrate her. Instead, he picked up another phallic object, long and slender with wiggling ticklers on the end, and inserted it into her lubricated asshole. The woman jackknifed her butt and moaned, sliding her lips further down Large-cock's thick rod. And the third man—

Wait. The third man! The breast-sucker. Where was he? He must have slipped away into the shadows.

Oh, shit. She had to get out of there, before—

Suddenly, whatever was keeping her there released its hold, and she felt a wave of energy. She could move. She whirled around and slammed into a wall of hard flesh. *No!*

Her scream never echoed through the graveyard. A masculine hand muffled the sound before it escaped her throat.

Dark. Muscular. Deadly dangerous.

That's all she could see. And feel. Black clothes, black hair, black eyes. Black stubble against lightly tanned skin. Massive chest. Solid. Over six feet tall, for sure. He loomed above her five-foot, seven-inch frame.

She tried to jerk away.

The man's fingers left her mouth and clamped onto her arm. He dragged her deeper into the shadows. This wasn't the third man. He had thick hair, and his lips were fuller, his jaw line stronger.

"Let go!"

"Quiet," he whispered harshly. "You don't want to be their next victim."

"I need to call the police. To help her, if she's being forced." *And get myself the hell out of here.* She tried to get a better look at the man holding her, but clouds had moved across the moon again, casting shadows along his face. She did notice his scent—hot and spicy.

"It's too late. They've already begun the Initiation." His voice rasped deep in his throat.

"Initiation?" Was this a college fraternity stunt? It couldn't be. She'd seen almost inhuman things. Been unable to move. Or so she thought. But then, a dark graveyard had a tendency to distort one's perception. Perhaps she'd just suffered a panic attack. That could temporarily paralyze a person and cause her to think she'd seen things she probably hadn't.

Alexa didn't know. She only knew that she'd stumbled upon something beyond her comfort level and understanding.

Escape was her only thought. The hell with anything else. She'd find another way to recover her mother's journal and unlock the secrets of her life.

As far as Alexa knew, the man who pulled her into the deep shadows could be part of the gang-bang group, too. Their lookout. Not about to trust anyone without a uniform and a great big gun, she drew back her boot and kicked him in the shin.

He released her arm. "Ye-ow! Dammit!"

She ran for her life. If the hounds of hell had been after her, she couldn't have been more afraid. No way was she going to become *anyone's* next victim or nocturnal plaything. Nor did she want to witness any more erotic, kinky, or fetish-type acts for the rest of her life.


Braden watched the woman flee the cemetery. Her honey-blonde hair, which shone like a beacon in the night, fell from its bun and swept out behind her.

He limped around in a circle, working out the pain she'd inflicted. His instinct was to go after her. Now. Before she ran into one of the Egesa.

She'd ventured too close to the Initiation Rite and gotten trapped in the paralyzing protection shield they'd erected. Luckily, he was able to release her by zapping the field with a pin-laser.

A chuckle in the darkness stopped him cold.

"She got away from you, Braden."

He stiffened and slowly turned toward the voice, his pain forgotten. "Checking up on me, Laszlo?" He hadn't expected the man to leave the ship and set foot on-planet. But then, he hadn't expected him to come on this mission at all, given the importance of his duties back on Xylon.

Taller than even Braden's six-feet, two-inches, he stepped out of the shadows. The smile faded from his face, and his lips tensed. "They didn't violate her, did they?"

"No. The decoy worked." Alexa was their intended target. But Laszlo had found a volunteer—or in Braden's opinion, a sacrifice—a similar-looking woman willing to take her place for the good of the cause, once Laszlo learned of the note they'd sent to lure Alexa out, their lie about having the journal.

Looking toward the crypts, Laszlo nodded. "Good. I did not like giving them one of our women, but she will make a good spy for us."

"Don't count on that, Laszlo. She's enjoying the fuck too much. I saw. They have a great deal of power over her already. She could very well turn and decide to serve them willingly. Rough sex has always been her weakness. They must have sensed it and are using her need to their advantage. They're going at her hard."

Another sharp cry into the night, and a woman's plea of, "More! Yes!" cut through the darkness.

"Rough sex isn't limited to the Egesa."

"No. But their particular nastiness is. That may be something she craves and is unable to get from us." Braden felt the need to charge in and drag her out, save her while he could. Volunteer or no, this situation didn't set well with him. Just because she wasn't a breeder didn't make her life any less valuable...in his eyes, at least.

Laszlo's concerned gaze swept the graveyard. His next words came out slow, but determined. "It's for the best. We can't lose Alexa.

Maybe our woman will fool the Egesa long enough for us to do what we need to, undetected. Very few females remain with the proper DNA to breed with us. We have to initiate as many as we can before it's too late."

"Alexa doesn't even know who she is. How important she is to Xylon."

Laszlo's attention drifted back to him, his blue eyes glowing in the night. "She will. Soon. But not by my hand."

Braden shivered at the intensity of the man's stare. "I don't understand." The Council had already given Laszlo permission to proceed.

"I want *you* to initiate her, Braden."

"Me?" The image of touching Alexa inside and out hit hard. He rubbed his fingers together, felt his temperature rise, his cock harden even more than it had when he'd only dreamed of fucking her. "Alexa was chosen for you, not only to initiate but to mate."

"I do my own choosing."

"Can you go against The Council?"

He smiled. "I do as I see fit, Braden. You should know that by now."

Yes. Laszlo followed his own will. This huge man, who resembled the golden-haired medieval warriors from Earth's past, had led the Xylon Warriors for as long as Braden could remember. He suspected the man could defeat the entire Council in one swoop if he so chose. His influence was that great, his followers that loyal.

That must be why Laszlo had assigned him to watch over Alexa. The man had already decided not to participate in the Initiation. And Laszlo knew he'd developed a fixation on her after researching the woman for The Council.

He'd gladly initiate Alexa, but only under one condition. "I initiate alone, Laszlo." He had no desire to share Alexa with others.

Ironic. He'd hoped to be one of the remaining two men picked to help initiate her. Now that he was the lead, instead of Laszlo, he didn't want anyone's mouth sucking those luscious tits, no man's cock pumping her pussy, no tongue licking her delectable ass, but his own. Only his.

A small grin tugged at Laszlo's mouth. "You think you can handle her by yourself once the appetite comes?"

"I'll figure out a way." During this particular Lair of Xylon rite, an initiate's sexual needs could be nearly impossible to sate until the cravings passed. Still, he couldn't bear the thought of other Warriors fucking Alexa, even if he chose The Alliance of Three.

"As you will. She is yours, and yours alone."

Braden glanced down the path where she'd disappeared.

"If she rejects you —"

"She won't." He imagined rolling Alexa's nipples between his fingertips, flicking her clit with his thumb. As a preview of things to come, he'd plunge two maybe three fingers inside her, just enough to stimulate her, until she cried out his name and demanded satisfaction.

Only then would he fill her with his cock. Spill his hot seed inside her. Brand her with his mark, so everyone knew she belonged to *him*.

And finally after she'd come, wild and hard, he'd take her again. Soft and slow. Bring her to the brink, then push her over into an orgasm that lasted so long she'd collapse from exhaustion. He could hardly wait.

He shook his head. What was he thinking? The dream must have affected his reasoning. He couldn't Brand her. She wasn't his to keep, unless The Council so decreed. He could mate with her, but that's all.

*Mate.* No. Again, wrong way to think about it. He rubbed the back of his neck. He'd have to seek The Council's permission to make her his mate. And he'd need Laszlo's approval, too. The man had only asked him to initiate her. Lead the *fucking-frenzy* as the Warriors called it. Ensure her protection and prepare her for breeding. Then he'd have the option of keeping her as his mistress, if he so chose and Laszlo didn't claim her, until The Council selected another breeder mate. Nothing more would be his right, simply because he wanted it to be so.

Sirens wailed in the distance, the sounds increasing as they neared. Alexa must have called the authorities.

"How long do we have before we leave orbit and head back to Xylon? I'll need time to gain her trust. I won't take her by force."

When he received no answer, he peered over his shoulder. Laszlo was gone.

# Chapter Two

Alexa pulled into the driveway and jammed on the brakes. The car jerked to a halt. She killed the engine and dropped her forehead onto the steering wheel.

Her heart pounded, her limbs shook, and her breath came in ragged pants. Her fingers gripped the steering wheel so tightly they ached. "Why did you involve me in this, Mother? What's the secret you've been so fiercely protecting me from all my life?" She shook her head. "Journal or no, I am never going back to that damn cemetery again. I'm getting out of this town as soon as possible."

When she'd reached her rental car in the cemetery parking lot, she had called the police on the car phone, but had refused to give her name. The last thing she wanted was to repeat what she'd seen to some officer. Let them discover the fuckers, literally, on their own. At least she knew if that woman had been a victim, instead of a willing participant, she'd done the right thing by calling for help.

For tonight, she wanted to go inside and forget. Soak in a hot bubble bath. Crawl between warm flannel sheets, watch some mindless comedy on television, and sip on a cup of hot chocolate with lots of mini marshmallows.

A slam into the windshield brought her head up with a snap. She sat stunned for a moment. "No!" The scream tore from her throat.

Lizard-man sat crouched on the hood. His long tongue swiped back and forth across the window glass, leaving a creamy substance behind. She remembered where that tongue had been, and gulped in a large pocket of air. This was not happening. "Go away!"

His yellowish eyes glowed in the night. A reflection from the street lamp, just like the light in the cemetery. It had to be. Nobody had yellow eyes.

She fumbled for the phone and dialed the emergency number. Someone answered almost immediately. *Thank you!* "I need — wait! No! Don't put me on hold! Shit."

She tossed the phone and fumbled with the car keys, trying to re-start the motor. She needed to get out of there! The grotesque man had found her, knew where she lived. How? He couldn't possibly have followed her on foot.

The driver's-side door flew open, as the engine roared to life. Another yellow-eyed man! She shifted into reverse and stepped on the gas. The wheels spun, but the car didn't move.

A pair of meaty hands grabbed her and dragged her out onto the pavement. She'd locked that door! And he had opened it as if the lock was no barrier at all. He spun her around and held her captive against his chest, her back to his front. Strong fingers dug into her arms, keeping her trapped against him.

She knew him.

The large-cocked man. She had recognized him before he'd turned her around. She felt his hard shaft pressing against her from behind. Images from the graveyard flashed through her mind, and her panic rose to a frenzied level.

"Please. I didn't do anything. I didn't see anything," she lied. "Whatever you're involved with is none of my business. I'm not going to tell anyone. Just let me go. I'll forget you were even here."

She fought the urge to struggle. He was strong, his grip painful. And there were two of them. It would be a waste of energy. She'd have to think her way out of this one.

*Do they know I called the police?* If so, they also knew her words were a lie. This could be some sort of retaliation. An attempt to shut her up permanently.

With a strange accent that she didn't recognize, Large-cock whispered in her ear. "We bring message from Daegal. He says you will serve him on Marid. We initiate. Take your body, Alexa. Make you sterile, so you are good for fuck-bitch only."

She shook her head. His words were a jumble of confusion that she wasn't processing.

"After so, we have fun. You will eat my pole. Lick and slurp 'til I spurt, then swallow spunk like graveyard whore."

Her stomach churned. If she'd had anything in her gut, she would have lost it. "Let...me...go!" Wait. He'd used her name. How did he know her name?

Out of the shadows, a third man awkwardly loped toward her, one leg shorter than the other one. The breast-sucker!

She kicked out at him, landing a blow to his thigh. "Stay away from me!"

He kept coming.

Large-cock twisted her arm, and she shrieked, the pain so bad she had a difficult time catching her breath. She sagged against his chest.

"No more fight, or we whip pussy — three straps. Hurt bad."

Alexa couldn't stop the whimper that escaped her throat. Images of them holding her down and beating her flooded her mind. How had her life turned from simple, safe, freelance photography to this? She sniffled, but was determined not to cry. Not now, when she needed her wits about her.

As the pain in her arm eased, she tried to relax, tried to regain some strength and control. Think, Alexa! There had to be a way out of this. There was always a way out of dangerous situations, if one could find it.

About equal to her shoulder height, Breast-sucker hovered, unhurt by her kick. He picked at the coat she wore, plucking open the buttons one by one. His nails were longer than her manicurist's! Except for his index fingers, which looked de-clawed and resembled thick, rough stumps.

"Please..." she begged. She never thought anything like this would happen to her. She hadn't planned for it. And she always planned for things, so she knew what to do if the situation arose. Sure, she'd thought she might have problems with a man at some point. But not three men! And especially not men who were so monstrously demented.

"Yes," he growled, the word barely recognizable. "I please." With his claws, he dragged aside her coat, then shredded her sweater and bra, like the material was made of paper.

The ripping of her clothes echoed in her ears. Pain raked her chest. "Stop!"

Her bare breasts hung exposed. Blood beaded, staining her flesh, from the scratches left by his claws. The cold air, plus her fear and pain, puckered her skin and hardened her nipples.

"No stop. You like. Have good, full titties. I feed. Suck hard." He pursed his crooked lips and blew a stream of fetid air over her nipples.

"No!" His use of the word *feed* struck her odd, since that was her exact thought in the cemetery. She twisted and tugged against Large-cock. Who were these creatures? Not college students, for sure, like she'd once thought. More like severely deformed, mental patient escapees with weirdly colored eye contacts. What other explanation could there be?

Atop the car hood, Lizard-man hissed. Alexa's gaze flew to him. He made an obscene gesture to her, and she immediately stilled. Her struggling only seemed to be exciting them more.

This situation worsened by the second. How could she fight three of them?

Large-cock whispered in her ear again. "He fuck you deep with scream toy. You purr good. We make you cunt-pet. Play with you long. Take you to Marid. Daegal fuck you wild, while Egesa watch and cheer. Sometimes help if Daegal want. Lots of fun."

Lizard-man flicked his tongue. He jumped off the hood of the car and shook a silver case above his head. Alexa knew what *scream toy* was in that case. And she didn't intend to become anyone's pet, or go to Marid, wherever that was, or submit to this Daegal person, whoever he was, not to mention the Egesa, whom she'd never heard of either.

Raving lunatics — that's what these three were! And she wanted no part of their sick plans. Even though her nearest neighbor was almost a mile down the road, Alexa screamed, over and over, until her throat felt raw.

Unmindful of the ear-splitting sound, Breast-sucker lunged for her exposed, left nipple. Alexa slammed back against Large-cock, trying to knock him off his feet. Anything to get away.

In mid-lunge, Breast-sucker shrieked like no human or animal she'd ever heard, and then disintegrated like confetti before her eyes.

All at once. Gone.

Lizard-man swung around. He clicked his tongue at something in the shadows and then scurried away into the night, dragging the case on the ground behind him.

Alexa felt Large-cock shiver, and he didn't feel so large anymore. His grip around her arms eased.

She took immediate advantage, twisted, and stomped on his foot with her boot. He wailed, then pushed her, or she fell, because the next thing she knew he was gone and she was on her knees, her palms scraping against the pavement.

Fat raindrops began to fall on the cement around her, and one plopped onto the back of her neck. The icy chill felt good, revitalizing.

She glanced up, in pain, but ready to flee. As soon as her legs would support her. She didn't know what had just happened and didn't care, as long as she got away intact. She'd let the police figure it out, after she was safe and sound behind locked doors.

In mid-crouch, a presence stopped her.

A man stood nearby, his hands shoved into a long, dark coat. Feet spread apart. Face obscured by the darkness. "You're hurt," he said, his voice tight, angry.

The other man! The dark one from the cemetery. She recognized the tone. This was not happening. Her vision swam in front of her, and she slumped to the ground.

Braden fought back his temper. He should have killed all three of those damn Egesa for daring to put their hands on Alexa.

The two survivors would return to their ship and transmit what happened back to Daegal on Marid. The man would know that Alexa was under a Warrior's protection, and that at least one Xylon ship was here in Earth's orbit, cloaked from detection. Maybe it would be a deterrent...for the moment.

He walked over to the car, shut off the engine, and grabbed the keys. Primitive transportation. He coughed at the noxious smell. Gas-fueled vehicles needed to be replaced with something cleaner and more advanced, if Earth hoped to progress beyond their current technological boundaries.

He scooped Alexa up in his arms. She curled into him, as if instinctively knowing he was there to help. Vaguely, he registered how good she felt in his arms, then immediately pushed aside the thought. He had a job to do. She wasn't his. He didn't have the right to feel anything. Even though Laszlo had relinquished her to him for now, the man still had the right to come back and claim her as his mate.

The rain began to fall harder, slowly turning to sleet. He needed to get her inside. The poison had already taken effect and caused her to black out. She'd be experiencing the pain soon.

With purposeful strides, he headed up the stone walkway toward the arched front door. Her mother's home. He'd been monitoring the residence for weeks, waiting for his chance. After the woman died—an unfortunate circumstance, he hoped Alexa would finally come home. "You should have done your job, Adrian, and not kept your daughter from us."

Alexa would need instruction and training to fulfill her destiny. Provided she survived long enough for him to get her back to Xylon.

* * * * *

A feeling of constriction stirred Alexa. Her eyes fluttered open. She was inside the house, tightly embraced, and someone was carrying her toward the master bedroom.

The stranger.

Would this nightmare ever end? "Let go!" She struggled, arching her back and pushing against his rock-hard chest. She'd have had more success pushing at a wall; he was that unmovable.

"Stop it, Alexa. You're hurt."

The use of her name, this time, was as calming as a caress. His voice slid over her, soft and determined. She stilled and stared up into his violet eyes. In the dark, his eyes had looked black, but they were really a dark violet. Menacing, compelling, eerily beautiful.

His hair was black—a military cut that had grown out. The stubble on his face was black; his clothes were black. A small scar on his left cheek, just below the eye, caught her attention. She had the sudden urge to caress the mark of imperfection.

Her weight seemed no problem for him to bear. "How do you know my name? Who are you?"

"My name is Braden Koll." He entered the master bedroom, pushed open the bathroom door, and set her on the counter between the double sinks. He flipped on the light. "Just sit there, please."

The word *please* sounded strange coming from the man's lips. His voice was soft and compelling, but his body was all hard and intense, wound tight.

Her chest began to hurt, and her hands, bringing back the memory of what had happened. "Those men…"

He took out a small tube of something, then shrugged off his coat and draped it over the side of the garden tub. "Don't worry about them right now." He glanced down her body.

Alexa followed his gaze and gasped. Her breasts were completely exposed. They looked raw, scraped, spotted with blood. She moved to cover herself, but the stinging in her hands made her wince.

Braden brushed her fingers away. "Let me tend to you."

"I don't even know you!" She'd found a gun in the nightstand last night. If she could get to it… She scooted forward to hop off the counter.

He grabbed her waist. "Listen to me. Those scrapes will become extremely painful and cause permanent damage if you don't let me put this cream on you."

She shook her head and seriously considered kicking him in the nuts. Unless she got in a good blow, she probably wouldn't have time to get the gun before he recovered. But she could flee the house. Hide.

Except…the other men might be lurking outside, waiting for her to come out. At least this man, Braden, hadn't tried to hurt her. Yet.

Leaning close, his voice came out low and velvety soft. "Alexa, you know what those creatures did. You saw what they were. And you can also see I'm not like them. Trust me."

Trust? He had a screw loose if he actually believed that. "I don't know what to think. What I saw. Who to trust." Her voice shook, but she couldn't control it.

Pain surged through her chest. She winced and flapped her hands in the air. "They're burning!" Her breasts felt like acid was eating right through the flesh.

"Let me help you."

She had no choice. The pain was too severe. She sucked in a breath, tried to control her tears, and nodded.

Braden helped her out of the coat and what was left of her emerald-green sweater and matching bra. At the sight of the wounds marring her beautiful breasts, his temper rose.

He should have followed her sooner, seen to her protection better. The Egesa had figured out the ploy with the decoy, and had tracked Alexa to the house.

She sat with her head against the mirror and her eyes squeezed shut, tears escaping the sides.

"It'll be all right," he told her, his voice steadier than he actually felt.

He flicked the top off a silver cylinder, set the dose, and waited for the white goop to fill his palm. If already initiated, she'd heal almost immediately with the help of the cream. In Alexa's current state, her body wouldn't recover until sunrise. He set aside the container, then rubbed his hands together to warm the substance.

With a light touch, his palms covered her soft, full breasts.

She jerked, then settled back with a sigh.

The cream would not only heal, but contained a drug that would seep into her system and relax her, so she could sleep. He gently caressed her breasts. Perfect. A little more than a handful each. And he had large hands.

"That's nice," she whispered dreamily.

He felt her body begin to relax. In response, his body tightened. The sight of his fingers massaging her breasts, the weight of the soft flesh in his hands, the feel of his palms rubbing against her hard nipples, made him want to open his pants, strip Alexa down, pull her to the end of the counter, and plunge himself deep inside her pussy.

"Your hands feel good."

Torture. The urge to fuck this woman, make her surrender to his will, was growing to an unbelievable need. He'd never felt like this with any of the other women he'd initiated. What was happening to him? He brushed his thumbs across her nipples, watching for her response.

"Oh..." Alexa's eyes popped open. "Braden?"

His throat felt dry, his cock hurt, and his hands twitched. He ached to explore her body. He knew he couldn't. Not yet. But soon. Very soon.

Her eyes rolled back in her head, and she slid down the counter.

He caught her in his arms and propped her up, then carefully tended to her hands. No poison there. The scrapes just needed cleaning and a regular antiseptic. The bruises on her arms where the Egesa had held her would soon fade. In time, all this would just be an unpleasant memory.

If she wasn't healed properly by morning, he'd call in a Xylon Healer.

"Come on, Alexa." He carried her into the bedroom and lay her on the mattress. He stripped off her black boots and socks and loosened the belt on her pants, so she'd be more comfortable.

She looked so innocent that something inside his heart twisted. He brushed aside the soft emotion and flipped the bedcover over her. Tenderness was not in his make-up, and he had no desire to discover that elusive, human emotion now. The problem was he knew too much about her from his research. If she were Xylon, he wouldn't even be giving her a second thought. She'd just be another woman to fuck into The Lair.

He walked back to the bathroom and took the vid-cell from his coat. He punched in a set of numbers and waited. The display flickered, then popped up an answer.

"Damn. Only ninety-six hours until we leave." If they waited any longer, they'd miss the entry point back to their star system. He'd have to work fast. He punched in some more numbers. "Kam, lock on my location. I need you and Erik to secure this perimeter."

A foul odor reached his nose, like rotting fish in stagnant water. He disconnected the transmission and stepped to the door. He glanced into the bedroom.

In the short time that he'd been gone, one of the Egesa had materialized inside the house and stripped off the bedcover, along with the rest of Alexa's clothes.

The creature sat crouched between her spread thighs, a blood-red initiator pulsing in his hand, ready to stab its poison into Alexa's unprotected cunt.

Braden had no time to think, only act. He drew his disruptor and fired. One second there. The next gone. So fast, the Egesa hadn't even uttered a sound.

Daegal must want Alexa sterilized bad to send someone back in for a second try so soon. Or maybe the creature had made the decision himself, not wanting to go back to the ship and report his failure.

Braden quickly moved to Alexa's side. He brushed his hand down her arm, along her abdomen, making sure she was okay. His gaze drifted over her naked body, taking in every detail. Her blonde hair lay tangled around her head, and dark circles stood out under her eyes. She'd been through an ordeal tonight. He wished he could remove her memory of the entire experience.

Her full breasts rose and fell with each breath. The nipples still hard; the buds a deep, sexy beige. Taunting him. Soon, he'd know their taste. And she'd squirm beneath his mouth and tongue.

His gaze slowly continued down her body, learning every dip and curve. The plane of her stomach flared out nicely at her hips. Further down, between her open thighs, his perusal stopped.

Dark-blonde hair covered her pussy. Damn. He wanted to touch her. Open her up. Put his mouth down there. Suck and bite her clit. Tongue-fuck her slow and thorough. Make her come. Lick her clean. Then do it all again.

"Braden?" a deep voice called from behind him.

Jerked out of his fantasy, he flipped the covers over Alexa's naked body. He turned. "Hey, guys."

His most-trusted friends, Kam Nextor and Erik Rhodes, stood near the bathroom door. Like him, they were part of the elite team of Warriors trained to protect the people of Xylon, and part of a special mission to search star systems for compatible women.

Those children born of Warriors and left on other worlds, if of age, were to be initiated for breeding and brought back to produce more Warriors for Xylon. Three ships were currently conducting searches, each responsible for a different star system, with more ships to be sent out soon.

Unfortunately, the Egesa were on a similar mission, except their orders were not to breed, but to sterilize these women, and to keep them from the Xylon Warriors at all costs.

Kam peered over Braden's shoulder. "Alexa?"

"Yeah. Laszlo gave her to me."

Erik's intense gaze snapped from the bed to Braden. "No shit? Can he do that?"

"Apparently."

"She's agreed to everything?"

"Not yet. The Egesa tried to get to her at the cemetery, then out in front of the house, and again just now in here. I need you two to stay close, while I take care of her. Help monitor for intruders. She'll wake in a few hours, and I'll explain things."

"No problem." Erik moved to stand over Alexa. He studied her face, then turned back to Braden. "Why don't we just get her back to the ship?"

"This is going to be hard enough on her as it is. I don't want to force her compliance. Familiar surroundings might make her more willing to cooperate. I think among the three of us, we should be able to keep her safe right here."

"Damn straight." Erik turned back toward her. "Why didn't the Egesa transport her up?"

"Their ship must be out of range. Or maybe they didn't have time to calibrate their hand-helds for multiple transport."

Erik smiled. "She is so fucking hot. We lucked out with her. I can't wait to watch her come. I can't wait to *make* her come." He rubbed his hands together. "When's the fucking-frenzy?"

Braden held his temper in check. Erik had simply made the logical assumption. They'd all initiated women together before. Still, it bugged the shit out of him. "I'm getting to hate that term."

Erik turned and cocked an eyebrow. "You're the one who came up with it."

Karma was a bitch. "Yeah, well. There will be no Alliance for her Initiation."

Erik laughed. "You're kidding, right?"

"No." Even though Kam and Erik were like brothers to him, he didn't want to share Alexa.

Kam drew Braden's attention with a touch on his arm. "You can't quell the sexual appetite she'll experience by yourself."

"I will."

"Braden, no one man has that type of stamina. Her mind could snap."

Braden brushed Kam's hand aside, avoiding his gaze. He didn't want to talk about his feelings or his decisions concerning Alexa. Especially when he didn't fully understand them himself.

He'd see to her. Somehow. *Alone.*

# Chapter Three

Alexa pried open her eyes. She felt groggy, sore. Disoriented. Where was she? She forced herself to focus.

Sunlight filtered in from partially opened window shades. Yellow-flowered wallpaper surrounded her. Vanilla scents teased her nose.

Okay…she remembered. Her mother's bedroom, her bedroom now, as long as she was in Black Marble.

She'd had the worst dream, or more accurately nightmare. Far worse than her normal ones. The only comforting part of it all was a handsome and sexy savior, who protected her from harm. She wouldn't mind him appearing in more of her fantasies.

A sigh eased from her lips, and she stretched languidly.

"Good morning."

Her heart jumped. She swung her gaze to the green and beige padded chair in the corner. Braden. He hadn't been a dream. She surged up on the bed, and the covers fell.

With a gasp, she reached for the sheet.

In mid-stretch, her gaze dropped to her naked breasts. Wait. They looked perfectly normal. How could that be? She clasped her hands over them, squeezing and caressing the smooth flesh. She couldn't believe it. No pain. No scratches. Nothing. If it all hadn't been a nightmare, then her skin should be raw with angry-red welts.

Braden groaned.

Her gaze flew to his. She suddenly remembered his hands applying some substance to her breasts and massaging them with tender care. Then he had flicked her nipples, and…

"You've healed beautifully, Alexa." His gaze honed in on the protruding nubs, and he licked his lips.

She snatched up the cream-colored sheet. As she moved under the covers, she could feel that the rest of her body was naked, too. Her face heated. Where were all her clothes? She scanned the room but didn't see them. Braden must have stripped them off her last night.

At the realization that he'd seen her completely naked, a tremble of nerves ran through her. Had he violated her? She shifted uncomfortably. She didn't *feel* violated. Of course, that didn't mean anything. Her stomach clenched at the thought that he might have taken advantage of her vulnerable position. He could have touched her anywhere. Done anything. "Did you...?"

"No." His gaze raked the outline of her body, and he rubbed his chin. "I didn't rape you, if that's what you're wondering."

He said it so casually that his words held the ring of truth. Still, she couldn't afford to let her guard down. "Thank you for what you did." He'd saved her from those horrible *things*, and the miracle cream he'd put on her was a generous gift.

A barely perceptible grin crossed his face, and he nodded.

She didn't know what to think of the man. Maybe he truly didn't intend any harm...only help. He *looked* like every woman's fantasy. Strong, sexy, dangerous. Her gaze swept him from head to toe and back again. She paused at his lap.

He shifted his hands to cover his groin.

She'd seen the massive erection. Oh, my! After she practically shoved her bared breasts up like an offering, she supposed she couldn't fault him for the reaction.

"What are you still doing here?" Had he simply waited for her to wake up, to make sure that she was all right? Would a stranger, with no ulterior motive, do that?

"I'm here to initiate you, Alexa."

Initiate! He might as well have slapped her. The shock would have been the same. The word's meaning speared through her. Fear chilled her to the core, and her stomach clenched. That's the word he'd used to describe what those three were doing in the graveyard. So Braden *was* a part of their group, as she originally thought.

Images of him doing those same erotic things to her flashed before her eyes. The idea was not so revolting with him in the picture.

Despite her fear, her body responded, and an intense need grew within her. Her nipples hardened almost painfully. Moisture gathered between her thighs, and her clit throbbed, needing a man's touch—his touch.

No! Shame rolled through her, and her temperature skyrocketed, as she experienced a full-body blush. It wasn't *her*, just her system that wanted him. He was a virtual stranger, not some lover from a dream. She knew that. It was her body that didn't understand.

Braden might be the most magnetic man she'd ever encountered, but she didn't want him to touch her intimately. Really, she didn't!

Her palms grew sweaty, and she quickly scanned the room, trying to figure out what to do. "You can't—"

A sound brought her attention to the bedroom door. Two large men, even taller than Braden, stood there studying her with apparent interest. Her heart slammed against her ribs. She was going to have a coronary. Any second now. Who were *they*?

One had dusty blond hair. His light blue eyes looked kind, and he appeared to understand her fears. One corner of his mouth hitched up into a gentle smile.

The second man was just the opposite. With dark brown hair and extra-wide shoulders, his intense green eyes held dangerous possibilities. He made her feel sinfully naked, even while covered by the sheet.

They were both dressed in black, just like Braden.

Three men. Like the three who attacked her, but not. They'd been dressed in black too.

These men were handsome and incredibly sexy, unlike the others. But that didn't change anything. She knew now they were all connected, and she understood what initiate meant. *Rape.*

A memory tapped at her mind. The woman in the cemetery hadn't actually struggled against what happened to her. Alexa still couldn't say for sure if what she saw was an attack or consensual.

Maybe they would just ask her if she was interested in some sort of kinky four-way. This *initiation* might not involve an issue of force at all.

Sex with a stranger used to be one of her favorite fantasies. Sex with three strangers she had never even imagined—oh, my! But rape definitely was not one of her fantasies.

Besides, this was reality. She needed to figure a way out of it in case they pounced.

What the hell was going on in Black Marble anyway?

A cult, maybe. Yes, that could be it. Cultists of some sort, dressed in black, going about in threes, recruiting women through sex and bizarre rituals.

Well, not her. She tried to appear calm and compliant. She didn't want to alert them to her plans, whatever they were. She had to think up something fast.

Maybe if she didn't get hysterical and outright fight them, she could buy some time. "Initiate? I see. Why me?" Ah, she knew. She *could* turn the tables. She was in the perfect position to do so.

"Your DNA is compatible."

Okay. *Whatever that means.* She rubbed her nose and pretended to sniffle, then casually reached inside the nightstand drawer, hoping it appeared she was searching for nothing more than a tissue. When they didn't immediately jump forward to stop her, she pulled out her hand, and the gun came with it.

The man with the intense green eyes chuckled.

Her hand tightened around the weapon and sudden irritation more than fear, flowed through her. She didn't get the joke. Maybe he thought she didn't have the guts to pull the trigger. If so, he wouldn't be laughing for long. Her mostly-absentee father had taught her to shoot when she was eleven, right before he permanently disappeared into parts unknown. And right about now, with these three hovering, she felt justified in doing whatever necessary to keep herself safe.

"I'll use this if I have to."

What kind of men didn't even flinch at the sight of a gun trained on them? She couldn't shoot all three of them if they decided to rush her. Nor did she want to, unless given no choice. But she *would* protect herself.

"Get out of my house."

She swung the gun around. She'd had the weapon aimed at Braden, who she figured was the leader, but somehow she couldn't shoot him. He'd helped her, after all. It was easier to target the largest man of the three. The one who had laughed at her. Since two of them stood close together, her odds of hitting at least one increased. Though she hoped not to hit the one with the kind eyes. He looked so sympathetic to her cause.

Don't make excuses for any of them, Alexa, a voice in her head chastised. But they haven't hurt me, another voice argued back.

That voice was right. They hadn't hurt her. But then, she didn't intend to actually kill anyone if she didn't have to, just wound. They'd run out. She'd call the police, and the authorities could take it from there.

"Are you going to leave?"

"I'm sorry, Alexa," Braden replied. "We can't do that."

"How do you know my name?" He never had answered her the first time she'd asked.

"I've been tracking you for a while."

Her heart sped up, thudding hard in her chest. Tracking. *Stalking.* "Okay." She swallowed. That's it. "I warned all of you."

The trigger clicked, and the gun fired. Almost to its target, the bullet stopped and crumpled, hitting some sort of invisible wall. It dropped harmlessly to the floor.

Alexa's mouth fell open. That couldn't happen!

"Put the gun away, Alexa," Braden ordered. "The bullets can't penetrate our shields. If you'd taken us by surprise, perhaps. But your actions were quite predictable for a human female, so we were prepared."

Shields? Human female? She stared down at the gun in confusion. Before she realized it, a hand covered hers. She jerked and tried to pull away. Her gaze flew to the man who was holding her, and her stare locked with his. The one with the kind eyes. He held her tightly and pried the gun from her hand. "It's all right, Alexa."

Braden grunted, drawing their attention. "Gentlemen, leave us. Alexa and I need to...talk."

Alexa sat frozen. Her brain refused to process what had just happened. She stared at her empty hand, as if it wasn't her own. She must be losing her mind. Hallucinating. None of this was real. It was impossible. Ever since she'd arrived in Black Marble, her world had changed for the worse.

After the door closed, Braden stood and approached the bed. Alexa shrank back against the pillows. "Who are you people? What are you?"

He sat beside her, his weight dipping the side of the mattress. "We're Xylon Warriors on a mission to bring back women to our planet for breeding purposes."

Alexa stared at him with a look of utter disbelief. "You're crazy."

He supposed that's how he sounded. Blurting it out like that wasn't the best plan of action, probably, but they didn't have time for him to ease her into everything.

She raised her palms to ward him off. The sheet clung to the tips of her breasts, barely covering her and threatening to slide completely off. Braden's pulse kicked up at the thought of caressing her soft, full tits again.

"This is all too much."

His attention returned to her eyes. He ached to reach out and touch her. Comfort her. Ease her fears. Though doing so might have the opposite effect and frighten her even more.

"You three are going to rape me, aren't you?" When he opened his mouth, she blurted, "I know you called it something else, but it's the same thing."

"No, it's not, Alexa. We won't touch you. *I* won't touch you unless you agree. We'd never force ourselves on you. In fact, I'd kill anyone who tried to hurt you in any way." His voice came out low and gruff. "You have to believe that."

The tenseness in her body eased somewhat at his words. Good. It was a start. Her look indicated faraway thoughts, and he wondered if she was remembering the man he had killed outside the house. The second man she didn't know about, but he was just as dead. And if the third came after her again, or any other Egesa or Marid assassin, he wouldn't hesitate to act.

Her focus returned. "Okay." She cleared her throat. "Unless I agree? Fine. I don't agree. Get out."

"It's not that easy, Alexa." He hated that he couldn't take the time to seduce her properly. He needed to explain how much the survival of The Lair of Xylon depended on her, how much her own survival rode on her decision.

Alexa clutched the sheet close, like a piece of armor that might ward him off. "But you said—"

"I know what I said. Please don't be afraid. We're not going to hurt you."

She chewed on her bottom lip, studying him. Probably wondering what to do. "If you're not going to rape me, if that's the truth, can I put on some clothes? I'm not comfortable like this."

Her hands fisted in the covers. She looked worried that he might strip them away. Getting dressed seemed a waste of good time to him. He wanted to initiate her here in familiar surroundings, where she'd be more comfortable. But if clothes made her feel more secure at the moment, he supposed it would be worth it. He stood and positioned himself in front of the door so she couldn't slip away. He widened his stance and crossed his arms over his chest. "Go ahead. Get dressed."

"Can I have some privacy?"

"No." He didn't dare leave her alone until they were safely on the Xylon ship. The Egesa might try to get to her again. And right now she was helpless, for the most part.

She looked ready to protest, then instead wrapped the sheet around herself and pushed off the bed. Watching him warily, she grabbed some gray sweats and pink underwear out of a dresser drawer.

He looked forward to slipping that pink lace off her body and tasting every inch of her soft skin. Somehow, he'd convince her to go through the Initiation. And not just because he wanted to fuck her. After spending months researching her, something about her tugged at his heart, and he wanted her heart to feel something for him in return. Shit! He gave himself a mental shake. Where had that thought come from?

*She's not mine.*

When she headed for the bathroom, he cut her off, grabbing her arm. "No."

Her eyes snapped to his. "I have to pee." Her voice snapped just as intently as her eyes. "I can't hold it forever. And you are *not* watching."

The corner of his mouth twitched in a barely-there smile. "Hold on." He walked over and opened the bedroom door. "Kam?"

A moment later, the man stepped inside the room. His gaze shifted from Braden to Alexa and back again. "Yeah?"

"She's going into the bathroom. Can you stand outside the door? Monitor the area. Make sure she's okay." Kam would be able to pick up any air movement on his detector and be able to identify an alien presence. He felt a little uncomfortable about her being in there alone, but he understood her need for privacy. And they'd be close enough to get to her if something happened.

"Sure. She'll be fine."

Alexa gave them both a strange look, then disappeared into the bathroom, shut the door, and flipped the lock. There wasn't a window in there large enough for her to get out, so Braden didn't worry about that. And maybe the time alone would do her good.

Erik appeared at the bedroom door. "What's going on?"

"She's getting dressed." Braden sat down on the bed and raked his fingers through his hair.

"Dressed? Why? You're gonna have her ass in the air and your dick shoved up her before the day is over."

Kam grunted. He made a few adjustments on the monitor in his hand.

"Did anyone ever tell you that you have no social skills at all?" Braden replied.

"Social skills? You're kidding, right? We're on Earth. Besides, I gotta be me." He laughed. "Hey, I could have been really crude about it." The grin on his face faded. "Did she refuse?"

"Sort of. But I haven't explained everything yet. She thinks we want to rape her."

"Geez." Kam shook his head. "I hope you put her straight on that one."

"I don't think she quite believes me." Braden took out his vid-cell. "I'm calling Leila."

Erik visibly stiffened. "Why? Alexa's fine physically. We don't need that Healer bitch's help."

Kam's eyes narrowed. "Just because she refused a public fuck with you at a Joining Party doesn't make her a bitch. You've been calling her that ever since she snubbed you."

"Why was she there, if she didn't want to get fucked? I watched her all night. She didn't choose anyone."

"Did you bother to ask her? Would you rather she *had* picked someone else?"

"Guys," Braden interrupted. "Enough. Alexa might be more willing to listen to a woman," he explained. "I think it's a good idea." He clicked on the cell and made the transmission.

\* \* \* \* \*

Alexa opened the bathroom door and peered out. Three sets of curiosity-filled male eyes swung her way. She tentatively emerged and walked into the bedroom. Funny how the room had always seemed fairly large to her, but filled with these three, even the air felt lacking.

"I'm glad you didn't decide to stay locked in there," Braden told her.

"I might have if I thought you couldn't get in." While in the bathroom, she'd decided to present a strong stance. Let them know she wasn't some wimpy female. At least she had clothes on now, which made her feel more in control.

She looked over at the other two men, but they said nothing. That unnerved her. She always found conversation comforting. The theory being that you don't hurt people you've gotten to know. Hopefully.

The tension in the room steadily grew, as everyone remained silent. They were all staring at her with too much interest. She felt like the special of the day or something. She hugged her arms below her breasts. "Um, what's a Xylon Warrior?" she finally asked, breaking the eerie quiet.

All eyes turned to Braden.

"A specially trained soldier from our planet."

"Planet? As in, not from Earth?"

"That's right."

Okay. Definitely insane. Them or her, she wasn't sure. But someone here was cracked.

The air in the corner shimmered. A woman appeared out of nowhere. Dressed in black. Alexa blinked several times. She lowered herself into the chair Braden had sat in earlier. Her knees were too weak to remain standing. If a two-headed elephant came crashing through the bedroom window right now, she couldn't be more surprised. Maybe they weren't insane. Maybe this was actually for real, after all.

"Thanks for coming, Leila," Braden greeted.

The slender woman, with extra long brown hair down to her butt, and cinnamon eyes, glanced around the room. She hesitated when her gaze fell on the man Alexa had tried to shoot. A frown marred her features. She immediately turned her head to look at Braden, and her expression softened. "Hi, Braden. How can I help?"

"Alexa needs to be initiated."

The woman stiffened. Her gaze flew to Alexa, then snapped back to him. "You want *me* to be part of the Alliance?"

"Now there's a visual," Erik replied. "I'd pay big to see that wicked tongue of yours between her legs, licking her out."

Alexa's stomach clenched. No! He wasn't serious. Was he? Her gaze met Braden's, and their eyes locked. He seemed to be studying her reaction to the sexually charged words. Her face heated, and she tore her gaze away.

"Shut up, Erik," Kam replied from across the room.

Leila's eyes narrowed as she stared at him. "Always the bastard, aren't you? You have no compassion for initiates."

His eyes darkened, and he stormed over to her. Alexa sank back in the chair. He looked ready to kill. Amazingly, the woman stood her ground. Alexa wondered where she got the courage to go toe to toe with a man like him. He towered over her and could probably crush her with one hand.

"Careful, Leila. I don't take shit from Class 1 Warriors, so I'm certainly not going to take any from a Class 3." A grin crossed his face. "I bet you'd love to do her."

"Get out of my face, Erik. My opinion stands, whether you want to hear it or not."

His smile faded. "Fine. I may not have much compassion, in your opinion, but I have enough *passion* to get even a frigid bitch like you hot and bothered and begging for some good, hard cock."

Alexa gasped.

"Hey!" Braden shouted. "We don't have time for this shit. Leila, I need you to explain the Initiation to Alexa. I think she'll be less intimidated if you're the one to fill her in on the details and importance of the ceremony. But I need to talk to you in private first."

Alexa stayed huddled in the chair while Braden and Leila went into the other room. From the way he spoke, it sounded like he expected her to agree to that Initiation thing. He was in for a surprise.

She warily watched Kam and Erik pace the floor. Erik frightened her. He was so intense and aggressive. Kam somehow made her feel safe with his caring eyes and calm voice. And Braden...well, his dark and mysterious aura got *her* hot and bothered, to use Erik's words, that was for sure.

Once she realized he wasn't going to hurt her, the initial attraction she felt had grown. And somehow, she did believe he wouldn't harm her. Regardless of what he seemed to think she would agree to.

"Why do you treat Leila like that?" Kam asked. "She's a good woman."

"Yeah? So why don't you try for a hump or suck?"

Kam glanced at Alexa with an almost embarrassed look in his eyes, then turned his attention back to Erik. "Because you want her, and for more than that."

"Like hell!"

Kam cocked an eyebrow and raised a small monitor. This one looked different from the one he had earlier.

Erik pointed a finger. "Don't try to analyze me with that sensor piece of crap."

"What is that?" Alexa interrupted. She hoped her question would diffuse the argument between the two men. Besides, the bluish panel caught her interest.

Kam walked over and crouched in front of her. "It monitors and analyzes emotions. You don't need to be afraid of us, Alexa. I know your fear has subsided a great deal. But you *can* completely trust us. We're the good guys. Really."

"And the three who attacked me outside?"

"Not such good guys."

Erik snorted. "There's an understatement."

"Braden said you were specially trained. Trained for what?"

That gentle smile of Kam's again crossed his face. "Let's just say that we're very capable of fighting our enemies."

"Those creatures…what are they?"

Erik muttered something under his breath and turned away.

"They're called Egesa. They're from Marid, one of the five moons of Xylon."

A planet with five moons. Like in her dreams. Could these people really be aliens?

"It's a slaving colony basically. But don't worry about them, Alexa," Kam answered, cutting his eyes momentarily toward Erik, who was still mumbling to himself. "You have enough to deal with, right now. You'll learn everything, in due time."

*Ruth D. Kerce*

# Chapter Four

Alexa watched Braden, Kam, and Erik file into the hallway, frowns on their faces, like a line of little boys banished from their playroom. If she wanted to try an escape, now would be the time. She glanced toward the window, gauging the chances of success. She'd have to kick out the sunscreen. That would take time, not to mention cause a lot of noise. She wasn't even sure she could do it. She'd have to incapacitate Leila first. The woman was smaller than she was, but Alexa didn't know what kind of training the woman might have. She could be a killing machine, for all Alexa knew. They did call themselves Warriors, after all.

Leila sat down on the bed. With an understanding smile on her face, she caressed the yellow and green pattern of the comforter, giving Alexa a moment to assimilate everything that was happening. "I guess you're a bit out of sorts with all this," she said, repositioning herself on the bed, so she sat between Alexa and the window.

Alexa nodded in response and inwardly sighed. So much for escape. Leila was no fool. The up side was that she felt more at ease now that all the testosterone was gone. She needed a break from the men, and she needed answers. Talking to Leila would be easier. Or at least less intimidating. "I came here to settle my mother's estate as soon as I was able. She died a couple of weeks ago, from a heart attack. Mostly, I've lived abroad with other relatives all my life. Shuffled from place to place, with no explanation why."

"It must have been a hard life for you."

"I didn't know anything different. That's just the way it was. Supposedly, her missing journal contains the answers. I received a call from a woman who said she had it, and I was supposed to meet her in the cemetery. That's where I came across Braden and a lot of stuff I don't understand."

"I'm sorry for your loss. And for the information obviously kept from you all your life. You're having the dreams?"

The question caught Alexa by surprise. "How did you know?"

42

Her nightmares were always of some strange red and green planet with five multi-colored moons. She'd had the images in her head for as long as she could remember. In the dreams, she was always running from some danger she couldn't see. And searching for someone she couldn't name. She had to do something, accomplish something vital. Carry something to, or for, those she loved. The dreams had gotten so powerful, so repetitive, that she often felt her sanity slipping away from her. Each time she awoke from one, it took her longer and longer to recover.

"The visions will ease off after the Initiation, then eventually stop altogether."

"What's their significance?"

"It identifies you as an off-worlder, half-breed Xylon—still unclaimed. Your father was one of us, Alexa. Our men used to be able to mate with any humanoid-type female from another world and produce children, but that stopped approximately twenty years ago, for reasons we don't understand. We no longer have that many females on Xylon. And many are sterile. So, we're now seeking females born from Xylon genes, particularly Warriors, left on other planets, in the hope of re-populating our own world with children who are strong and can help us fight the Egesa, who are at this point threatening our very existence. Not to mention causing problems on other worlds, including Earth. Your dreams simply prove you have the correct DNA to carry a Xylon child in your womb. I'll run a test to be sure, but I already know what the result will be."

Alexa sat there, staring at the woman. This was unbelievable. Even after everything that she'd already seen and heard.

Leila pulled a small book from inside her jacket. The gold lettering on the front stood out from the brown, suede cover.

"That's my mother's journal!"

"Yes. Braden retrieved it from the house before you arrived."

"Braden. He was the one who lured me to the cemetery with that note, not the woman?" Anger filled her. He'd manipulated her, and she'd fallen right into the trap. "Why? To witness that woman being fucked, or initiated, or whatever you want to call it? Did he think it would turn me on so much that I'd beg him and those other two out there to do the same thing to me? Who was the woman who called me on the phone? You?" Unable to control her tone, her voice rose with each question.

"No, Alexa. It wasn't me. Braden took the journal for safekeeping. He found it when we came here looking for you. He didn't send the note, though he did know about it. We suspect Daegal ordered it sent to lure you out where the Egesa could get to you easier."

"Oh." The common sense of Leila's words sank in. She kept hoping they'd trip up somehow, contradict something already said, so she'd know for sure they were lying. But no such luck. "Daegal. I've heard that name before. He's associated with those others who attacked me."

"Yes. The Egesa serve him."

Egesa? She kept hearing that term too, but remembered what Kam had told her. "The bad guys. Is Daegal one of them? I mean, you referred to him as separate from the creatures, it seems like."

"We're not sure what or who Daegal is, other than their leader. No one who has seen his face has ever betrayed him and lived long enough to tell the secret."

Alexa bit her bottom lip. "What do they want with me?"

"They were in the graveyard, hoping to capture you. Make you sterile, so you would be incapable of producing Warrior children. That's the Egesa Initiation. The Warrior Initiation is almost identical, except instead of making a person sterile, it prepares their body for breeding."

Alexa shuddered at the thought of going through what the woman on the slab had experienced at the hands of those vile creatures. They weren't sexy and sinfully hot, like—

She gave herself a mental shake. *Focus.* She had to stay focused. "Braden killed one of them." She rubbed her arms, suddenly chilled.

"Two, actually. One came back after you passed out. They thought that other woman was you. Until they spotted you in the shadows, I guess. They must have figured out then they had the wrong target and followed you home. I don't really know the complete details."

"Why go through the trouble of luring me to the cemetery? They could have just come to the house to begin with."

"They probably wanted to get you someplace where you couldn't get any help from neighbors or other passersby, someplace even the authorities don't normally patrol. After they missed you at the cemetery, they must have gotten desperate though. Time is running short."

"Short? Braden said something like not having time, too. I didn't realize he meant it literally."

"We can't stay on Earth much longer. If we do, we'll miss the entry point back to our star system."

"Which would mean what?"

"We'd be stuck here for several more months, and we don't have the necessary fuel to orbit our ship for that long. We've been in space too long and have regenerated our power to its limit. I'm assuming the same is true for the Marid ship, since they've probably been shadowing us the entire time."

"Okay." Alexa's head was spinning with more questions, and from trying to understand what answers she'd already received. She had the sudden urge to search every cubbyhole just to see if she was being set-up and taped for some new, weird television show. She could see it now, *Stupid Woman Convinced She's Part Alien*, Wednesday nights at 8:00pm. "So, I'm supposed to be some sort of breeder? Half-human and half-Xylon. Is that it?"

"Yes."

"Mmm hmm." If it weren't for everything that she'd already seen with her own two eyes... "How did you find me?"

"Braden found your mother through some careful research. That wasn't too hard. A few computer and database cross-references, along with the info we already had, produced a hit. But he couldn't find you, not your exact location. Lots of information, but no current address."

"I'm a photographer. I move around."

"Once you entered the city, he was able to track you through your implanted computer chip. It's short-range only, so it couldn't pick you up prior to your entering California."

"Chip? I have a chip. Where?" Alexa blew out a heavy breath of air. She felt like jumping into her rented car and driving until she was as far from Black Marble as she could get.

"It's in your brain, very small, very hard to detect, unless you've had an MRI. Implanted at birth. At least your father *did* see to that."

She sat stunned. Now every time she had a headache she'd wonder if it were normal or if her head was about to explode due to some malfunction. She also didn't like the idea that she was basically a tagged animal, even if the thing only had short-range capability. "Where is my father?" she asked, barely above a whisper.

"We don't know. I'm sorry."

Disappointment, then suspicion, flowed through her. "If he's really one of you, how can you not know?"

"He disappeared shortly after leaving Earth and returning to Xylon. The Council, our ruling Board, has sealed the information on his whereabouts. I don't know why."

"How come I've never heard about you people before? Why wouldn't my parents have told me? And can I have the journal, please." If it held the answers she so desperately needed, the book would settle everything, once and for all.

Leila gave her an indulgent smile. "I don't know what's in the journal. I'll have to clear it with Braden before I can give it to you. He did want you to know it was safe though." She slid the journal back into her jacket. "As far as your parents telling you... would you really expect them to? They obviously chose the human life for you to live, as opposed to bringing you to Xylon. And they moved you around enough to make you difficult to find, if we came looking. But we need you, Alexa. And all the women like you that we can locate. Not only to ensure the safety of Xylon, but also to make sure the Egesa can't spread their evil to other planets and systems. No more than they already have anyhow. Earth *is* one of those planets, Alexa. You should know that."

Earth might be in danger? Her stomach clenched at the possibility. "I'm not agreeing to anything," to say the least, "but if I did agree, then that would mean I'd have to have sex with Braden, Kam, and Erik in order to be initiated, so I can breed and have these Warrior children. Right? Do I have a grasp on the situation here?" How convenient for the men that the Initiation was sexual in nature. It didn't take a genius to figure out which gender had come up with the specifics for this rite.

"Braden will attempt to initiate you by himself. I'm not sure why he made that decision. It's not standard. But it's what he wants."

Alexa wasn't sure if she should be flattered or not. Though if it were only Braden... Geez! Was she actually considering this?

"And, yes, you do need to be initiated in order to breed with our men. A lot is riding on this, Alexa. We need you. The future of many free planets is in jeopardy. We need our numbers to remain strong, so we can continue to fight the Egesa."

This was all too much. However, if Leila was telling the truth, then a lot did rest on her decision.

"Would Braden be my husband then, or whatever you call it?"

"Breeder-mate." Leila wouldn't meet her eyes. "Yes."

She got the uncomfortable feeling that Leila wasn't telling her the exact truth with that answer. The woman looked too nervous, all of a sudden, sitting there, chewing on her thumbnail.

In their favor, these people hadn't hurt her, even when she had tried to hurt them. Braden had saved her, in fact. The circumstances were just all so strange and confusing that she wasn't sure what to do or believe. She needed more information. Anything to help her figure all this out. "Can you explain the ceremony?" Her voice lowered. "From what I know, it's very erotic."

"Yes," Leila answered, her gaze returning to Alexa, and her voice lowering in kind.

She stood and lifted a case that was leaning against the wall. Alexa hadn't even noticed it there. It looked a lot like the one Lizard-man carried. That did *not* calm her. Leila brought it back to the bed and pushed it open.

She took out what looked to Alexa like a clear, glass dildo with a tube encased inside, along with some wires. And she saw buttons located on the base.

"This is the first part of the rite. The tube contains a vaccine of sorts that will protect you from any diseases the other side might try to infect you with. The Egesa sexually transmit diseases, and they often inflict various poisons through torture techniques. It's how they sterilize or incapacitate their victims."

Alexa shuddered, thinking about the now-healed wounds to her breasts. What she'd experienced could have been a lot worse. "Those creatures did say they planned to make me sterile."

"It's one of the ways they're trying to extinguish our race. We can protect you from that. You'll be stimulated with the dildo, then when you orgasm, the fluid will be ejaculated into you. Your orgasm will pull in the medicine, so to speak, and your system will absorb it."

The dildo looked huge. She had to be kidding. "Um, can't the vaccine be administered through a shot or a pill?"

"This is an Ancient Rite, Alexa. It's a protection and bonding ceremony, full of tradition and very powerful. We're looking for alternate ways, but so far nothing has worked effectively."

"What if a person can't orgasm? Is that required?"

"Why do you ask?"

She shrugged. "I've...never had one." She averted her eyes when she felt her face heat at the admission.

"Never? Are you a virgin?"

"No." Though she might as well be. Her past relationships were, well, unexciting. "I've just never been able to do it."

"Hmm." Leila chewed at her thumbnail. "It might present a problem. I'll talk to Braden about it."

Alexa's gaze snapped to hers. "I haven't agreed."

Leila studied her a moment before answering. "Okay. I understand that." She set the dildo into the case and withdrew a much smaller dildo with feelers at the end. "Are you still willing to at least listen and consider what I say?"

Warily looking at the object in Leila's hand, Alexa hesitated, but then nodded. She might as well hear it all. It would buy her time to think, if nothing else.

"This is the second part of the rite. The tiny feelers are coated with the protective vaccine and inserted anally." She pulled on the base, and the feelers disappeared inside the dildo. Then she pushed, and the feelers re-emerged, shiny with liquid.

Alexa shivered. Oh, no way! "I've never done anything like that. I don't think I could." The understatement of the year. She should get a trophy for keeping her voice much calmer than she actually felt. Why would anyone agree to that sort of bodily invasion?

"Braden's very skilled. You wouldn't have to worry. He won't hurt you."

Alexa wondered if the woman's knowledge was first-hand. "Did he initiate you?" The thought of him initiating who knows how many women bothered her. It was such an intimate act. And did that mean he bred all of them, too? She didn't like that idea. Of course, being a man, he probably got off on it. Or was she judging him unfairly?

She tended not to give men the benefit of the doubt much. Because of caution or self-preservation, she wasn't sure. That's just the way she was. Maybe her mother's constant mistrust of the opposite sex rubbed off on her in her formative years. Or maybe she simply always knew, deep down, that she wanted a different sort of man.

Wait. No. Her thinking must be wrong. Because if he initiated Leila, then they'd be mates. Unless she lied about the mate part. Or unless they could have more than one mate, which kinda made sense, since normally three people performed an Initiation. This whole thing was so bizarre.

"What makes you think I'm a breeder?"

"Oh! I'm sorry. If that's an insult or something…"

"No, it's a compliment. I am a breeder, but unmated so far. And, no. He didn't initiate me. My ceremony was…different." She slapped the dildo back inside the case and slammed it closed.

Whoa! Distress and anger were clearly visible on Leila's face. Maybe Leila had feelings for Braden and *wanted* him to initiate her. Then didn't get her way. Why hadn't she produced children if she was a breeder and there was such a need? And if Leila went through the initiation, then how could she be unmated? Something was wrong somewhere. "You're lying."

Leila's head snapped up. "What?"

"You said that Braden would be my breeder-mate. If you're a breeder and went through the initiation, then you can't be unmated."

Leila stiffened, and Alexa swore she saw tears in the woman's eyes, before she got herself back under control.

"My situation is a special case. It has nothing to do with how yours will play out."

That's all Leila said, and it was obvious that's all she intended to say, much to Alexa's frustration. "Is that everything then? I mean, everything I need to know about *my* situation?" Alexa asked, though she really wanted to ask more about Leila's situation.

"Not quite. The third part of the rite is voluntary, but highly recommended. Your mother might still be with us if she'd gone through it, but she decided against the act. This last part will allow your body to heal spontaneously when injured in some manner. It's ninety percent effective."

"What is the third part?" It had to be worse than the first two for her mother to refuse it.

"It's, well…we don't know exactly where it originated, but male and female Warriors and breeders who have gone through all three parts contain this healing ability and can transfer it during an Initiation."

"Wait a minute. Men go through this, too. Just Warriors or also regular Xylon?"

"All breeders go through the ceremony. The ceremony for men is somewhat different, of course, given their anatomy. Warriors are the strongest breeders and produce the most children. Almost all Warriors are breeders. Not all breeders are Warriors."

Alexa fidgeted. For that to be true they *must* be allowed more than one mate, otherwise Braden wouldn't be available. She did not like the idea of multiple mates, and wondered who had initiated the man these people had chosen to initiate *her*. Or had Braden even gone through the ceremony before? He must have, or he wouldn't be able to perform the third part. She needed a damn handbook for all this stuff. "Who initiated Braden?"

"I don't know. Three women from what I've been told."

Well, duh. She could've figured that out. Unless... Something Leila said earlier came back to her. She had asked Braden if he wanted *her* to be part of some Alliance. And Erik's reaction seemed to suggest that Leila could be part of the Initiation. That would mean opposite sexes weren't necessarily paired up for the ceremony. If that were so, then they couldn't use this method to select breeder mates. A society so desperate for children would frown upon same-sexed partners as mates, she was certain. Perhaps Leila had lied to make her more comfortable with giving her body to a virtual stranger, an alien species. Or had she missed something somewhere?

"Um, the women ultimately chose other mates."

That caught Alexa's attention. "So, he's not mated?"

"No."

A surge of relief swept through her. She did believe Leila about that. The honesty shone in her eyes. She suddenly felt more energized. Not only because there weren't other women in Braden's life, but also because apparently women actually were given a choice in the matter. She needed to know more. "So how is that healing ability transferred?"

"Orally."

"Orally? By kissing, you mean?" More memories returned in a rush, and she knew the answer.

"No."

The woman in the cemetery on her hands and knees sucking the Egesa's cock played through Alexa's mind. "You mean I'd need to swallow Braden's semen, don't you?" she asked with a strangled voice. "I remember that from the cemetery."

"Yes. Some women can't handle it. Warrior semen, especially, is particularly thick and heavy. And for it to work, you need a large amount taken in a short period of time."

"It could be pumped into a glass and drank, right?" That sounded so unappealing she almost gagged. But, she'd never sucked a man's cock.

"No. Ingested directly is the only way. If it comes in contact with non-living tissue, the protective elements neutralize. It *is* your choice, Alexa."

*Her choice.* And if she chose not to do it? Any of it? "I'm just one woman out of who knows how many. You've made it seem like the future of your world, and mine, rests completely with me."

"Well, maybe not completely. But we can't afford to lose more women. We're in a desperate situation."

"It's a little hard to believe all this."

"I understand. But you can't deny what you've seen and experienced. And what would we gain by lying?"

"A cheap thrill?"

"It's a lot of work for a cheap thrill, Alexa."

That was true. And she had seen unexplainable things. How could she continue to doubt their words?

"Also, you should know, there's a *reaction* to being initiated."

She raised an eyebrow. A reaction. Any *reaction* couldn't be good. "What's that?"

"It's an uncontrollable sexual appetite, which is why three people generally form an Alliance. To be able to deal with it."

"I don't understand."

"You'll become sexually starved for several hours. You'll need sex repeatedly. If the appetite isn't satisfied, the imbalance in your brain waves will become so severe that the result could cause insanity or even death."

"Peachy." She hugged her arms around her middle. She'd always wanted to be more sexually aggressive. Somehow, this wasn't how she'd envisioned accomplishing that. So, for several hours she'd be some sex maniac. If she understood correctly, only Braden would be touching her, satisfying the hunger. She could think of worse fates. Still…

Something suddenly tugged at Alexa's mind. She gripped the padded armrests of the chair. A wave of nausea hit her, then faded. The room darkened. An orb of light grew, starting as a dot and expanding rapidly.

She saw another room as if from above. She blinked, but nothing changed. *She* was on a bed, naked. Her ass up, her head down. Braden was aggressively pumping his cock into her from behind. Oh, my!

Braden's face held a look of complete concentration and need. The erotic image pulled a moan from her throat.

She watched her mouth open in ecstasy. The pleasure on her face caught her attention and seemed to transfer directly to her body — the one looking down.

Braden grabbed her hips and thrust harder, faster, moving with such speed and force that the sound of their bodies slapping together echoed in her ears.

No man had ever taken her like that. So wild. She couldn't look away from his complete, sexual dominance of her. They were like pure, hot sin together.

Her breasts tingled. Her clit throbbed. Her whole body tightened. She was right on the edge, ready to tumble.

"Alexa? Alexa?"

Her vision cleared.

Leila stood and approached her, an odd look on her face. "Are you all right?"

"What?"

"Are you all right? You zoned out."

"Oh, sorry. I'm fine." Where the heck had that vision come from? Her body teetered on the edge of unfulfilled passion. She wanted to go back to the vision to see how it ended.

Leila placed a hand on her forehead. "You're strangely pale and cool."

Alexa laughed, but the sound held very little humor. "Considering the circumstances, I'm not surprised."

Leila took a small, flat panel out of a pocket in her jacket. "Can you raise your sweatshirt a little and let me put this against your skin? It won't hurt. It's just a medical monitor."

Alexa raised her shirt. Leila stuck the monitor against her skin. It looked like one of those flat night-lights, except with buttons along the bottom. The little machine clung to her flesh, but she felt no pain.

The monitor clicked and whirled, then beeped. Leila removed it and studied the display.

"Am I okay?"

Leila put away the monitor. "You're fine. Will you excuse me?"

"Of course."

Leila opened the door. "Kam. Can you come in and sit with her? I need to talk to Braden."

# Chapter Five

"So?" Braden approached Leila. Another moment and he'd have stormed the bedroom. He hadn't thought she was ever coming out. "Did Alexa agree to the Initiation?"

"Not yet."

A string of expletives exploded inside his head, and it took all his energy not to let them fly. The hope he'd held drained out of him, and he felt like collapsing from exhaustion right there on the beige and green area rug. With a sound of frustration, he scrubbed his hands over his face. "We don't have time for these delays."

"She didn't refuse."

"What's the problem then?" Erik barked from the sofa. "If she doesn't want Braden fucking her, I'll do her. But let's get on with it."

"Can't you even *pretend* to have some compassion?" Leila shot back with a snap.

Braden shook his head. "She's still scared. Unsure of our motives. Unsure of what to believe." He had to look at things from Alexa's point of view. He knew she must feel overwhelmed, rushed, and probably completely confused as to what was the right thing to do. "What can we do or say to convince her, Leila? Any ideas? A female perspective?"

"I don't know, Braden. It's a sensitive situation. You know it's not the same type of Xylon pre-initiation when we're dealing with another species. I don't think there's any clear-cut path that will ensure her agreement. However, I did run a test on her, and I made an interesting discovery."

"There's a plus," Erik replied in a sarcastic tone. "We're all ears, sweetheart. Spill it. Maybe it'll invite some *compassion*."

"What did you find?" Braden asked, ignoring Erik's comments. The man needed a definite attitude adjustment where Leila was concerned. He always turned cranky when she was around. A story lurked there somewhere. When he had more time, he wanted to explore it. As for now, Braden really hoped Leila's *interesting* discovery meant good news and not bad.

"She not only has the right DNA for a breeder, but she's a super breeder."

"Damn!" Erik surged up from the sofa. "You shittin' us?"

Braden couldn't find his voice. A super breeder? Unbelievable! He couldn't stand still. Not with news like that. Nervous energy forced him to pace, while Leila's words sank into his weary brain. "Neither of her parents were super breeders."

"I know. This is almost unheard of."

If Alexa was a super breeder, then that meant she'd bear twins or triplets at each birth. Super breeders were so rare that maybe only one in fifty million women attained that status. "Are you sure, Leila?" He heard the excitement in his own voice.

"Yes, I'm sure." Leila placed a hand on his arm. "I think she does want to help us, if she's handled correctly. The sexual aspect of the Initiation is what makes her uncomfortable, for the most part. I kind of led her astray a little and told her you'd be breeder-mates."

"Leila, you know that's not true. Not unless I can arrange it."

"I know. But being from Earth, I thought she might feel better believing there was some sort of commitment in this. She…" Leila glanced over her shoulder at Erik, then looked back at Braden and lowered her voice. "She's never had an orgasm."

"I heard that," Erik replied. "She wouldn't have a problem with me. I'd give her all she could handle."

"Shut up!" Braden and Leila shouted at the same time.

"I don't think she has that much sexual experience, Braden. This is all alien to her, literally. You can imagine her reaction to the ceremony. Talk to her. She's better prepared now. I think she'll listen. Just be nice…and charming. And hopefully, she'll respond."

"Charming?" He sighed, then nodded. "Okay. Fine. I can do charming." He paused and rubbed his chin. "I think." Braden turned to stare at the closed bedroom door. His heart pounded so hard he thought it would burst from his chest. A super breeder.

Somehow, someway, he'd arrange it with Laszlo to make sure he didn't take Alexa as a mate. *He* wanted her. Needed her. His own mother had been a super breeder, and he knew they had very special, sexual needs. He refused to let another man fulfill those needs for Alexa. He considered her to be his and his alone now. Leila was right.

This ceremony *should* be a commitment. For him and Alexa, that's exactly what it would be.

A thought struck him. And it made sense. Laszlo somehow knew. That's the reason the man chose him to research and track Alexa. It would be too much of a coincidence otherwise, and he'd never much believed in coincidences—not of this magnitude. With his own latent super breeder genes, he and Alexa could produce more powerful Warriors than Xylon had seen in generations. Plus the odds of passing on the super breeder genes to at least one of their children were quite high.

As soon as he could, he was going to set-up a meeting with Laszlo and get things settled. Given the circumstances, The Council would surely revise their decision and officially allow Alexa to be *his*.

He started toward the bedroom. "Stick around, you two, okay? And try not to kill each other."

Erik grunted.

Without bothering to knock, Braden opened the door and stepped inside the bedroom. He stopped short. Kam was holding Alexa in his arms. Her face rested against his friend's chest, and her eyes were half-closed. Kam caressed her hair, and she looked totally at peace. Both blonde, both blue-eyed, both with skin tones so much alike. They looked good together. Too good. Like a perfect, freakin' match. Jealousy shot through him, right to the core.

Kam glanced toward the door. He gently untangled Alexa from his arms. "It's not how it looks, Braden."

"Oh?"

Alexa's gaze swung from him to Kam and back again. When he stalked forward, she met him halfway, a determined look on her face. She pushed her palms flat against his chest, stopping him. "You'd better not be planning to hurt him. He was helping me."

"Of that I'm sure." It took all his restraint not to grab her, toss her on the bed, strip her bare, and plunge deep into her pussy right there in front of Kam. Just to show the man that Alexa was his.

"I'm going to join the others," Kam said. "I'll get us some food. None of us have eaten today."

"Kam?" he called.

"Yeah?"

"Alexa's a super breeder. Leila tested her." In case his friend had any ideas about making a play for Alexa, he wanted the man to know that he'd have a fight on his hands.

Kam's gaze drifted to Alexa, then back to Braden. One side of his mouth quirked up into a grin. "That's great news." After a last look in Alexa's direction, Kam made his exit.

Braden remained quiet until the door closed him and Alexa into the room alone. Kam's casual response to the news confounded him. He didn't think he'd ever understand the way that man's mind worked.

"Why the sudden change?" he finally asked, turning toward Alexa. She'd stepped back, but still stood close enough for him to touch if he wanted. And he definitely wanted.

"Change?"

She crossed her arms under her breasts. He'd seen her do that in the cemetery. Was she chilled or was that a sign of some other source of discomfort? Not fear certainly, but something else. He saw it in her eyes. He just wasn't sure what *it* was.

"Your fear is gone." He had to state it, to be certain.

"Not…completely. Kam just helped me go over everything. He's very understanding. He shared secrets with me." She stared at the closed door.

Braden wondered at the look in her eyes. Kam had calmed her. That was obvious. But his friend had apparently also disturbed her in some way. He could see that, too, in her eyes. She wasn't very good at hiding emotions. He didn't like the sound of secrets though. He didn't want her bonding with any other man through confidences he wasn't privy to. "What secrets?"

Her gaze returned to his, and she smiled slightly. "If I told you, they wouldn't be secrets."

Jealousy warred with relief inside him. She was definitely more at ease, but still, he wanted details. She apparently intended to offer none. "So, you're ready to be initiated then?" he asked in a sharper tone than intended.

Her spine stiffened. "I didn't say that."

"Then what are you saying?" He knew he sounded impatient. He couldn't control it. He needed her. Now. He saw the suppressed passion in her, and wanted to set it loose. Her body, curvy in all the right places, turned him hard as steel. Her full mouth called to his baser instincts, urging him to take that mouth with his, then in return have her taste his body, his cock, drawing deep until he filled her with his essence. He practically groaned at the thought.

Above it all—even the sexual element—Alexa was a strong woman. He needed a strong woman in his life. And they all needed her to continue the species. Now more than ever.

She tilted her head and hugged her middle tighter. "What's a super-breeder?"

She was stalling again, dragging this out, instead of addressing the issue at hand. Certainly, she wouldn't refuse the Initiation, knowing how much her participation meant to Xylon. And if she did intend to refuse, or refuse *him*, he wished she'd just do so. Then he would know where they stood. "A super breeder means that you can get with child easily and will bear more than one with each birth." He tried to make his explanation sound as casual as possible. He didn't want his growing feelings of urgency, possessiveness, and lust to cause her fear to re-surface.

"A regular baby-making machine, huh?"

He raised an eyebrow at her irritated tone.

"Well, what do you expect, Braden?" She relaxed her arms to her sides. "A bunch of strangers show up and tell me I need to let some man do all sorts of sexual things to me. That I'm supposed to pop out a herd of children. And if I refuse, life on your world, and possibly mine, changes forever."

"It's not that simplistic. You'll be claiming your heritage, your place in *our* society. It's a great honor. And, yes, you'll be saving a way of life at the same time."

"Whether I want to or not."

"I already told you that you wouldn't be forced." If their system entry point wasn't approaching, and if they had more reserve fuel, they could remain on Earth longer and take plenty of time to acclimate her to their ways. Alexa had a more pivotal role than most breeders, which made her submission a must. Somehow, he had to convince her.

"Not physically forced maybe. But mentally I feel like I have no choice. How can I really refuse? If I do, then I find out everything I've been told is true, and worlds end up destroyed, I'd have to wonder whether I was at least part of the reason it happened."

Braden shrugged. "Then agree, and you won't have to wonder. I can't change the situation, Alexa. It is what it is. I've done all I can to make it easier for you."

Alexa didn't respond. She simply stared at him.

He'd try another avenue. "What do you want? Kam and Leila must have calmed you enough to get you this far. What can I do to get you the rest of the way?"

"To give my body to a stranger? Allow him, you, to do things to me that I've never allowed another man to do. To agree to bear children I'm not even sure I want."

"I'm sorry. That's the way it is. If it makes you feel any better, the Initiation won't get you pregnant. That doesn't come until later. You'll have time to adjust." Agony at the possibility shot through him, but he had to ask. "Would you rather Kam initiate you?"

"No!"

Her immediate response, and wide-eyed look, took him aback. She almost seemed panicked. "Okay," he answered, slowly drawing out the word. "Then what's holding you back? I won't hurt you. And I'll make it as enjoyable for you as I can."

Alexa laughed, but her voice held little humor. "Yeah. That's what men always say when it comes to sex, isn't it?"

A distracted look crossed her face, as if she was remembering something, and her skin flushed. Interesting. Maybe it really wasn't *him* that caused her hesitation; maybe it was the sex as Leila had said.

He wondered how many men Alexa had been with. And what kind of idiots they were to have turned this beautiful woman off the idea of sex. He didn't know what to do anymore. He just knew that this was not going well. He raised his hand, needing to caress Alexa's cheek, only wanting one soft touch. To calm himself. And show her that he did care.

He sensed, rather than heard, the breath she sucked in when she realized his intent. Her eyes dilated, and he saw something new. Interest? Or maybe that was just wishful thinking on his part.

A knock interrupted him, before he made contact. Braden lowered his hand, and frustration surged through him. He stalked over to jerk open the door. "What?"

"Sorry." Kam wedged a picnic basket into the crack in the door. "Leila already had this started. You and Alexa need to eat."

Braden opened the door wider and took the basket. "Thanks," he said, but his voice still held an edge. He lowered his tone. "Any advice? She's not responding well."

"Show her your feelings. She just needs to know that she can trust you, Braden." He grinned. "She *is* sexually and emotionally attracted to you. She told me that when I spoke to her about you."

Braden's heart leapt in his chest. Now that was information he could use. Maybe he had seen interest in her eyes, after all. "Thanks, Kam." Braden closed the door and turned, basket in hand. Be charming, Leila had said. Okay. A smile tugged at his lips. "Food."

"I'm not hungry." Alexa's stomach growled in response, loud enough for him to hear. She crossed her arms over her middle, and a blush crept up her neck.

"You're such a bad liar." He set the basket on the bed and almost laughed at the wary look on her face. "Why don't you sit down on the other side, get comfortable, and we'll have a picnic."

She stared at the basket as if expecting a poisonous asp to emerge. "You want to have a picnic? Now?" Her gaze snapped up to his. "Have you gone completely mad?"

\* \* \* \* \*

Kam snatched up the bag of potato chips sitting next to the prepared food and made himself comfortable in one of the plush living room chairs. The bag crackled as he ripped it open and reached in for a chip.

He hoped Braden didn't blow his chance with Alexa. If he did, someone else would need to step up and try to initiate her. *He* couldn't do it. And he doubted she'd accept Erik. They'd have to contact Laszlo. He really didn't want to go that route. With the limited amount of time they had, the situation could escalate into something ugly and get out of control.

"What are the chances of Alexa getting screwed anytime soon?"

Kam glared at Erik. "Just eat. Braden will handle it."

Erik grabbed a ham sandwich from the plastic tray on the coffee table, then flopped on the couch. He licked some mayonnaise off his thumb. "Well, if Braden wants us here until after the Initiation, we've got a lot of time to burn for just sitting around." His gaze shifted to Leila, who was relaxed in a cushioned chair across from him, her legs tucked up under her. A sly smile crossed his face. "How about some strip poker? I saw it on an Earth satellite feed, and it looked fun."

"Geez," she replied with a scowl, then crunched down on a sour pickle. "Is sex all you ever think about?"

Kam studied his friend. Something was eating away at Erik. Each year he became more and more uncivilized and moved closer to the edge of self-destruction. He might just tumble over if someone didn't pull him back.

"Who said anything about sex? Naked and sex are not the same." Erik bit into the sandwich. "Of course, if that's what *you* want, I'm sure that Kam and I can—"

"Me! You live for sex. I don't think anything else is important to you."

He took another bite of ham. "Food. It's a very close second. Ever had food sex? Cocoa-covered tits, topped with berry-berry cream, and a thick syrupy-coated pussy, are real delicacies. Ever tried it? It's a lot better than this crap they call food on Earth."

"Please." Leila shuddered. "Give it a rest, will you. You're making me ill. Besides, you seem to be downing that sandwich pretty well, for something you consider crap."

Kam shoved a chip into his mouth. Erik needed to eat more and speak less, before Leila popped him.

"I need energy. And you're not fooling me, Leila. I've heard the sex stories about you in The Lair. I know you love it rough."

She fell silent, and pain briefly flickered in her eyes.

When she remained silent, Kam wondered at her reaction. It wasn't like Leila to back down so easily. He wasn't sure what sex stories Erik was referring to. He'd never heard anything about Leila. Erik might just be yanking her chain and trying to get a rise out of her.

Leila sucked on the end of the pickle until Erik laughed lustily. She scowled and then ate the piece in two quick bites.

"Ouch," Erik replied. A huge grin remained on his face. When she stuck her tongue out at him, he slapped his hand over his heart. "Is that an invitation to lick and make it better? Please tell me it is."

Kam watched their exchange with interest. Anger, desire, frustration, longing. He didn't need his sensor to see the emotions flying between the two. A beep drew his attention. He picked up the detector he'd set on the table.

"Anything wrong, Kam?" Leila asked, leaning forward to grab a napkin.

He set the bag of chips on the floor. "We're not alone, guys."

Erik swallowed. He tossed the rest of his sandwich on the tray. "Where? And how many?"

"Um…one. Doesn't seem to be Egesa, but I can't be sure. The readings are strange. Something's causing interference. He's…moving around the house, back to front. Trying to scope out how many of us are in here would be my guess."

Erik surged to his feet, a mask of seriousness on his face. "I'll slip out the back door and circle around."

# Chapter Six

Erik pulled the cream-colored, slatted shade away from the back door window just enough to peek outside. He didn't see any movement, except for one black bird searching for worms around the base of an elm tree.

He'd bet the intruder was one of Daegal's highbred assassins — a former Xylon Warrior turned and now serving on Marid. Egesa usually only ventured out under cover of darkness when off-planet, the lowly cowards.

He turned the knob and cracked open the door. The lone bird lifted its head, hopped away from the tree, then flew off toward the adjoining empty lot.

No other motion caught Erik's eye. Seeing nothing out of the ordinary, he slipped out, staying pressed close against the house. His heart thudded, and his pulse raced. The thrill of the chase always excited him. Hunting ran very close to sex and food in his book.

With luck, he'd be able to take out this spy quickly and efficiently. The closer Alexa's Initiation got, the more attacks Daegal would likely order. They'd have to stay sharp. If Daegal's people got their hands on Alexa, they'd sterilize her, then bond her as a sex slave for the Egesa to play with. Death would probably be preferable for her. He followed the line of the house and turned the corner around the side. Still nothing.

He stopped and listened. No wind to cover any sounds. He heard birds. Cars in the distance. An airplane overhead. Nothing much else. He continued forward and turned the corner to the front of the house.

Movement! There he was, the intruder, peeking into the front, bay window. Wait. There *she* was. Damn. A woman. Definitely not Egesa. She held herself like a Warrior. He recognized the stance. Not one of theirs though. She hadn't been on the Xylon ship. He knew that. She must be a Marid assassin, as he'd originally thought.

She slid into a crouch beneath the window and took a vid-cell off her belt. She seemed about average height, too skinny for his tastes, and he never much cared for short hair on a woman either, which she had.

He aimed his disruptor and the cell disintegrated right in her hands. He didn't have a Class 1 ranking for nothing.

Her mouth gaped open as she stared at her empty fingers. Her head snapped in his direction. When their eyes connected, she bolted to her feet.

He pointed his disruptor. "Drop your weapon and your transport-connector to the ground."

She slowly did as ordered.

This would be easier than he thought.

After discarding the instruments, her eyes darted from side to side, as if trying to figure out her next move. Her short, black hair framed her face in such a way that made her look so vulnerable. He almost felt sorry for her.

"Don't bother running, if you were considering it." He drew nearer, moving only a few inches at a time. "I'd be on you within five paces."

She assumed a fighting stance.

"Ooo, now I'm scared." He re-attached the disruptor to his belt and mirrored her wide-stance, hands in a defensive position between their bodies. He cocked an eyebrow, wondering why she hadn't spoken yet. He had to admire that. Someone who could hold her tongue. That was something he never had much success at. She was either scared to death or highly trained not to reveal any information or weaknesses. "It's your move."

She kicked out, aiming for his side.

He easily sidestepped the blow. He needed the physical release. Hand-to-hand was becoming a lost art. No sense in passing up an opportunity to work out the body. "You gotta do better than that."

She punched forward with her fist, connecting with his jaw this time.

He flew backward and pain wracked his frame. He hit the ground with a thud. "What the hell?" he muttered, following the curse with a groan. His whole body tingled. It took him a moment to clear his head and figure out what had happened. "Damn. I don't believe it." After disarming her, he hadn't thought he'd needed to keep his shield activated. But then, the field only stopped non-living tissue, like a bullet or disruptor beam, so his shield wouldn't really have helped anyway. She hadn't transferred her power along the airwaves.

At that moment, Kam rounded the opposite corner in a rush. The woman immediately spun toward him, ready to fight. He skidded to a halt, his gaze targeting first her, then Erik, and back to her again.

Erik raised himself onto his elbows. "Careful, Kam. She's wired for electrical transfer." The current she'd hit him with still sizzled through his body.

Cautiously, Kam took a step backward. "That must be the interference I'm getting." He glanced down at his hand-held sensor. "It shows she's scared."

The woman visibly stiffened.

Erik pushed to his feet. "Could've fooled me." After that blow, he'd have assumed she was highly trained and not one bit afraid of combat.

She glanced back and forth between the two men.

"We're not going to hurt you," Kam told her in a soothing voice.

"Speak for yourself," Erik muttered, scanning their surroundings for something to incapacitate her with. His disruptor wouldn't penetrate her wire-grid. He'd need a surge-rifle, and they hadn't brought one down from the ship with them.

"Who are you?" Kam asked.

He received no answer.

"Hey, sweetheart. Look over here," Erik called, drawing her attention. "Kam, back up. Now."

She turned just as Erik threw a flowerpot in her direction. She raised her arm to block the clay planter. It hit her forearm and exploded. Sparks flew, and the air crackled. A loud pop split the air. She screamed and stumbled backwards.

"Dammit, Erik!" Kam yelled, reaching for the porch railing to steady himself. "What the hell was that?"

"I hid an energy ball in the dirt, so she wouldn't know it was coming. I figured she wouldn't dive and roll from a pot."

"An energy ball? You could have killed her…and me, too."

Distracted by their argument and the shock wave, the woman's guard dropped. Erik saw the opening and grabbed her from behind, binding her arms to her sides. "It was low-grade, at best. And it neutralized her electrical field. You're too soft, man. This bitch will kill any one of us at the first opportunity."

She struggled against Erik's hold. He shifted to trap her legs between his. When she was unable to get free or land any effective blows with her hands and feet, she gave a sigh of defeat and relaxed in his arms.

Erik was too smart to think she'd willingly surrendered and knew her fight wasn't over, so he didn't relax his hold. Too bad that ball was low frequency. "It would have been a lot easier, if she'd been rendered unconscious."

Stepping forward, Kam grabbed one of her legs, then the other, and lifted. He opened the front door. "And a lot more complicated, if she'd been killed. She doesn't have a jacket shield like we do." He led the way inside. "We can do this without hurting her."

"Hey, don't make it sound like I enjoy hurting women. I don't." Erik kicked the door closed behind them. "But I know the risks."

"And I don't?"

Leila met them inside the entry. "A Warrior?"

"Not anymore," Erik answered. "Be careful. She's tougher than she looks." He wondered why she wasn't struggling more. Maybe she thought she could acquire additional information from the inside. Fine. Let her. The knowledge wouldn't do her any good. She wasn't going anywhere and wouldn't be able to pass anything along that she found out.

"Bring her into the spare bedroom. It has a wrought-iron headboard and footboard we can secure her to. I noticed it earlier."

"My kind of bed." Erik chuckled. "I bet she'll talk once she's bound and spread-eagle."

"Maybe she can't talk," Kam responded. "She's been quiet, so far. Except for the scream."

"I'll check it out." Leila led the way to the bedroom. "In here."

When Leila pulled out restraints, Erik was barely able to stop himself from making a sexual comment, but decided against it at the last minute. None of them could afford to get distracted right now.

He stood staring down at the tied-up woman, while Leila checked her over with a medical monitor. Leila's round ass caught his attention as she leaned over the woman. He'd love to get *her* bound and spread-eagle. At his sexual mercy. One of these days...

"Nothing wrong with her that I can find." Leila put away the monitor. "She should be able to talk."

Erik leaned over the bound female. "Who are you?" he demanded.

She raised her head, and he leaned closer. She looked prepared to talk. She had to know she was defeated. Better for her to cooperate.

"Well?"

She spit in his face.

He jerked back. "Son of a bitch!" He wiped his cheek.

"What's your monitor show, Kam?" Leila asked.

"Nothing. Her electrical field must have shut it down. I'll need to fix it." He rubbed his temple.

Leila's easy gaze turned to concern. "Are you all right?"

"Yeah. I think I got a stray jolt when Erik tossed an energy ball at her. I was shielded, but still too close. I'm going back into the living room and sit down for a while."

"You want me to check you over."

"No. I'll be fine."

A surge of worry struck Erik. He should have been more careful, and made sure Kam was well back before trying to kill her electrical set-up.

After Kam left, he turned to stare at the captured female. "Leave us, Leila. I'll find out who she is and what she's doing here. Her disruptor and transport-connector are out front. Secure those. We don't need some stranger or child coming across them."

Visible fear crossed the woman's face. Good. Fear worked for him.

Leila touched his arm. "No. Let's leave her for now. She's not going anywhere. Let her think about things. She might be willing to tell us what we want once her arms and legs get numb and her body starts to protest."

"I'll make her body protest now." Let's see what she'd make of that statement. Put some real fear into her. He rubbed his palms together for added effect.

Leila tugged on his arm. "No you won't. Now stop pretending you're such a hard-ass. Come on."

* * * * *

Alexa popped a grape into her mouth. She watched Braden's throat work as he drank deeply from a bottle of water. Somehow, the action seemed very erotic to her.

She had to make a decision, and quickly.

Before Kam dropped his bombshell, her decision might have been different. Everything they'd said was so outrageous. Their words were at least partially true. She'd seen that for herself. But now, after what Kam revealed, she believed it all, and actually felt the need to help. How could she not?

"Where would I have to be initiated? Would we need to do it immediately?"

Braden spewed water over himself. He coughed to clear his lungs. "You're saying yes?" he rasped out.

"Maybe."

"Most initiations are performed on Xylon in The Lair, but we need to get you protected as soon as possible. We prefer to do off-world rites either on-ship, or we can do it here, if that's more comfortable for you. I, um, kind of already planned it that way actually, if you agree." He wiped the water from his chin. "It'll be okay, Alexa. Really. Like a date...sort of. Or a fantasy. Anything you want."

The eager look in his eyes and sound of his voice drew her in and made her feel all soft inside. She liked the fantasy of believing it meant more to him than just something for 'the cause.'

"Yes. I'd rather do it here than on some ship." So, she'd decided. If she didn't agree and something horrible happened because of her, she'd never be able to live with herself. There was one last item though. She hadn't asked about it again, because she'd been afraid it would confirm everything they said. But now that she had made her decision, she needed that last piece to fall into place. Just to be absolutely sure. "I want to read my mother's journal, Braden, before we do this."

Braden cleared the bed of the food and other picnic items in record time. Then he just stood there, staring down at her, apparently still in shock by her decision. "Of course. I'll get it for you."

Alexa drew her knees up to her chest and wrapped her arms around her legs. Even though Kam had tried to reassure her, Braden was still a stranger. She felt self-conscious about having sex with him. But also intrigued, especially since having that vision. He was such a powerful and sexy man. She watched him leave the room, admiring his tight ass.

This might work out better than she thought. Leila went through the Initiation but remained unmated, so she figured that if she wanted to, she could do likewise. Go through the Initiation, then refuse to bear children, if she decided enough was enough. *She* would ultimately choose her future. Not anyone else.

Braden returned in record time, probably still not comfortable with leaving her alone. "Here it is. I'll sit over there in the chair while you read."

She nodded and opened the journal to the first page.

Page after page, she read. All about how her mother was initiated by two women and one man—oh, ick. How the man, her father, a Warrior from Xylon, had later gotten her pregnant. Her mother's belief and fear that the Xylon aliens would take Alexa.

In the journal, drawings of Xylon and five moons filled several pages. The images just like in Alexa's dreams. Finally, passages appeared about her mother's inability to handle what her father was. She'd suspected he had another mate elsewhere, probably on Xylon. The stress of that belief had affected their relationship so adversely that eventually he left, and she never saw him again.

Additional pages held specifics to various ceremonies and life on Xylon. Those she skimmed, planning to re-read them in more detail later. But she found out what she needed to know. Alexa closed the journal. She ran her hand along the front cover and took in a large breath. "Okay. Let's do this."

"Are you sure, Alexa?"

His softly spoken question touched something inside her. She could see the caring in his eyes, and an unfamiliar excitement started to build in her. Desire? "You'll...you'll help me through, right?" Stupid question. He was as excited as a man with a new gadget to get on with it. She could see that. Men always seemed ready to make love. No. This wasn't making love. It was fucking—damn, she really hated that term sometimes. It was sex. Just sex. No matter what Leila had tried to convince her of, she knew the truth now, and was willing to deal with it and the consequences of her decision.

Her life was about to change in so many ways. But she couldn't turn her back and simply walk away. Not with a clear conscience. And

Braden was the first man in her life that she really felt attracted to and excited about. She didn't want to lose that. Or what might be...

"I'll be right there with you, Alexa, every step of the way."

* * * * *

The woman looked up at her bound hands, then down at her bound ankles. She stared at the closed bedroom door.

Two men—both Warriors. One woman—a Healer, maybe a Warrior, too. She didn't know. Three. The right number for an Initiation. She knew Alexa was in the house somewhere, waiting for the ceremony to begin. She doubted the rite had taken place yet, otherwise they'd have been dealing with Alexa's sexual appetite and never would have noticed *her* presence.

There was still time to stop this.

She pulled at her hand bindings. Too tight to work loose. She had to get out of there and back to the Marid ship. Tell them what she had found.

The Healer would be easy for the Egesa to defeat, Warrior or not. She was delicate-looking and couldn't be that strong. The two male Warriors would be harder to bring down, but it was do-able with the right force and element of surprise. Then Alexa would belong to Daegal to do with as he pleased. And *she* would have paid her debt to The Dome of Marid.

She twisted her foot, trying to loosen one of the ankle ties. She just needed enough leeway to—

A light knock sounded at the door. It cracked open a couple of inches, then a couple of more. Kam, she thought his name was, stepped inside. She was surprised that he'd come back. This time, she wouldn't blow the opportunity.

He stood there staring down at her, a confused look on his face. If she played the pathetic female, maybe he'd unwittingly help her out.

"Are you all right?"

She shook her head, then pointedly looked down at her ankle.

He bent to examine the skin. "You've rubbed it raw." He glanced up at her. "Can you speak? You don't have to. I'd just like to know if you can."

Knowing better than to get distracted by his pretense of caring, she ignored the question. Forcing out a couple of tears, she tried to look and feel shaken, which wasn't difficult, given the circumstances. He might even think *that* was an answer of sorts to his inquiry and feel sorry for her.

His fingers hovered over her ankle. Then he pulled at the tie. "I'll loosen it a little, but I won't take it off. Don't rub against the other restraints. I can't help you any more than this."

* * * * *

Erik glanced toward the closed bedroom door, where Kam had gone to check on the woman. He and Leila had tried to stop him. The man still looked pale. But Kam always worried more about others than himself and insisted on looking in on her.

Clearing his mind of his friend, he instead gave the woman, who so frustrated and fascinated him, his full attention. He needed the distraction. "Hard-ass?"

Leila shrugged. "I thought the word fit."

He crowded against her until her back bumped against the wall. "It does. And it's not pretend, sweetheart." His lips brushed hers when he spoke. "I am a hard-ass. And I don't like being ordered around by a woman." A smirk touched his lips. "Unless she's ordering me to fuck her harder. I'm always willing to comply in that situation."

"That's not funny."

"It wasn't meant to be."

Leila turned her head, no longer meeting his eyes. "Back off, Erik."

He saw the pulse beating rapidly at the base of her throat. His beat just as hard. "No."

Her gaze snapped back to his. "What?"

"You heard me." Her shocked expression was exactly the reaction he had expected and hoped for. He was pushing her. On purpose. But he didn't care. Or maybe he cared too much. He stroked the length of her brown hair, so long. Visions of that hair tangled in his fists with him pumping into her hot, wet pussy had him hard in a flash. He pressed closer, so she'd feel her effect on him.

At the pressure of his body, she bit down on her bottom lip, then released it. "If you don't back off, I'll—"

"What?" Erik glanced over his shoulder, hoping Kam would stay put for the moment. He turned back and cocked an eyebrow at her. "What are you going to do?"

She went completely still. Somewhere nearby the ticking of a clock counted off the seconds. Leila tilted her head, then reached up and caressed his cheek.

It was absolutely the last thing he expected of her. He jumped back as if she'd burned him with her touch. He wanted her submission, her desire, even anger or outrage was fine. Tenderness or compassion was the last thing he wanted. From any woman. "Forget it." He turned and flipped on the television. "I wonder if Alexa gets NNN," he muttered.

Several silent moments passed before she spoke. "NNN?"

Surfing the channels at record speed, he didn't even spare her a glance. He didn't dare. He was afraid of what he'd see in her eyes...and how he'd react. "The National Naked Network. It's the only thing on this damn planet worth watching."

* * * * *

She studied Kam as he stared out the bedroom window, lost in thought. *Good. Stay that way.*

With small movements of her foot against the mattress, she slowly worked her shoe off, and in the process, loosened the tie until it gave way. She'd learned the little escape trick from a long-dead companion, but it came in handy from time to time. Now she'd be able to get out of there.

She tried to push the shoe over the edge of the bed to draw his attention, but it stuck in the footboard. She made a whimpering noise instead—something small and pathetic, helpless sounding, until Kam finally turned toward her.

"What?" He sat down beside her. "Damn, you got the tie off." He frowned and reached for the restraint.

She scissored her leg up and over, aiming for his face with her foot.

Kam grabbed her leg. His fingers curled tightly around the material of her pants.

Damn the man!

He bent her leg to a comfortable position, and his features hardened. "How stupid do you think I am?"

Apparently not as stupid as she had hoped. But she wasn't stupid either. She still had a plan.

"I don't like my kindness being repaid by an attack."

*Too bad. Poor baby.* She completely relaxed her muscles. When she felt his grip ease a little, she jerked her leg back and kicked forward hard, catching him in the frontal lobe. This time she didn't underestimate him or hold back.

Kam shot to his feet. He grabbed his head and staggered to the door. Without a word, he slipped to his knees and toppled over backward.

She tapped her foot against the other ankle restraint. A spark flew, and the tie fell off. The energy ball had neutralized the main electrical current wired into her clothing and set up for body-to-body transfer on forceful contact, but she still had enough residual current left for a minor spark or two. It wouldn't work through her rubber-soled shoe though, so she'd had to get that off first.

When she had kicked Kam, thankfully, he'd gotten enough of a jolt to make him fall. She hadn't transferred the first time, hoping to be able to knock him out without using what precious little current she had left. But he'd surprised her with his agility and strength. He was only a Class 2 Warrior from the markings on his jacket. She had been a Class 1, before betraying her people. A quick glance at the man showed he was definitely out, but she didn't know how long it would last.

Thank goodness, she was limber. She kicked her leg over her head and took care of one hand restraint with another spark, then tugged loose the other. Now she was completely out of current and basically helpless. She'd have to rely on her wits from here on out.

She sat up and quickly put her shoe back on. She didn't have her transport-connector or vid-cell. She couldn't get out through the window. She'd make too much noise, and it would take too long to get the screen off. She couldn't sneak through the house unnoticed.

Desperation had her reaching for her only escape. Kam's transport-connector. She also lifted his disruptor. She might need that. She fiddled with the connector readings. Both ships were in transport range now, but his control wouldn't open the shield cloaking the Marid ship from Earth's detection.

She couldn't stowaway on the Xylon ship. They'd be monitoring the air movements too closely and had probably placed her on Xylon's most-wanted list by now. So she couldn't even materialize aboard and pretend she was a stranded Warrior who needed help. There *was* a Marid sub-station in the city — right near the cemetery. She'd materialize there.

If she didn't complete this mission, she was dead.

# Chapter Seven

Braden tugged off the covers on the unmade bed to reveal cream-colored flannel sheets topped with slightly darker-covered pillows. The lighter color reminded him of Alexa's skin. The darker, the color around her nipples. His cock immediately hardened.

*Hold it together, man.* His fingers were actually shaking. He couldn't remember the last time he'd been this excited around a woman. He felt like a young man about to get his first lay.

He set the Initiation case on the padded bench at the end of the bed and opened it up. Everything looked to be there. He snapped off one of the night-table lamps to dim the lighting. The overcast sky outside helped add to the intimacy.

Alexa's nervousness filled the room as she paced behind him. "Should I lock the door?" she asked.

"No. That's not necessary." He didn't say, for fear of making her more nervous, but he and Alexa needed to remain accessible in case any Egesa decided to materialize. They might need help from the others. With so many Warriors around, the creatures probably wouldn't chance it, but Egesa were unpredictable.

He drew a deep breath and rubbed his palms together. His hands felt like all the blood and heat had drained out of them. Why did he feel so awkward? He'd initiated many women. He'd just never initiated one alone. And certainly never one whom he wanted to take as mate. That upped the seriousness of the ceremony.

He still needed Kam and Erik for backup in case he couldn't handle Alexa's sexual appetite himself. He seethed at the thought of them touching her. Images of their hands and mouths exploring and pleasuring her body filled his brain.

Earlier, he'd spoken to Leila about his concerns, and she agreed to make the decision if it came down to it. As a Healer, she'd be able to tell if Alexa needed more sexual satisfaction than he could supply. Even so, he'd left specific instructions about what they could and couldn't do to Alexa's body.

"Can you hurry it up?" she snapped, then lowered her voice. "Sorry."

Her words brought him out of his thoughts. A woman doing what she believed was her duty, was his first thought. He hoped that wasn't the case, and it was just that she was filled with as much nervousness as he was. "It's all right, Alexa. Relax." He needed to heed those words himself. On his part, the nerves weren't based on not knowing if this was the right thing to do, but on his anxiety that he might not be able to make it an orgasmic experience for her. He wanted her to want this, want him. He certainly wanted her, with a fierceness he'd never known. He would use all his sexual skills to bring her the greatest pleasures, so she wouldn't regret what was about to happen.

He wasn't going to conduct this ceremony like some cold, impersonal rite. And he'd be damned if that's how she ended up remembering it. He turned and sat down on the side of the bed. "Come here, Alexa."

Tentatively, she approached him. "Do you want me to take off my clothes now?" Her gaze settled somewhere along his shoulder and stayed there.

The question contained no enthusiasm. She seemed lost in her own thoughts. Kam's words gave him hope. Sexually and emotionally attracted to him, the man said. He kept those words close to his heart. She was just nervous. That's all. Even though she'd agreed to the Initiation, she still had to be wary. And he understood that. It was time to take control. As soon as he touched her, everything would be okay. If not, he'd back off and find an alternate plan. "Look at me." His voice came out low, husky.

She raised her gaze to lock with his, and tangled her fingers together. She looked a little pale. He wanted to take her in his arms, hold her tight, and tell her everything would be all right. Except that would be putting too much emotion on the line. And emotions weren't something he dealt with well, not his own anyhow.

"You will do everything I say. Understand?"

Silence greeted his question. She pulled some more on her fingers, interlacing and releasing them.

"Alexa…it's necessary. I promise you will feel only pleasure. You need to let go of whatever is holding you back and trust me. Can you do that? If not, we need to stop this right now."

"No. I want to do this."

Still, she looked uncertain as to what to expect. He didn't blame her for that. But he knew how to fix it.

Time to get her thoughts away from her worries and onto her body. He skimmed his fingers down the front of her covered breasts, watching for her reaction.

She gasped at his touch. Her nipples pebbled beneath the thin sweat shirt and bra. Her whole body trembled, and surprise crossed her face. He smiled at her reaction. Good. She liked his touch.

This wasn't going to be two strangers completing a rite. This was a man and a woman bonding themselves together forever in the deepest way possible. Alexa just didn't know that...yet.

Alexa's heart pounded. She had to calm down. But Braden's touch was as no other. So sensual, like in the erotic vision. She wanted him to touch her again. And again. The explosion of desire that raced through her when he brushed her breasts was unexpected and more powerful than she thought possible. Braden was the sexiest man she'd ever known. And behind the intensity of his eyes, she saw his tenderness. He let it sneak out from time to time, and she wondered what would happen if he ever allowed that emotional wall to completely crumble.

Deep down, she needed everything the Initiation represented. To break free. Experience what it would feel like to be wild and unfettered. To live a different, more fulfilled life. Braden, and the group he was a part of, could bring her that. She was still undecided about the breeding part. But she'd deal with that later. She wanted to visit their world, explore, and learn everything she could about Xylon and other planets. And most of all...she wanted Braden, fiercely.

"I'll do as you say." The tearing down of her own emotional and sexual walls, letting go, actually made her feel stronger. *Let the adventure begin.* She almost laughed at the unconventional-for-her thought.

"Take off your top."

She pulled the soft, sweatshirt over her head and let it drop to the floor. The pink bra still covered her breasts, so she didn't feel overly exposed. He was going slowly, and she appreciated that. At least for now. Braden's eyes dilated as he looked at her. He made her feel so sexy and desired. Like a tasty morsel he couldn't wait to sample.

He scooted back a little on the bed, but kept his feet flat on the floor. "Come up here and straddle my lap."

Awkwardly, she mounted him, her thighs on either side of his on the mattress. She sank down and felt the ridge of his cock press against her. Her excitement grew, though she tried not to show it. That would make her too vulnerable. She needed to retain a modicum of control, at least until she knew for sure exactly what Braden had in mind. She rested her hands on his shoulders for balance.

His fingers eased up her back and drifted over the bare skin of her chest and arms. Back and forth, his fingertips slid, making her skin and muscles shiver in delight. He slipped one strap of the little pink bra down her shoulder, letting the back of his fingers caress her skin. Then he slipped down the other strap. "Take this off."

She reached behind her and fidgeted with the closure. Her move thrust her breasts precariously close to his mouth. She could feel his need to touch her, it matched her own, and she tried to hurry. Her fingers wouldn't cooperate and felt more like thumbs. Finally, she got the hooks loose. She held the bra cups in front of her. Would he like what he saw? Silly. He'd already seen her. It's just that this time seemed so much more important. She released her hold and let the bra fall to the floor.

He sat perfectly still, staring at her breasts. He didn't speak. Didn't even twitch a muscle.

She could see and hear his increased respirations. The beating of her heart increased in response, and her nipples grew hard at his intense scrutiny. He'd seen her breasts before, when he applied the healing cream. Even so, he was looking at her as if for the first time. No man had ever been so enthralled with her body. It was a major turn on.

"Absolutely beautiful." He licked his lips, leaned forward, then paused to look up at her.

He wanted to use his mouth on her. She saw the unspoken question in his eyes. He was giving her the choice. In that moment, she thought she might melt at his feet. "Yes," she squeaked out, barely audible to her ears, but Braden heard, or more likely read her lips.

Leaning into her, his tongue touched her left breast directly below the nipple. Lightly. Gently. Barely there. He drew up slowly, with the tip of his tongue, in one long lick.

She trembled and closed her eyes. The feel of his tongue was incredible. Slightly rougher than a human male's, the stimulation made her whole body ache with need. He was a man who certainly knew how to lick a woman. His hot breath wafted across the wetness he left behind.

He eased the tip of his tongue around her nipple, not touching the sensitive flesh this time, just teasing the skin surrounding the hard bud. Slow, lazy circles.

Her fingers burrowed into his hair, trying to guide his mouth. She wanted him to suck her. She needed to feel the pull of his lips, but Braden continued on his own path, much to her frustration.

Again and again, he circled the nipple, stimulating her, drawing her closer to the edge. When she didn't think she could take anymore without screaming out her need, he finally stopped. He kissed the hard bud ever so softly, then rasped his tongue across the center one time.

She jerked, the jolt of pleasure was so intense. A moan escaped her throat. This on-the-edge excitement was completely alien to her—no pun intended. No man had ever made her this horny after such a simple touch.

Though with Braden, nothing was really simple. She was beginning to understand that. He lived more intently than anyone she'd ever known and had drawn her into that same world right along with him.

"Your breasts are a man's wet dream. I don't think I'll ever get enough of them, or you, Alexa." Settling his mouth gently over one mound, he applied barely perceptible suction.

The muscles in her vagina tugged in tandem with each slow draw of his lips. This was torture. Pure torture. She pushed her hips forward, needing relief.

He raised his head, releasing her, and massaged her breasts. He tickled the outside fullness with his fingertips. "Lovely." He gently squeezed one then the other, repeating the pattern several times. His thumbs rubbed back and forth along the soft flesh, but not once did he touch her straining nipples. "A man's never given you an orgasm?"

She shook her head.

"A woman?"

Shocked breath caught in her throat. "Of course not."

A small smile tugged at his lips. He studied her in silence for a moment, then blew on her wet nipple. "You've never given yourself one?"

A blush heated her cheeks. She hadn't expected conversation. The other men she'd been with never talked much during sex. Mostly just a few moans and the occasional grunt. They'd certainly never questioned her orgasmic history. "No," she whispered.

His lips again circled her nipple. He drew it into his mouth. Slowly sucking once more. Feather light.

She couldn't take this endless seduction. She never had been good at delayed gratification of any sort. With sex, it hadn't ever been that big a deal. But Braden made her not only *want* it, but also *need* it. She shifted again, hoping to ease the tension between her thighs.

Braden's fingers clutched her hips, digging into her skin, even through the sweat pants.

She stroked his hair, letting her nails graze his scalp. "I'm not going anywhere." He must think she was going to jump up at any minute and run away, or change her mind about all this. "I'm yours. To do with as you please." She clamped her lips shut. Where had that last part come from? It didn't even sound like her—so full of passion and desire.

In response, his hold on her eased, and his tongue slashed across her nipple. Batting and rolling the hard flesh.

Alexa gasped and grabbed onto his shoulders. When his teeth scraped the bud, she squealed and bucked against him.

He soothed her with his tongue, then licked again, wildly, frantically, squeezing her breast. He clamped his lips around her nipple and sucked hard, drawing deep.

"Yes!" Pleasure exploded inside her; raced from her breast to her vagina. This was what she wanted, what she needed.

He tossed her onto her back on the bed. His breath came out heavy and labored. He stared into her eyes, trying to penetrate her deepest thoughts and fantasies. "What do you need sexually that you haven't been getting, Alexa? Tell me. All super breeders have one special thing they *must* have done to them to experience the ultimate fulfillment sexually."

The withdrawal of his mouth from her breast was almost painful. She heard his question—or command was more like it, but her mind wasn't functioning on all levels right now, after his sensual attack. She wasn't able to formulate any kind of an answer. For the first time, she'd been close to losing complete control. Cool air drifted over her wet nipple, keeping it puckered. She loved the attention to her breasts, and couldn't help but wonder what his mouth would feel like between her legs, his tongue lapping at the thick cream pooled there.

"I have a theory," he finally said when she didn't answer, his voice rasping over her. He caressed her breasts. Flicked his thumbs over both nipples. "I bet the men you've been with were very polished, very proper—not only in public, but in bed, too." He pinched the fleshy buds until she gasped. He released them, then pinched both again, harder this time, until she squirmed on the mattress.

Alexa teetered right on the edge of things she'd never felt before. And she wanted to feel those things. Everything he could bring her. She did *not* want to talk about her old boyfriends.

"You should know, Alexa...when it comes to sex, I'm not proper. So don't expect me to be."

His words caused her thighs to quiver. The blood raced through her veins, and her eyes locked with his. "What are you?" she asked, barely above a whisper. All the breath had left her. She couldn't fill her lungs, no matter how hard she tried. Her nipples ached. Her clitoris ached, even though he hadn't touched her there. Every inch of her body, inside and out, screamed for his attention.

Braden leaned down and licked her ear. He chuckled low and deep. "I'm nasty, Alexa. I like my sex that way, my women that way when they're in bed with me—or wherever we're fucking. I don't play fair. But, with me, you'll come harder, longer, and more often than you've ever dreamed possible. And I'll do *anything* you need to get you there."

Her heart jumped, then pounded hard. He wasn't bragging. She had no doubt that he spoke the absolute truth.

Braden stood up and stripped her pants and panties off in one move. Before she could respond to the abrupt action, he flipped her onto her stomach.

"Wait!" She tried to turn back over. Naked and on her stomach was too vulnerable a position.

His fingers tangled in her hair, and he held her steady. "Stay put," he ordered and smacked her bottom hard.

* * * * *

Leila stared at the guestroom door. "Erik? Erik?"

A grunt was the only response she got. He was sitting on the couch, trying his best to ruin his eyes. He tilted his head back and forth, straining to make out the images on the scrambled NNN television station.

She stepped in front of the screen.

"Hey! They were just getting to some good girl on girl action. I can see partial tits and ass."

"Turn that shit off. Kam's been in the guestroom too long. Don't you think?"

"Maybe he's getting some action in there."

"Cute. I think we should check on him."

With a scowl, Erik flipped off the television and tossed down the remote. "Yes, mother."

He surged to his feet and headed for the bedroom door, mumbling something under his breath that she couldn't make out, but sounded suspiciously like he thought she needed some body-on-body action herself.

Leila followed behind him. She could have checked on Kam without his help. But she wanted to reconnect with Erik and bring him out of the shell he always retreated to. He was a real jerk a lot of the time. But she didn't consider him a hopeless case — no matter their heated exchanges.

The man was simply scared to death of any emotion between a man and a woman that bordered on intimacy. Her heart actually ached for him. Some woman must have hurt him badly. She didn't know that for certain, but the alternative was that his arrogant, sex-crazed, often times bastard-like personality was simply his nature. And that didn't sit well on her heart.

* * * * *

Braden stared down at Alexa's bare body stretched out on the bed. He loosened his grip in her hair and glided his other hand down her back and over her beautiful ass, still pink from his smack. *All mine.*

When his palm settled on her shapely butt, she trembled beneath his touch.

Good. Let her wonder about his plans. He'd shocked her so much with the spank that she'd sucked in hard and apparently was too surprised even to speak, because she hadn't said another word. Or maybe she'd enjoyed it so much she hadn't wanted to do anything to dissuade him. That was a tantalizing thought. Maybe *spanking* was her need. He'd soon find out. "Are you going to do as I say?"

One heartbeat passed. Two. Three. "Braden..." Her voice came out low, and her tone sounded uncertain. Had she changed her mind?

He refused to let her retreat. She needed to, once-and-for-all, fully commit or tell him to stop. There was no middle road. And he wasn't going to sugarcoat what was about to happen, because once the ceremony started, he'd have to finish it. He smacked her ass again, harder this time. The sound of the slap bounced off the walls.

She yelped. "Yes, yes. Okay. I'll do as you say."

He smiled. She'd done it. Made her final decision. He heard it in her voice. His heart softened. She wouldn't regret it. He squeezed her ass cheek. He knew the slap hadn't hurt her. That yelp had been surprise that he'd done it again, not pain. He recognized the difference. Sure, her butt probably stung, but he suspected now that she liked it. He'd remembered watching her at the graveyard, and her reaction to the Egesa spanking the decoy. If she hadn't liked it, hadn't wanted what he intended to take her through sexually, she could have told him to stop. And he would have done so immediately. His hand caressed her bottom, and he dropped a soft kiss right above where her ass cheeks joined.

Alexa squirmed.

Very slowly, he allowed his tongue to touch the sensitive skin he'd kissed. Then he drew his tongue just barely between her ass cheeks.

"Oh, oh."

"Easy." He sucked at the flesh leading to the valley between those luscious mounds. He intended to take her right to the edge of her sexual limits.

"What are you doing?" Her breath came hard and fast. She again tried to turn over.

He tightened his hold in her hair. "Don't move, or I'll have to spank you again." He watched for her reaction, wondering if she'd give him complete control over her body, or if she'd try to level the field somehow.

A long, tense moment passed before she responded. "Promise?"

Braden about choked on his tongue, and his cock jerked. He hadn't expected *that* response. Sweat actually broke out on his brow. His hand hovered above her ass, until he noted a small smile on her face. She'd done that on purpose just to shock him — the little minx. When she chuckled, he knew it was the truth. "Okay, you managed to surprise me. Let's see if I can return the favor."

"Mmm," was her only response.

Spanking might still be her special need, but she was bound and determined to test the limits. That was okay. He dropped his hand to his side. Two could play that particular, sexual game. "I want you to spread your legs, Alexa. Do it right now." He wanted to fuck her like a rutting bull. But he had to restrain himself and do this right.

She opened her thighs about a half inch. He chuckled. Orders did not set well with this one. Or, at least, she pretended they didn't. But in bed, he had a feeling she would enjoy being sexually dominated. Otherwise, she wouldn't be pushing him. Seeing what he would do when she didn't comply.

He'd put her off-balance by flipping her over on her stomach. And definitely by spanking her. But it had excited her. He could feel the energy humming through her. She needed some nastiness in her life. In her bed. And he was more than happy to provide it.

"Wider." He spanked her again. His hand made contact with her soft flesh, and the sharpness vibrated through both of them. His cock twitched again, as his excitement grew. Damn, this felt good.

She murmured something he couldn't understand. Not a protest certainly, for she pushed her ass up as if wanting more. Fine with him.

After a third sharp spank, she complied and spread her legs appropriately. He knew she was drawing this out on purpose. She was going to drive him mad with lust before the night was up.

He knelt between her thighs, pressed his pants-clad cock against her ass, and leaned over her back. Time to see just how far she was willing to go.

She wiggled beneath him, but he held her steady. Any more stimulation might send him over the edge. His lips grazed her ear. "Has a man ever pushed his dick up your ass?"

She stiffened beneath him, but said nothing.

Her lack of protest spurred him on. *Okay, Alexa. Let's see what you can handle.* He reached between their bodies and popped open the top snap on his pants.

\* \* \* \* \*

Erik pushed open the guestroom door. "If anyone's naked, we're coming…in." He stopped in his tracks, and Leila smashed into his back.

"Ow." She grabbed his arm. "Don't stop like that."

"What the hell happened?" Erik barked.

"What? Let me through." Leila pushed past him.

Kam sat in the middle of the floor, rubbing his forehead. "Sorry, guys, she got away."

Leila's hands fluttered over him, checking him out, while Erik stormed across the room and inspected the window and screen. Still intact. "How'd she get out of here?"

"My transport-connector. She took my disruptor, too."

*Freakin' perfect.* Erik pulled out his vid-cell. He punched in some numbers. "Erik 301085466. I need a transport destination check. A woman, within the last hour — thin, short black hair. Using connector 66678."

"Can you stand?" Leila asked Kam.

"Yeah. I'm okay." He pushed to his feet. "I just feel stupid. She was more powerful than I expected."

"Thanks. Self-destruct that connector. It's been stolen." Erik ended the transmission. "No record of her. She didn't use it."

"She had to," Leila said. "There's no other way out."

Kam sat down on the bed. He rubbed his forehead again. "Maybe she did something to mask her usage. We've underestimated her abilities from the beginning."

Erik sat beside Kam and studied the man. He seemed okay. Just shaken. "It's a possibility, I suppose. You're lucky she didn't kill you with your own weapon."

"How'd she get loose to begin with? Did you untie her, Kam?" Leila asked.

"Of course not. I just loosened the restraint on one ankle. She'd rubbed it raw."

Erik looked from Kam to Leila and back again. "You both are too damn trusting. Next time, we do things my way."

# Chapter Eight

"Braden, you're not going to…" She couldn't say the words. Alexa's heart pounded harder than she thought possible. "You're too big."

He chuckled low, close to her ear and pushed his groin against her ass. "You'd be surprised how much the female human body can stretch to accommodate." He rocked against her once, twice.

Her fingers curled into the mattress. She couldn't believe it. He was actually going to do it! Should she protest or submit? Was she ready to experience something she'd never even fantasized about?

"However, that's not what I have in mind…for now."

She breathed a sigh of relief. He'd taken the decision out of her hands. She knew it was part of the ceremony with the small dildo. But Braden's cock felt excessively big. He was just taunting her sexually, teasing her, trying to drive her over the edge of control.

Suddenly, his weight was gone from her body. She waited for his next move, but nothing happened. Too uncomfortable just to lie there exposed, she rolled onto her side and sat up. He stood at the foot of the bed, fiddling with the large Initiation dildo. The muscles in her vagina tightened. It was time. The next step. Or the first actually. He'd gotten her all worked up, now he intended to fuck her with *that* monster.

The thing looked huge. Eight, nine inches. She didn't know. She never was any good at measurements. Maybe it was only seven. She reached for the sheet to cover herself.

"Leave it," he ordered without looking up.

The flannel slipped from her fingers. Even though she'd complied, she wasn't sure she liked the way he kept issuing commands.

After the Initiation was over, things were going to change. She wondered how he'd feel about getting *his* ass spanked. She snorted. With Braden's unpredictability, he'd probably get off on it.

If she were honest with herself, his control of her, and the sharp smacks to her butt, had soaked her vagina. A secret pleasure she'd never admitted to with any other man. One hand eased down to touch the skin, which still felt a little warm. She actually wouldn't mind him doing it again, once her ass cooled off.

She suddenly realized that she had no idea what they expected of her, after the Initiation. Would they want her to produce children continually? If so, no way.

After all this was over, if she decided that she wanted nothing more to do with these people, she would just leave. Disappear. And she'd have some decadent memories to keep her warm at night. Except she had a real connection now, and not only with Braden. Could she really leave?

He looked up, dildo in hand. "Ready?"

After a moment of hesitation, she nodded.

"Good." Braden moved to the side of the bed closest to her and held the object at an angle. "Lick it."

"What?" That wasn't what she expected. Once more, he'd surprised her. A common occurrence it seemed. She'd have to stop trying to analyze what he might do next, because nothing he did was in her realm of normalcy.

"Lick it like you would my cock."

His cock. The thought of tasting him heated her blood. She'd never had her lips around a man's penis. Plain old, boring missionary position was all she'd ever experienced up to this point. Well, there was that one guy who gave her a quick lick between the legs while she was in a doggy position, then came all over himself. She didn't figure that counted. There were so many sexual things she'd never tried. But all this seemed terribly out of order. "You haven't even kissed me yet. Do you realize that?"

He smiled and lowered his head to hers. His mouth gently brushed hers, then he pulled back.

Frustration built and spread. She was about ready to tackle the man. "I'm not made of glass, you know. Not my lips, not my ass, and not my…" She waved her hand toward her breasts.

"They're nipples, Alexa." His lips quirked.

"I know that." What did he think? Maybe she wasn't some sex queen, but she wasn't a porcelain doll either. "I want to experience everything…with you."

"Everything?"

"Yes."

He dropped the dildo on the bed and pulled her tight, crushing her breasts against his chest. His fingers tangled in her hair, and he covered her mouth with his, forcing her lips apart with his tongue.

She didn't resist. Her tongue dueled with his. Sliding, tasting, exploring. He reminded her of molten fire and pure sin. She pressed closer, aggravated that he was still fully dressed. It wasn't fair. She reached around and pulled the shirt from his pants, needing to touch his bare flesh.

Abruptly, he broke the kiss and staggered back a step. He stuffed his shirt back in place. "Don't do that again," he grumbled.

What? Don't? She froze, completely stunned.

"I'm sorry." The harsh lines on his face softened. "It's just that we have to complete the ceremony first or we'll never get to it. You're too damn sexy. I'll lose control and all sense of time."

Alexa couldn't believe his words. Not coming from someone as sinfully handsome and obviously experienced as he. The confession made her feel powerful, more confidant, and still feminine at the same time.

He reached for the dildo. "Now, let's get on with it, while I'm halfway sane. Lick it."

"I've never…"

He stroked her hair, then cupped the back of her head. His eyes filled with understanding. "That's okay. Tonight will be a first for many things." He drew her head down to within an inch of the object.

Her tongue darted out and touched the fat tip. Some substance stuck to her tongue. It tasted slightly salty, slightly sour. She licked around the tip, down the underside, and back up again until she'd covered the entire length.

A near groan escaped Braden. His fingers tightened in her hair. "Very good. Now I want to watch you suck it."

\* \* \* \* \*

Kam's head snapped up. "The detector's working. And there's trouble. Two more. Definitely Egesa this time. In the kitchen."

"Damn." Erik glanced outside. With the approaching storm, the sun had faded earlier than usual. And now the creatures were coming out. He headed for the door. "Leila, stay put. Kam, you up to helping?"

He stood, staggered, and plopped back down. "Not yet. Sorry. You want to call in reinforcements?"

"If there's only two, I can handle it."

"Be careful," Leila said, her voice soft and full of concern.

Erik hesitated, ready to spit out a quick retort. Instead, he came back and brushed her cheek with his fingertips. She cared too much about people. One of these days, that selflessness was going to get her into trouble. He drowned a moment in her concerned eyes, then turned and left the room.

* * * * *

Alexa pulled back. She'd completely covered the dildo, which gleamed from her mouth's wetness. She hadn't thought she could take its length down her throat without gagging. But after a couple of attempts and Braden's direction, she managed several inches.

He handed the dildo to her, then stepped back to the foot of the bed. He crossed his arms over his chest. "Okay. Insert it into your pussy. Make sure you're wet first."

Alexa's jaw dropped. "Excuse me?" Certainly, he didn't mean that like it sounded. "You want *me* to do it?"

"Yes."

"No." The idea of him standing there watching and giving 'stick Tab A into Slot B' instructions was not happening. It was one thing while she was sucking. This was quite another.

His hands dropped to his sides, and his eyes filled with something she couldn't identify. She didn't care. She wanted him involved in this. Not just an observer. She wasn't some odd science experiment. She wanted to feel the heat of Braden's body, his sexual power.

Slowly, he approached her. She could almost see his mind working overtime, trying to figure out what to do.

"You're pushing me on purpose, I think."

Was she? Seemed to her that he was the one pushing.

"Get up on your knees." Instead of waiting for her to comply, he clutched her arms and pulled her up.

*Oh, my.* His strength gave her pause, but excited her at the same time.

He reached between her thighs. She expected him to touch her intimately and held her breath, waiting for the contact. But then, Braden never did the expected. He rolled his fingers along the inside of her thighs, in the wetness there.

Raising his hand, he studied the sticky moisture on his fingers. He brought his hand to his nose and inhaled deeply of her scent. Slowly, he licked his fingers clean.

She stared, unable to speak. Sweat from a hot flash trickled between her breasts. Then she shivered when a chill hit her.

Braden gently wrapped his hand around hers. Both of them now held the dildo. "Together?"

The tenderness he put into that one word threw her off balance. She nodded, unable to do or say anything more.

Slowly, they inserted the dildo into her, one thick inch at a time.

\* \* \* \* \*

Erik stepped inside the kitchen. Empty. He opened the back door. Nothing. The Egesa couldn't have gotten by him. Unless… Maybe Leila hadn't locked the front door after she'd retrieved the woman's disruptor and transport-connector. The creatures could have circled around the back and then entered the front after he'd already passed.

He rushed into the living room. Nothing. He tried the front door. Nope. Locked. He headed down the hall. The bathroom was empty. He paused at Alexa's bedroom door and listened. He heard a few murmurs. Nothing strange. He continued to the guestroom. "There's no one here."

Kam's eyes narrowed. "They're here. The detector is showing their presence."

"Maybe in Alexa's room?" Leila suggested.

"I didn't hear anything unusual coming from in there."

Kam shook his head. "Egesa are here in the house. Somewhere. Given all the electrical current shooting around this thing, maybe there's a glitch in the locator. Let me fiddle with it a little."

"I searched the whole damn place."

A silent moment passed, then Leila and Erik looked at each other at the same time. "Master bath," they said in unison.

Kam looked up. "That could be it. That must be it."

"Are you sure?" Leila asked. "You need to be sure."

His brow furrowed. "No, I'm not sure."

"We need to alert Braden." She looked to Erik as if seeking confirmation. After Braden, he was ranking Warrior down here.

He wasn't sure what to do. If Kam was wrong…

Kam shook his head. "We shouldn't interrupt, unless we're certain. Alexa might bolt. I don't want to disrupt the Initiation. I just need a few more moments to make some adjustments to the settings. Then I can probably get you an exact location, down to the foot."

Erik pulled out his transport-connector. He couldn't wait. Alexa and Braden might not have a few moments. "I'll materialize into the master bath and check it out, discreetly."

Before anyone could protest his idea, or offer an alternate plan, he was gone.

* * * * *

"Relax." Braden brushed Alexa's hand off the dildo and worked it in another inch himself. He thought she'd feel more comfortable inserting the object herself, but had misread her. That was okay. He'd rather participate than watch anyhow. He nuzzled her neck and licked at the sensitive skin there.

Her whole body purred and seemed to relax.

Given her history and his experimentation, he was piecing her needs together as fast as he could. To ensure her continued climb toward orgasm, he knew he needed to keep surprising her. Not let her get too comfortable or complacent. He cupped her breast and rubbed his thumb roughly across the nipple. The callus on his thumb tip caught and sandpapered across her skin.

She shuddered and grabbed at his shoulders. Her eyes closed, and a sigh escaped her lips.

Amazement flowed through him as he watched her response. She'd obviously denied herself so much sexually. Probably things she had never even known she craved. His fingers rolled and tugged at the nipple. She bit her bottom lip and the dildo pushed back against his hand as her internal muscles clenched in response. Good. He'd give her all the stimulation she could take.

He had to bring her to orgasm, so the fluid would inject and absorb into her body. The first time would be the hardest. After that, she'd know she could climax and would be more relaxed during the rest of the Initiation. In one smooth move, he pushed the length of the dildo home.

"Oh!" Alexa tensed. He'd completely inserted the glass-like cock. It filled every ounce of space inside her.

"Feel good?"

She gulped and nodded. The thing was pulsing! Not a lot, but enough to make her inner muscles quiver.

He helped her down onto her back, easing a pillow under her hips at the same time. He was so careful with her that her heart melted. He flipped some sort of switch, and a light vibration started between her legs. Ooo, yes!

"I can't wait any longer, Alexa. I have to taste you. And not on my fingers." He spread her vagina wide, bent over, and touched her clit with his tongue.

"Ah! Oh." Her hips bucked and pleasure speared through her. The warm, wet sensation was like nothing she'd ever felt. This wasn't a quick lick, but a total sensual assault. His slightly roughened tongue slid over her bud of nerves until she sobbed from the intensity. He varied his licks, driving her right toward the edge. As his tongue moved, she realized he was spelling out something on her clit. Over and over. B...r...a...d...e...n...s. *Braden's.*

Alexa swallowed hard and rode the rising waves of pleasure. She felt branded, possessed, and totally at this man's mercy.

\* \* \* \* \*

Erik materialized inside the master bathroom. Two Egesa were crouched at the door, staring into the bedroom. Weapons drawn. They looked back at him, then materialized out before he could draw his disruptor.

"Shit." He had the worst luck. But at least the creatures were gone. This had been a rotten decision on Braden's part. He should have initiated Alexa on the ship, no matter her feelings. They would have been safer. Relocation wasn't an option now, so they'd just have to deal with whatever came along.

He peered out the bathroom door to make sure the two of them hadn't been hurt. He had to stand a little inside the room to see the bed.

The only thing in their favor right now was the Egesa's determination to take Alexa alive. Otherwise, they could have killed her numerous times already. Braden was lucky his own ass hadn't been fried. The man didn't have on his shield coat or jacket. Another moment and the creatures probably would have disintegrated him.

Damn. What a view. Alexa lay on her back with a pillow raising her hips. Her back arched, her breasts thrust up, and Braden was tugging on one nipple with his fingers.

Erik's eyes traveled down to lock on Braden's tongue as he licked Alexa's pussy. The smell of sex wafted through the air, exciting his senses. A low growl escaped him. He and Kam should be in on this. No one initiated alone.

His cock twitched when Braden curled his fingers around the dildo and slowly began to pump it inside her.

Alexa's back arched even more. Her hips jerked. Man, she was responsive. And so beautiful. Her head turned toward him, and he couldn't move away in time. Their eyes locked.

He heard her sharp intake of breath, even from where he stood. Shit.

Braden's head jerked up. His eyes narrowed.

Erik knew he'd better get out of there. Braden felt differently about this woman than others. Right as he was about to step away, Alexa pushed Braden's head back down.

"Don't stop, Braden." Then in a barely audible voice, which Erik wasn't even sure he heard correctly, she added, "With him here watching, it's...nasty."

Braden's eyes widened. He looked at her face, then back toward *him*. Erik's knees locked, not believing this.

Braden lowered his head and lapped wildly at her cunt.

She bucked and moaned, clutching at his head, spreading her legs wider. "Yes, more, more."

Erik's eyes snapped to hers. Her heavy-lidded gaze traveled down his body, hesitating at his cock. She sucked a finger into her mouth, moving it slowly in and out. Damn. He shifted, his pants growing tight.

She was getting off on him watching and growing excited. Well, well, well. Alexa wasn't so vanilla after all.

Or...*nasty* was Braden's word. They were as close as brothers; he knew the man almost as well as he knew himself. Maybe Alexa really wasn't doing this for herself, but for Braden. A lump caught in his throat at the thought.

He rubbed his aching cock, trying to get a little relief. Just how nasty was Alexa willing to get in her desire to please Braden? Possibilities flashed through his mind, and he almost came right there in his pants.

\* \* \* \* \*

Daegal adjusted the picture on the closest monitor of a wall filled with screens. Was he seeing correctly? He zoomed in for a closer look. "Well, this is a surprise." He chuckled.

Gabriella, his mate, shifted on his lap. Her hand caressed his chest in lazy circles. "I thought you said Braden had a possessive streak toward Alexa. Why's he letting Erik watch him fuck her?"

"I don't know. But it'll work in our favor. The Egesa took care of their part. Everything's set. And I've gotten in a preliminary report from the woman we sent. We'll be able to get this show on the road real soon now."

"What road?"

"It's an Earth expression. I heard it on one of their television broadcasts." He flipped a button, opening his private moon-to-ship transmission channel. "Send the two specially-selected assassins to the breeder's home. Take out the lone male Warrior not participating in the Initiation. They can do what they want with the Healer, as long as they make sure she can't cause us any trouble."

"Why don't you just destroy them all and take Alexa?"

"We will. But don't underestimate Braden and Erik, my dear. They are quite deadly on their own. Together, they're almost invincible. There's a better way than a direct confrontation. We can't afford to lose too many more of E-Team 30. They've already killed two, and another is currently missing."

Gabriella snorted. "You are just toying with them, I think."

Daegal chuckled and squeezed her bare thigh. "You know me too well." The woman knew him not at all. And that's the way he liked it. The element of surprise had always served him well. Soon, he'd have complete control of Marid *and* Xylon. Then he could concentrate on his pet project, the enslavement of Earth.

\* \* \* \* \*

Braden knew Alexa was right on the edge. He just needed to push her over and let the orgasm take care of the rest. This would be a first for her, and a special moment between them. He wasn't sure how he felt about having an audience.

He pushed against the dildo, getting it into her a little deeper. He rotated the angle to a better position. While caressing her breasts, he moved to lick and kiss her stomach.

Glancing across the room, he saw that Erik still stood there watching. The man's cock looked ready to bust open his pants. Not that he could fault him for that. His own cock hurt so much he doubted he could even walk upright.

Personally, he wasn't uncomfortable with Erik being there because they'd initiated women together many times. But the fact that the woman was Alexa sent pricks of jealousy along his nerves.

He'd been ready to bark an order for Erik to get out. Until Alexa stopped him. Nasty, she'd said. Throwing his own word back at him.

Damn. He didn't know what to do. But then, maybe this wasn't such a bad thing, after all. If Erik being here fed her excitement, she might be able to orgasm easier.

Braden sucked her nipple into his mouth. He scraped his teeth along the fleshy bud, knowing she liked that from his earlier experimentation.

Alexa whimpered. "Yes, yes, yes."

Her pleasure meant more to him than anything else right now. He flipped off the vibrator, then pumped the dildo fast to keep her stimulated. He gave her nipple a small bite and a lick.

Making a decision he hoped would benefit them all, he looked over at Erik and motioned him closer.

# Chapter Nine

"Where is he?" Leila asked, a snap of irritation in her voice. "He should have been back by now." She paced in front of the guestroom window, chewing on her thumbnail at each turn. "Do you think something's happened to him?" She paused beside the nightstand, took in a shuddering breath, then paced anew. Worry crossed her face and remained there.

Kam shook his head. "No, I don't think so." Erik was such a fool not to realize how much Leila cared about him. He should be *here* with her. "He's okay from what I can tell. He's on the detector and the sensor. Nothing abnormal." Just highly sexual readings.

His brain had to be fried, and Braden's too. It had already been decided, just as he knew Braden would want. Not that it was really a problem for him personally. Braden and Erik were both good men. But Leila was bound to be hurt. And Alexa would probably want to crawl into a hole after it was all over. Once her rational senses returned. She wasn't accustomed to their type of lifestyle, and it would take time for her to adjust.

"Is he still in Alexa's room?"

"Yes."

"And the Egesa?"

"Gone." Kam stood. "We should go back in the living room and wait. It might be a while."

"*You* should lie down. You still look pale." Her brow creased. "If the Egesa are gone, then what's Erik doing?"

Kam arched an eyebrow at her, but didn't respond. He'd let her come to the conclusion herself.

She stopped pacing and just stared at him, seeking some kind of answer. A moment later, after he said nothing, her eyes widened. "Wait. You think he's...but, I thought...geez!" Her lips clamped closed. She turned and stalked from the room, slamming the door after her. The whole room shook in response.

Yep. Erik was definitely a fool.

* * * * *

Alexa's body throbbed. Braden worked the dildo with precision and skill. His fingers tugged on one nipple then the second. So good. He seemed to know exactly what she craved.

A hand settled warmly on her stomach. Wait. That's three hands. Her eyes popped open.

Erik! What was he doing? She thought he was only going to watch. The idea had rather excited her, and she wanted to please Braden by upping the intensity level. But for Erik actually to participate…

She looked over at Braden and wondered if the panic she felt shone in her eyes. She tried to get her voice to work, but nothing more than a squeak came out.

A smile of understanding crossed his face.

She relaxed. Good. She trusted him with her body and well-being. He released the dildo and made a few hand signals to Erik, who nodded in return.

Erik would leave now.

She never should have started this. Something had broken down all her normal behavior patterns. She seemed to weave in and out of the erotic spell. Doing things that she never imagined she would ever do.

Erik looked her directly in the eyes, raised one of her hands, and gently kissed the palm. That bit of tenderness was a nice gesture. He flicked his tongue against her sensitive skin.

An unexpected jolt of passion hit her. Not real passion. Just a physical thing. That erotic craving deep inside her. She knew that. Anyone would have felt it. Well…that's what she was choosing to believe.

Braden stroked her brow with light brushes of his fingertips. His lips grazed her cheek, then lowered to her ear. "Trust us," he whispered.

Us? Her heart lurched in her chest. Erik *wasn't* leaving? "I-I..." Now that the two men were staring down at her, heightened excitement in their eyes, the dildo inside her felt like a tree trunk. She watched Erik's fingers slowly curl around the object.

Oh! Alexa held her breath. Just say the words. That's all she had to do. She could stop this right now.

But do I want to stop this?

Braden would never force her to do anything that she didn't want to. Even after such a short time, she knew that. But Erik? Despite the tender kiss, he always seemed so...aggressive. Sexually stimulating for sure, but also uncontrolled.

"Remember, only pleasure." Braden moved to her breast and began licking her nipple.

Erik kept his eyes locked with hers. His hand tightened on the dildo, and he mouthed something.

It took her a couple of tries to read his lips. Braden's tongue kept distracting her.

*I...fuck...hard.*

Her whole body flushed. Too much. A threesome was nowhere in her realm of manageability. And certainly not with this man.

Braden's tongue slid between her breasts, down her ribs, over her stomach. He pulled one of her thighs wide.

Erik pulled the other one wide, opening her completely. He pushed on the dildo once, twice, as if testing her resistance.

He was really going to...no way. She couldn't do this. "This is too—"

Braden's tongue curled around her clit, and the erotic sensation stole her voice. Erik's eyes glazed over, and he pumped the dildo into her. Short, strong strokes.

Her hips jerked.

Braden lifted his head, and his eyes locked with hers. "Faster, Erik."

He nodded, his face turning into a mask of concentration. He thrust the glass cock into her with greater speed.

"Ah!" Her body tensed, and her fingers dug into the mattress. Pleasure built, curling deep inside.

"Make her squirm, Braden."

Braden broke eye contact. He lowered his head, and once more tongued her sensitive bud.

The feeling was beyond her wildest imagination. She no longer thought about what was happening. Her need to climax took precedence over everything else.

Braden's tongue slashed her clit, and Erik continued pumping. A few more seconds… When Braden stopped licking, she almost sobbed at the loss. She'd been so close.

"Come on, Alexa. Let go."

"Come for us, baby," Erik encouraged. He worked the dildo with even more aggressive and demanding thrusts.

Alexa's back arched. He sure knew how to manipulate a cock. She slid her fingers into Braden's hair. "Don't stop."

Both men's lips quirked into a grin. Braden lowered his head and repeatedly flicked her clit with his tongue. Erik continued to fuck her with the dildo.

The ecstasy grew and expanded inside Alexa, then exploded, shooting through every muscle and pore. She cried out, bucked, and thrashed on the mattress. Her body arched. She screamed, moaned, then screamed again when the feeling intensified.

"Yeah!" Erik responded. "Keep licking her, Braden. She loves it. She's coming hard!"

Alexa's voice keened high. Wave after wave rolled through her in one continuous explosion. Surely, she would die if this feeling didn't stop soon. It was so intense. Too intense. But so good!

Finally, her body collapsed against the mattress. She trembled as Braden tenderly swiped his tongue back and forth over her quivering clit. Erik worked the dildo easy now, in and out.

*Oh, my!* She'd had her first orgasm. And it was a massive one. If all orgasms were like that one, she didn't know how people survived them.

Braden moved up and licked her lips. She tasted herself for the first time and licked back. Their tongues moved together in sensual rhythm.

The dildo was eased from her vagina.

"We're going to roll you over, Alexa," Braden said, his lips sliding across her cheek. "You came beautifully."

She couldn't move or respond. She felt like liquid. All she could do was lie there while they put her on her stomach.

Someone readjusted the pillow, raising her ass in the air. Her eyes fluttered closed in exhaustion.

Their conversation floated around her, sounding far off, even though they were right next to her.

"Hand me the other dildo," Braden said. A moment later he mumbled, "Thanks."

Someone's hands massaged her butt. It felt good. Right.

"Open her up." Again, Braden's voice.

Which meant it must be Erik's hands on her. He gently spread her ass cheeks.

Something wet and slightly rough touched her opening. She jerked. A tongue? Yes, that's what it was.

"Relax, Alexa." This time it was Erik who spoke. His voice was gentler than she would have expected from him.

She didn't know whose tongue had touched her, because it left when she jerked and before Erik spoke. The sensation had been so new to her that she couldn't lie still. She didn't know what was going to happen next, but she was looking forward to finding out.


Erik leaned over and again tongued Alexa's ass, getting her ready for the second part of the Initiation.

She squirmed beneath him, but didn't try to pull away. She liked getting her asshole reamed. He knew she did, so he did a thorough job. Otherwise, she'd have screamed a protest at the first touch. Did she even know it was his tongue? He wanted her to know.

He couldn't get the sight of her orgasm from his mind. She'd been so beautiful, just like Braden said. His friend was a lucky man. Maybe someday *he'd* be lucky too, and find a woman as special for himself.

The image of Leila's face flashed through his mind, until he forced it away. She wasn't for him. She'd always made that perfectly clear.

"Hey," Braden said, interrupting his thoughts.

Oops. He'd spent a little too much time licking Alexa's rear entry. He pulled back and cleared his throat. "Sorry."

His mouth moved to the base of Alexa's spine, and he sucked on the nerves located there, while Braden slowly inserted the small dildo.

Alexa barely twitched. But then, the thing was so slim that he doubted it would cause even a virgin asshole any discomfort. He heard Braden's sigh of relief. He must have expected her to protest. Erik massaged one of her ass cheeks. So soft. He suspected Alexa had more passion and eroticism built up inside her than either of them knew. Probably more than she, herself, even realized.

He slid his tongue slowly up her spine, enjoying the small tremors it caused her, until he reached the back of her neck. The smooth skin there sent thoughts racing through him. Braden needed to Brand her. Here. Now. Not wait for approval. It was the only way to ensure she would be his.

He let his tongue touch her ear as he whispered to her. "Did you like the feel of my tongue up your ass, Alexa? Maybe I'll do it again. Maybe I'll use something other than my tongue."

She moaned and bit her bottom lip.

He dragged his fingers through her hair, smoothing the silky strands. He wished he could stroke the hair between her thighs to see if it was just as silky, but he suspected Braden wouldn't allow that. He hadn't thrust the dildo deep enough, earlier, to graze her curls. His mistake. He should have shoved it in to the hilt, let her juices coat his fingers, so he could have gotten a taste of her. "Do you want to come again?"

After a moment of hesitation, she answered, "Yes." The word was barely audible, as if she felt embarrassed to admit her need.

He was glad that she did admit it. By the look on Braden's face, he was about ready to teach her another lesson in the pleasures of power fucking.


Braden pushed a second pillow underneath Alexa's hips. The dildo in her ass had already done its job, and he could have eased it out, but he let it remain for the moment. Alexa didn't need to come for it to work. He intended to make her come anyway. She was much too pent-up sexually, and needed the release.

Erik had settled in beside her and was stroking her hair and back, whispering in her ear. Not once had his friend taken advantage of being here. Braden respected the fact that Erik only touched Alexa to *his* specifications and hadn't pushed for more. He grabbed a soft-bristled hairbrush off the dresser and handed it to him. "Use this. Full body."

She'd love the sensation. The men in her past were fools not to have realized her need for intense stimulation, both physical and emotional.

When the bristles touched her skin, Braden felt her shudder and sigh. Erik dragged the brush down her back, across her ass, along the inside of her thighs—back and forth, until she couldn't lie still anymore.

"Please…"

"What do you want, Alexa?" Erik asked, nodding at Braden.

Braden flipped on the slim vibrator and adjusted the feelers on the dildo to stimulate her more.

She jackknifed her hips, then settled down with a hum of excitement. Erik continued stimulating her with the bristles.

The sight of Alexa lying submissively between them, on her stomach, letting them touch her any way they wanted, was an experience he'd never forget. This wasn't how he'd planned it, but compromise went a long way. "Erik asked you a question, Alexa. What do you want?"

"Say it, baby," Erik encouraged.

"I—I want to come."

Braden's heart softened. That sounded so hard for her to admit. And it really shouldn't be.

"Louder," Erik replied. His voice held a demanding tone this time that didn't surprise Braden, but must have shocked Alexa.

She didn't respond to the near command. She'd come a long way sexually. But she still needed to submit completely to the desires of her body and mind. Admit and acknowledge what they were without shyness or hesitation. He made a hand signal to Erik. His friend cocked an eyebrow, then visibly swallowed and nodded. His eyes dilated in excitement and anticipation.

Braden clenched his hand into a fist, then stretched his fingers wide.

"Now, Braden. Do it."

He brought his palm down, slapping Alexa's ass. Once. Twice. "Tell me when to stop, Alexa. Tell us what you want. What you need. Is this it?"

She buried her face against the pillow. Her fingers gripped the sheet, released it, then gripped it again and held on tight.

He made contact a third time, smacking her butt more sharply.

She jerked and moaned.

After a fourth swat, he hesitated, giving her ample chance to speak. "Do you want more?"

She remained quiet, not acknowledging the need, nor protesting the action.

"Smack her again, Braden." Erik stared at Alexa's pinkening backside and groaned. "Damn, she's got a spankable ass."

Braden saw the man's hand twitch. He knew Erik wanted to spank Alexa himself. But that was his pleasure alone. His hand connected with her ass a fifth and sixth time, the sharp slaps echoing in the room. His cock was so hard he was about ready to spurt.

Erik gathered her hair in his fist and gently pulled her head up. His voice was anything but gentle when he spoke. "Do you like being spanked, Alexa? Tell us."

Braden smacked her ass a seventh time—only a little harder. One word from her to stop, and he'd back off immediately. But he knew better. His hand made contact again.

Alexa squeezed her eyes closed. "Yes, I like it! I like it all. Now make me come! Make me come!" Then in a lower voice, "Please, make me come." Erik released her, and she collapsed on the mattress.

"Good girl," Erik responded, stroking her hair.

A surge of triumph filled Braden. She was panting heavily, her back rising and falling with each breath. But when she didn't say anything else, didn't move in any other way, the feeling turned to apprehension.

Maybe he'd pushed too hard and gotten her involved in something too sexually potent. He hoped not. He wanted her to remember this experience and grow stronger, more assured and comfortable with her sexual needs. That was important if she were to be happy with the Warrior lifestyle.

"Do her, Braden," Erik growled, rubbing his cock. "She's ready."

More like Erik was ready, he suspected. Nevertheless, when Alexa didn't issue a protest, Braden slowly pulled the dildo from her ass and inserted the tip of his tongue into her wet pussy from behind. She was soaked, her juices thick and heavy, coating his tongue and lips.

"Do you like that, Alexa?" Erik asked. After a silent pause, he reached down, squeezed her ass, and held it firm.

She mewled and squirmed.

Braden raised his head, wiping his mouth. "Easy, Erik," he warned.

Erik frowned, but loosened his fingers a little. "From now on, Alexa, you *will* tell us everything that gets you off. Now, do you like Braden's tongue licking your pussy? Don't make me ask again."

Braden bent down and licked her once more, pushing his tongue up inside her.

Alexa pushed back against the invasion. "All right. Yes. I like it. Deeper, Braden. Deeper." She bent her legs, spreading her knees wide to give him better access.

"Damn." Erik groaned, releasing her ass.

Braden's response would have been the same if he could have spoken. This was a turn around. She actually *was* telling them what she needed. He pushed his tongue deeper. He wanted nothing more than to rip open his pants and plunge his cock into her, but he had to wait until after the third and last stage of the rite. Even though he didn't think he'd survive that long.

Instead, he stimulated her with his tongue, mirroring the movements he wanted to make with his cock. Soon, he'd be inside her. And he could finally take her without having to restrain his actions and needs.

Alexa felt her climax building. She couldn't hold her body still. She glanced up at Erik who sat next to her. He was almost as sexy as Braden. He was definitely more aggressive. The memory of his tongue penetrating her ass made her muscles clench. She reached for his hand and sucked two of his fingers into her mouth.

"Yeah. Suck me, baby. That's hot."

Braden immediately stopped licking.

"No…" she moaned.

Erik looked down at him and wiggled the fingers of his free hand to show Braden exactly *what* she was sucking. He smiled, then leaned over and whispered nasty things in her ear that made her squirm.

A moment later, she felt Braden back between her legs, again eating at her pussy.

While he did wicked things to her body with his mouth and tongue, Erik did wicked things to her mind, stimulating her with descriptive words and images of sex acts so provocative that she never wanted this to end.

Braden's spanks, though they'd stung like crazy, had made her whole body ache with need. His and Erik's demands, along with her own admission, aloud, of what she wanted and needed, seemed to release a power inside her.

Braden's tongue moved shallow then deep. He thumbed her clit, and a flutter started within her. It built as he continued the stimulation, then spread up her body with alarming speed.

"Spill some more cream for him, baby," Erik whispered in her ear, as Braden's tongue curled inside her, magnifying the pleasure. Erik's tongue circled her ear, and his warm breath teased her. "You love being tongue-fucked, don't you? I bet you'd love another tongue licking your clit, and two more licking your tits, at the exact same time, all making you come at once, wouldn't you?"

The forbidden image filled her mind. "Yes!" she screamed and shattered, climaxing hard.

Braden stayed with her, rubbing and licking, until the last spasm disappeared. He pulled away, then kissed her bottom where he'd slapped it earlier. "Rest."

Erik gently kissed her cheek. "You were great, Alexa. Try to sleep a while. We'll be back for more."

*More.* She didn't think she could take any more. She felt them move away, but didn't know how far. She was too exhausted. The third and last part of the rite was still to come. A sigh escaped her, and as she started to wonder how she'd face herself later, after everything she'd allowed them to do to her, sweet oblivion set in.

\* \* \* \* \*

Leila circled the couch. Once, twice, three times. She couldn't deny it. She was mad. She just didn't know why she was mad. So what if Erik was in there with Braden and Alexa? By all rights, Kam should be in there, too.

If Braden changed his mind about Erik participating in the Initiation, she had no right to care one way or the other.

But, somehow, she did. Dammit.

Those three had initiated plenty of women. So why was it getting to her this time?

Maybe because she'd never been in the next room while they'd been going at a woman. Listening to Alexa's screams of pleasure had gotten her more than a little agitated. And she couldn't help but wonder if it was Braden or Erik who made her scream like that.

She needed a drink. Anything to dull this unexpected and unwanted pain. Certainly, Alexa had some liquor somewhere in the house.

She spun on her heel toward the kitchen and smashed into a hard chest. She gasped and staggered backward. Two massive hands clamped around her arms.

"Hey there, sexy she-bitch. Remember me?"

\* \* \* \* \*

Braden led Erik into the master bath, where they could have a little privacy to talk, but still keep an eye on Alexa.

Erik raised his hands in mock surrender. "I swear. I didn't plan that."

Braden clapped a hand on the man's shoulder. "I know. I didn't expect this turn of events either. Not with Alexa."

"Are you mad?"

After thinking how best to answer that, he said, "No. It's an Initiation. Unexpected things happen when the chemicals coating the dildos get into a person's system. Even before the liquid releases. We all know that. And I had her lick and suck some of it before we got started."

"Alexa doesn't know."

"If I need to, I'll explain it to her later so she doesn't get crazy about everything that happened. What's going on? Why'd you materialize in here?"

"A couple of Egesa popped up. No big deal."

"Any other problems?"

"One Marid assassin, a female. We took care of her. Sort of."

"Sort of? Do I want to know what that means?"

"Probably not. Is Alexa going to complete the optional third step of the rite?"

"I didn't ask. She didn't say. So, I'm just going along with it. I want her to be fully protected." He recognized the concentrated expression on his friend's face and apprehension filled him. "What is it?"

Erik peered out at Alexa, then turned back. "Brand her, Braden. Now. While you have the chance."

The shock must have shown on his face, for Erik used their hand-signal for *do it now* to display his seriousness of the subject. Braden dragged his fingers through his hair. "I do want her. And I intend to have her. But I can't Brand her as mine without The Council's approval...and hers. She still technically belongs to Laszlo."

"Does she know that?"

"No. She doesn't know the specifics about the Breeder Program."

"Maybe things will work your way, Braden. Especially if Laszlo is okay with it. But maybe not. Tip the scales. Do it while she's lost in the sexual appetite. It'll take a lot out of her, which will make it easier for you to service her through the rest of the ceremony alone, without Kam's help and mine; if that's the way that you still want it to go. In the long run, it'll work in your favor all the way around."

"Until she sees it on the back of her neck. She'll go ballistic."

"Handle it."

"And the Warrior Council?"

"Don't let them know. Talk to Laszlo. Then pretend to go through channels. If it all works out...great. If not, you can reveal what you did to make her yours. They might banish you both to one of the lesser moons, but at least you'd be together."

Braden considered his friend's words. Banishment together was better than living the lonely life he'd been living, unable to find that one special woman to truly connect with. This might be his only chance. "You'd have to stay and hold her down for me."

"Not a problem."

# Chapter Ten

Daegal fastened his pants as Gabriella cleaned between her legs with a moist cloth. Even though sated, the sight of her pert breasts made his mouth water. Beautiful.

He glanced toward the monitors. Braden's threesome performance was a classic. He'd be sure to keep that file in the computer for future viewing.

Not often did a remote feed get him that hard and horny. Watching Leila's Initiation was the last time he'd been able to come twice so closely together as he'd just done.

In fact, Leila's performance was his all time favorite. But Braden's was a close second. The only reason he rated Leila first was that her sex show had been one of the raunchiest he'd ever seen.

Her dominance by the three Warriors initiating her had been complete. And she never fully recovered, which was probably why she always refused a mate. He didn't think she'd even taken a lover since. The Warriors involved eventually were dismissed from The Lair of Xylon for their excessive sexual behavior. The Council had no tolerance for such abuse. All the better for him. He'd taken immediate advantage, and now those Warriors turned assassins, served *him*.

"What's happening with the others?"

At Gabriella's question, his focus changed to study the screens. All quiet. "We only have surveillance in the bedroom. The other feeds aren't transmitting. Some sort of interference."

"Should I send in more assassins for you, darling? We can overpower them. They won't expect a full-out assault, given our normal pick-them-off, one-by-one strategy. If we act fast, they won't have time to organize an effective resistance."

"It's all been taken care of, Gabriella. We just need to wait. Wait, and watch, and be entertained."

She tossed the cloth into a nearby receptacle, then ran a comb through her tousled blonde hair. Her gaze drifted to a monitor showing some woman collared and stripped naked.

Daegal smiled at the view of the punishment chamber on the Marid ship, presently in Earth's orbit. "Don't bother getting dressed," he said when Gabriella reached for her clothes. "We're not through. I'm suddenly in the mood to watch you whimper and squirm, while we both watch *her* whimper and squirm." He reached into a cabinet and pulled out a bag of his favorite fuck toys. "Lean over the console and spread your legs."

"Ooo, yes, please." She placed her palms down on the free space on either side of the console. "That's the woman who was sent to the breeder's home to spy for us, isn't it?" she asked, staring up at the monitor again.

"That's right. The Egesa sent a preliminary report earlier. Now they're making sure she didn't hold anything back. She actually believed we'd let her and her sister go if she brought us information."

Gabriella laughed. "Stupid whore."

He switched on his personal recorder and positioned Gabriella for the best view. She always gave a mouth-watering performance. His loyal Egesa loved to watch him do her. He allowed them the files, and other privileges, as a reward for their service.

She glanced over her shoulder at him, and a sly smile crossed her face. She wiggled her ass and laughed.

So sexy. He felt his dick twitch. Impossible. So soon? This was better than expected. He grabbed a butt plug and a thin, leather switch. Braden didn't know how to do a woman's ass right. *He* did. "You ready, my obedient fuck-pet?"

\* \* \* \* \*

Leila pulled back, trying to get away. This wasn't happening. She thought she'd left this nightmare behind her long ago. She bumped into another hard body standing directly at her back.

The man holding her chuckled. "You didn't think I'd come alone, did you?"

She glanced over her shoulder and almost choked on the gasp that leapt to her throat. The second man she'd hoped never to see again. She looked around for the third monster from her past, the one who'd issued all the orders during her Initiation.

"It's just us. Lucky you. Or you'd really be in for a *hard* time." Dare drew her closer. "Now where's the third Warrior, the one not fucking the breeder?"

The other man—the one behind her—pressed against her spine, sandwiching her between him and Dare. "Where is he, Leila?"

Somehow, she found the courage to lie. "He left. The woman from the Marid ship, the one wired with electrical current, hurt him. He returned to the Xylon ship for treatment."

Dare cupped her chin and squeezed. "You're lying. I can see it in your eyes. I'm a Pain Master now. You can't fool me, Leila."

A Pain Master. She wasn't surprised. It suited his personality. It also meant that she was in real trouble. Deadly trouble.

Dare's long black hair, beard, and mustache, along with his nearly black eyes and black outfit made him look like he'd come straight from the bowels of Xylon. And he was quite capable of inflicting pain. In fact, she knew he loved to hurt others.

The man behind her, known as Shear, grabbed the transport-connector and vid-cell from her belt. He also lifted the Marid disruptor and connector she'd retrieved from out front. She couldn't escape or transmit for assistance now.

"Where's *your* disruptor?" Shear demanded.

"She's a Class 3," Dare answered. "They're not issued weapons."

Damn regulations. She was as capable as the higher-ranking Warriors. Not that a weapon would have done her any good, given the present situation. They'd materialized in too close and too fast.

Dare reached inside her jacket and yanked out her shield control. It would have only been of use if they shot at her. Still, she felt exposed without the added protection.

She felt Shear's hot breath next to her ear. If she screamed for help, she'd be dead before anyone arrived. She had to be smarter than they were. It was her only chance to survive.

Shear grabbed her breasts and squeezed.

She squealed in response.

"I remember these tasty tits. Want to relive old times, Leila? We're much more skilled now. It'll hurt *so* good."

She shuddered and jerked against his hold. "Take your hands off me."

When he did remove his hands, she almost stumbled forward in surprise.

Dare laughed. "Entertain yourself with her, Shear. I'm going to look around."

A gag circled her mouth before she could stop it. That's why he'd released her—to put on that filthy thing. She stood still while Shear's arm slid tightly around her waist, almost crushing her ribs. She could barely take a breath. If she didn't come up with a plan, she would never survive.

"I've got her. Don't waste time, Dare. *This* is our party."

"Don't I know it. Try not to wear her out before I get back."

*Think.* She couldn't give up. There had to be a way for her to escape and get the two assassins out of Alexa's house.

Shear ran his tongue down the side of her neck. The revulsion of his touch made her want to heave, but she wouldn't give him the satisfaction. She knew better than to fight. Shear was also a Pain Master. She'd heard the rumors of his conversion shortly after her Initiation. He would love for her to fight, so he could torture her. She'd learned that the hard way, years ago. Nothing had changed; she was sure. And she still had the scars to prove it.

"No reaction, sweet thing? You've grown hard, have you? Well then, I'll just have to do you harder, won't I?"

\* \* \* \* \*

Kam heard the door click open. The slow entry about killed him. Leila was in trouble. He'd picked up her terror on the sensor. But he couldn't help her. Not yet. Without evening out the odds, he'd die, and she'd be alone.

He had tried to transmit for backup on his vid-cell, but the electrical jolt he'd gotten from the woman must have shorted it out. He didn't have his transport-connector, so he couldn't get to Braden and Erik for help. If he ever came across that electrical-trained beauty again, she would suffer the consequences. She'd put them all in danger with her betrayal of their people.

The giant of a man stalked toward the lump on the bed, his heavy-booted feet making the wooden floor vibrate. "Cowering like a little girl, Warrior?" He whipped back the covers to reveal a mound of pillows and a male, blow-up doll. "What the—"

Kam smashed him over the head from behind with a heavy crystal vase. The woman must have reported in to the Marid ship; otherwise, this intruder wouldn't have known another Warrior was in the house.

The man crumbled to the floor.

"That's what happens when you get overly confident. You also get overly stupid." Kam rolled him over. "Damn. Dare, the Pain Master." No wonder Leila was projecting terror on all cylinders. Dare could scare even the toughest Class 1 Warrior. The man wasn't the brightest orb in the system, but he knew how to hurt better than any assassin.

There was someone else with Leila now. He was picking it up on the detector. Only one man though. Good. She stood a chance. *Hang on, Leila.* As soon as he secured Dare, he'd figure out what to do next.

* * * * *

Braden grazed his fingers over Alexa's ass. His handprint was clearly visible on her tender flesh. He swallowed the lump in his throat. He hadn't realized how hard he'd smacked her. He knew he'd given her some good swats, but...

What was wrong with him? He could have seriously hurt her.

A tug on his arm drew his attention. He glanced over at Erik, but couldn't drudge up enough enthusiasm to say anything.

"She's okay, Braden. She just has pale skin."

"Mmm." All the more reason why he should have been gentler with her. He'd let his own excitement cloud his judgment.

"She liked it, Braden. You know she did. She needed it. She's a strong woman. She would have told you to stop if she really wanted you to. The mark will fade in an hour, probably less."

Perhaps. He still felt like a bastard. In the future, he'd be more careful. He leaned over and placed a gentle kiss on the pinkish mark. "I'm sorry, Alexa," he whispered. "I'd never intentionally hurt you, sweetheart."

Erik shuffled his feet, then cleared his throat. "Do the tender shit later, Braden. She's not in a right mind to appreciate it anyway. Now get undressed." He dropped a pillow on the floor beside the bed. "I'll get her into position. It's time."

Alexa felt a hand on her arm. She was so groggy and couldn't remember if it was day or night. Her butt hurt, her nipples ached, her leg muscles were sore, and she felt completely drained.

Sounds from outside reached her ears. A storm had moved in. She could hear it growing in intensity. Rain pelted the windows and roof. Wind slapped tree branches against the side of the house. The room seemed darker now than earlier. Only the small lamp in the corner threw out any light.

With the help of someone behind her, she dropped to her knees onto a pillow. Her mind vaguely registered that it must be Erik, because Braden stood on the other side of the bed taking off his clothes.

Talk about a perfect body!

A chiseled chest, lightly sprinkled with dark hair, caught her attention first. Strong and capable of anything was the thought that came to mind. Her gaze drifted down his six-pack abdomen. Nice. And…oh! His cock. Hard, long, and thick, it rose out of a thatch of coarse-looking, black hair. If he knew how to use that thing, she was due for a mind-shattering, orgasmic time. Powerful thighs, indicative of strong thrusting power, made the view picture-perfect.

She wanted him fiercely. Her clit throbbed, and her nipples hardened in anticipation.

Then a wave of dizziness hit her.

She would have fallen against the bed, if not being held. Why did she feel so out of it?

Rough hands caressed her stomach and hips. Firm lips grazed her neck. Who? Erik. Yes, that's right. She couldn't think. His hard erection pressed against her through his pants. Were they both going to…?

"The appetite is slowly taking hold of her, Braden. We have to complete the ceremony *now*, while she's still able to follow instructions."

Braden walked closer. He stood proud and naked before her. He slowly licked the palm of one hand, never taking his eyes off her, and fisted his already-erect penis. He pumped hard until the erection looked massive to her. She wanted that hunk of flesh inside her. When he sat on the edge of the bed in front of her, disappointment hit. She pressed back against Erik. Anything for some relief.

Erik's voice rumbled in her ear. "Careful, Alexa. Don't tempt me. I only have so much control. You're going to need to suck Braden's cock. Make him come in your mouth. Swallow as much as you can. Do you understand?"

She understood. She spoke English. She just couldn't understand or remember how she'd gotten herself into a sexual situation with two men. This was *not* like her. And her brain seemed to be growing foggier by the minute.

Drugged? No, it was something else. Wait. Yes, somewhat like drugged. They told her, but her mind couldn't grab onto the memory.

The scent of sex filled her senses. Somehow, she thought she should protest being naked with two men, but she couldn't muster the energy.

A hand pushed on the back of her head. Before she even realized it, her lips were sliding over that big, hot, slick cock. She could barely get much more than the head in her mouth, it was so thick. She automatically sucked.

A groan filled her ears, while musky flesh filled her mouth. Had that been her groan or one of theirs?

Her body grew warmer, and her need increased. She *had* to suck. She couldn't stop. As she relaxed, she was able to take another inch or two. His flesh tasted so…decadent.

Two hands cupped her breasts in a firm hold. Ah. Her nipples twisted in pain-pleasure from tugging fingertips, manipulating the hard buds. She jerked and moaned. *Yes.*

More. She needed more.

At the first touch of Alexa's lips on his cock, Braden almost lost it. He had to hold out as long as possible. The more he let the pressure build, the more self-protecting elements he'd spew down her throat, and the better she'd be able to heal herself internally if the need arose.

The way her eyes halfway glazed over, he knew she'd be completely out of it soon. He stroked her hair, letting the silky strands caress his fingers.

At the same time, Erik was doing something to Alexa with his hands that Braden couldn't see. She kept twitching and whimpering. And Erik kept pressing hard against her ass. His tongue was liberally bathing her from ear to neck to shoulder, and he left an occasional love bite on her skin. Braden could tell he was getting too excited, and soon wouldn't be able to stop if he continued stimulating her. "Erik," he forced out, trying to keep his mind off Alexa's sucking for a moment. "Erik, stop."

The man looked up. Surprise crossed his face, then his gaze skittered away as if he realized he'd gone too far. He released Alexa and scooted back. Without a word, he staggered to his feet and toward the master bath.

Braden felt bad for Erik but having him leave during this third step was for the best. He didn't want to come to blows with his friend over a woman. And now he could concentrate fully on Alexa.

She sucked him deeper, and he groaned. Her tongue and mouth demanded he come. And he couldn't deny himself any longer.

His fingers tightened in her hair. "Yes!" he shouted and came hard and long in her mouth. "Ah!"

She sucked and swallowed, over and over, until she'd completely drained him. Her enthusiastic response surprised and pleased him. For a woman who'd never sucked cock, especially Warrior cock, she was a wonder. He was sure being almost completely under the influence of a raging sexual appetite helped. The delay had worked in their favor.

He collapsed on the bed, worn out and unable to move. Her mouth on him, her tongue and lips hungrily taking all he could give, had been a trip into paradise.

*  *  *  *  *

Shear's head snapped around at the sound of a shout. Leila panicked. That was Braden. If Shear and Dare burst in on them now, the ceremony might not be completed. And if Braden and Erik ended up killed, Alexa would be at the Pain Masters' mercy.

Leila felt Shear's hold loosen. She broke loose and ran in the opposite direction from Alexa's room. "Stupid freak! You're no match for a Xylon Warrior."

"Get back here, bitch!" He thundered behind her, his massive body like a boulder on a mission of destruction.

Good. Now if she could just keep him occupied, maybe that would allow Braden and Alexa to finish what they'd started. She hoped Kam would spot Dare before he stormed Alexa's room. If Kam could keep Dare busy, or if Dare would come back and check on Shear, that would give Braden and Erik the time they needed to get Alexa protected against any Marid sterilization procedure.

The thought of both Pain Masters being so near sickened her, but eventually, either Kam or Erik would check on her. She just prayed that would be sooner rather than later, and before she lost her sanity.

* * * * *

From just outside the master bath, Erik watched Alexa crawl up on the bed next to Braden. She was fully lost in the sexual appetite now. He saw it in her glazed eyes.

He watched her breasts sway as she moved. Damn, he needed to fuck, to come. He could barely stand straight. He popped the top button on his pants.

Alexa's mouth traveled up and down Braden's body, trying to revive him. She needed to fuck. Erik saw that in her eyes, too.

He'd had to put some distance between them while he could, before helping Braden put his mark on her. He was too excited to control his actions and responses. And Braden had known it.

Regret tugged at him. He'd already overstepped his bounds by pinching her nipples. She really liked it though when he tugged and twisted them between his fingers. She'd rubbed that soft ass of hers back against his dick and purred like a contented feline.

If allowed, he would have sucked her nipples hard and deep, until she screamed and her juices ran down her thighs. He'd have slowly licked every drop of that thick cream off her body, then gone right to the source for more. The thought alone made him hard as steel.

He'd already seen for himself what a great fuck she was. Hot, but also sweet. An irresistible combination. He knew her pussy would taste so good he'd want to eat her again and again.

Her mouth drew his attention. She'd done a pretty good job eating Braden's dick. She had some technique to learn in his opinion, but still, she'd done well. Too bad she couldn't service him the same way. He'd teach her everything she didn't know.

He leaned against the door and unzipped his pants. His cock needed to breathe. He groaned when Alexa, apparently frustrated with Braden's lack of response, reached between her own legs and rubbed her clit.

"Yeah. Twiddle it, baby," he whispered, pulling his shaft free. In her present state, self-gratification would barely take the edge off. She'd soon find that out. But he had no problems watching her try.

As she pleasured herself, he gripped his thick flesh and pumped. His hand was a poor substitute for a tight, wet pussy. But it was all he could do. "Make yourself come, Alexa. Make me come." He knew she couldn't hear him, he spoke too low, but his words fueled his own desire.

* * * * *

Kam rolled Dare, now trussed and gagged, into the closet. The blow-up doll wouldn't fit. He needed to ask Alexa about that thing. Later… Right now, he had to get to Leila.

Luck had been with him. When he searched Dare, he found a Pain Inducer. The small, taser-like gun induced compliance or punishment on prisoners. It would make a good weapon, if he could get close enough to his target to use it. Dare had a disruptor on him, too. But it was a modified model, and he couldn't figure out how to switch the damn thing on. He stuck it in his belt anyway.

He slipped out of the room and quietly made his way down the hall. He peered around the corner. The living room was empty.

He heard Leila's whimpers coming from the kitchen, and he moved quickly. Please, let luck remain on his side. He hoped that whoever was with her was facing *away* from the door.

"You love it, you little bitch. You know you do." Shear positioned his Pain Inducer between her legs. "It's so much more powerful against bare skin, especially with the power adjustments I've made. This is just a tease. Soon, you'll really scream good. Let's get you stripped and strapped. I'm sure you remember how I love to belt-whip a woman's body before shooting my come all over her."

Remember? The man's words incensed Kam. Had he done such a horrible thing to Leila at one time? He'd never known about any abuse she had suffered in the past. But then, she never spoke of her past.

Kam wrapped the belt he'd taken from Dare around Shear's throat. Let's see how *he* liked a belt used on him. The man rose up with a roar right before his voice cut off.

Leila kicked the Inducer from his hand. It smashed against the wall and broke.

Kam tightened the belt, hanging on for dear life. The man had a neck like a mastodon. "Leila, get the Inducer from my belt."

She jumped up from the kitchen island, where Shear had pinned her, and whipped off her gag. She grabbed the Inducer from Kam's waist. Without waiting for instructions, she pressed the unit to Shear's groin and hit the activator full blast.

The shock reverberated throughout his body.

"How do *you* like it, you bastard?"

He gurgled in pain, the belt still around his neck, and slumped to the floor.

* * * * *

Erik's heart pounded. Watching Alexa touch herself, with him right there so close, made jacking off much better than any fantasy he could make up in his head. He just hoped she didn't finish before he did.

Her eyes still looked glazed and would remain that way for quite a while. She probably didn't even realize what she was doing—not really.

And she might not even remember any of this. Some women did, some didn't. She'd probably be better off not remembering.

She spread her pussy, and he moved so he could see every wet, intimate inch of her. Her fingers circled her clit, then she teased her entry with a finger positioned at the opening.

"Do it." He groaned, his hand pumping faster over his hot, straining flesh.

Alexa pushed her finger inside.

"Ah. That's right, baby. Yeah. All the way in." He moved his hand to the same rhythm as hers. His gaze took in each beautiful move she made. She bit her bottom lip, and he could tell she wanted to come desperately.

"Not yet, baby. Keep fucking yourself. Wait for me." She inserted a second finger inside herself, and he felt his balls tighten. "Oh, yeah. That's hot." When Alexa moaned, and her eyes locked with his, he came in a massive rush. She climaxed almost at the same time.

Both their voices mixed with the raging storm outside and filled the room.

*Ruth D. Kerce*

# Chapter Eleven

The sound of voices, along with the storm, brought Braden out of his stupor. Damn. How long had he been out? He hadn't crashed like that in years. *Crashed.* They'd been away from Xylon longer than prudent. His thought and speech patterns were becoming too alien. He'd noticed it in the others as well. They normally tried to mimic the speech patterns of whatever planet they were on. But when the majority of one's thought patterns followed, that's when he knew it was time to go home.

He glanced over at Alexa. She had sucked all the energy out of him—figuratively and literally. He stretched his arms over his head, working the muscles loose. After his rest, he felt revived.

He reached for her, pulling her down beside him. She pressed a kiss to his shoulder. Her skin felt good against his. Cool and soft. She draped a leg between his thighs and snuggled against his side.

He caressed her hip, rolling slightly toward her. "How are you feeling?" She still had a while before her sexual appetite would ease.

She rubbed his chest. "I need you inside me."

Her words stirred his emotions and his cock. He was ready. Ready to penetrate her. He rolled over, trapping her beneath him.

She clawed at his back. "Now."

He felt between her legs. Wet and creamy with her juices. He brought his fingers to his mouth and licked her essence from his flesh, delighting in the taste of her. With deliberate ease, never taking his eyes from hers, he pushed his cock into her, one slow inch at a time. He felt ready to explode, but held back, needing this moment to last.

Her eyes closed, and a smile of pure bliss crossed her face.

His heart pounded, and his pulse raced as he stared down at her. She was the most beautiful woman he'd ever known. "Look at me, Alexa. I need to see your eyes."

She opened her eyes, and he captured her gaze with his own. Their fingers interlocked as he lowered her hands down to the mattress, holding them above her head. He pushed deeper inside her. Braden marveled at the tight, lush heat of her body — her willingness to trust him, and give him every part of herself. Her soft folds held his cock lovingly, while her inner muscles caressed the length, squeezing his hard flesh.

"Deeper, Braden."

He gritted his teeth and, in one smooth move, buried his cock deep into her pussy.

"Ah!" Her legs circled his hips, and she pushed up against him.

The perfect fit of her around his thick flesh was almost his undoing. He hadn't expected the intensity of penetration to be this strong. "Oh, geez! Alexa. You feel incredible."

"I need you so much, Braden. Fill me up." She pulled her hands loose and raked her nails down his chest.

He shuddered, his muscles contracting beneath her touch. He slowly pulled his cock almost completely out of her, then pushed back home. Slow. Tight. Wet. Stretching her to fit him.

Her tongue found the pulse in his neck, and she licked at each beat against his skin. One sensual stroke after another. Her fingers tangled in his hair. "More! Faster." She pumped her hips.

He grabbed her wrists and held them against the mattress again. Her eyes practically glowed from her intense need. With a low growl, he drove into her.

"Again!"

Having gone through the cravings himself, he knew what she needed and gladly continued to give it to her, increasing his rhythm until he was pounding into her body.

It didn't seem to be enough. She whimpered and undulated against him, trying to get closer.

Braden dropped his control. The sexual animal in him took over. Only raw need existed. He moved like a wild man, untamed, undisciplined, with only one goal. Mindless pleasure — pure sexual satisfaction for himself and his mate. He thrust into her with abandon.

Alexa pulled her hands free of his grip. She pinched his nipples and called out his name in a needy voice. He roared in ecstasy. Nothing had ever felt this good. Grunting loudly with each thrust, he continued pumping into her.

The squeaking of the bed. Their ragged breathing. The smell of musk. The banging of the headboard against the wall. Their bodies slapping hard against each other. The aroma of sex. It all fueled his excitement.

An orgasm rushed through Alexa, then another. The muscles inside her pussy pulled at his cock.

"Yes!" she sobbed.

Pure ecstasy. He rolled them over onto his back, not ready to release her or take his own pleasure yet.

Alexa rose up on his body. She threw her head back, arching her neck and spine. He wondered if she'd ever been on top before.

If not, she caught on fast. She rode him hard, bouncing on him as if her life would end in the next five minutes if she didn't make him come. Damn! Now this was fucking! A true fantasy. His dick would be sore for a month. But he didn't care.

She looked down at him and squeezed her breasts, pushing them together. Her tongue swiped along her bottom lip.

Words spilled from his throat before he could stop them. "You're everything to me, Alexa. I'm all yours. Forever, if you want me."

In that instant, time seemed to stand still.

Her eyes cleared and locked with his. She slowed her movements. Her fingers slid down her body and across his hot flesh, until her fingers curled in his chest hair, then straightened.

Keeping eye contact, she moved her hips almost completely off him, then sank back down to the hilt. Over and over. Slow and steady— a complete seduction of his senses.

As he stared up at her, amazed at the change, something beyond the physical act gripped him inside. A deep, emotional joining weaved around them. The physical and emotional feelings grew and took hold. This wasn't fucking. Something more was bonding them.

When she sank down the next time, taking all of him inside her, he held her hips steady, pushed up, and poured himself into her. A cry of pleasure escaped him, and he came harder than he believed possible, pulling her right over the edge with him.

Looking up at her, he drowned in the blueness of her eyes and felt closer to her than he'd ever felt to a woman. She collapsed on his chest, and he wrapped his arms around her, holding her close to his heart.

He had heard about this happening during an Initiation, but it was rare, and only occurred between perfectly matched breeder mates. She was now a part of him, an equal part. And he intended to cherish her forever.

\* \* \* \* \*

Kam and Leila pushed a duct-taped Shear into the garage. He rolled up against the wall, crashing into some paint cans.

"Thanks, Kam. What happened to Dare?"

"He's out cold in the guestroom closet. Are you all right?"

She took in a large breath. "Yes, I'm fine."

He saw her trembling and knew she was lying. But if she didn't want to talk about it, he wasn't going to push. The best thing he could do for her was be her friend. "We need to get out of here."

"Shear took my transport-connector and vid-cell. I don't know what he did with them. What about your vid-cell?"

"It's not working. I didn't find your equipment on Shear. He must have dumped them in the house somewhere."

"Let's look."

They made a quick search of the kitchen and living room, but turned up nothing.

Leila sighed. "What now?"

"We make sure the others are okay. Braden and Erik both have transport-connectors. We need to get out of here as soon as possible. When Dare and Shear don't return, they'll send more assassins and Egesa, if they have the crew for it. We can't take the chance. They're more persistent than I expected they'd be."

"Do you think they know Alexa's a super breeder?"

"Anything's possible. They do seem overly-eager to take her alive."

"Should we interrupt the ceremony?"

"Given the circumstances, we have no choice."

Leila nodded and followed him toward the bedroom.

Before they took more than three steps, an Egesa materialized next to the fireplace. He pulled out an energy ball and tossed it across the room.

"Down!" Kam turned and tackled Leila to the ground.

* * * * *

Erik let the warm water of the shower roll over his sated body. He'd jacked off again after stepping into the stall, his climax so hard he imagined the ground shaking beneath him. He had never seen a joining like that of Alexa and Braden. Their union went beyond that of mere sex. Although the sex had been hot to watch, too.

For Braden to have allowed him as much freedom with Alexa as he had awed him. Would Braden regret his leniency? He hoped Alexa wouldn't hate both of them for it, but instead would embrace the Xylon lifestyle. It probably depended on how much she ultimately remembered, and how much she felt able to trust them.

He didn't want her to feel uncomfortable around him. And he didn't want to lose Braden's friendship should he have any regrets later over the turn of events. They were brothers in spirit if not blood.

His current plan was to stay close. Help with the Branding and make sure everyone stayed safe, until transporting up to the ship. After that, they'd all return to Xylon, where Alexa would receive the best of protection. She and Braden could then spend all the time together they wanted.

* * * * *

The low-grade energy ball had rolled under the sofa and exploded. The cushions contained most of the blast, but that sofa was history. Better it, than them, was the thought that rattled through Kam's head.

Another man materialized inside the living room.

Kam couldn't believe his eyes.

The man drew a disruptor, catching the Egesa off guard. The creature screamed and materialized out, taking a severed arm with him.

Leila gripped Kam's arm like a lifeline. Her nails digging into his skin.

"It's okay." He loosened her grip and helped her to her feet. "How'd you get here?" After ten years, the man's appearance had changed, but not enough so that he wasn't recognizable. Still dark and dangerous. And something more glinted in his eyes now.

"I heard there might be trouble."

"Be careful. He's an assassin," Leila whispered to Kam.

"He doesn't work for Daegal."

"But he wasn't on the Xylon ship. I'd have known. I cleared all the male Warriors; my assistant did the females."

The other man laughed.

Kam didn't think he'd ever seen him laugh before. Maybe banishment had done him good. "Leila, this is Torque. He's on our side. Torque, this is Leila. She's one of our Healers."

"Torque? Interesting name."

His gaze slid down Leila's body.

Kam stepped in front of her. He hadn't forgotten about the man's habit of *collecting* women. Leila would not be one of them. "What are you doing here? I thought you were still on the Sand Moon. Banishment doesn't allow travel privileges."

Torque raised an eyebrow. "Territorial, Kam? Is she yours?"

Leila pushed him aside. "Step out of the Dark Ages, guys. I belong to no one. How do you two know each other? What's going on here?"

Kam sighed. "Leila, this is Braden's brother."

* * * * *

Braden grabbed a bottle of wine off the dresser. He didn't remember it being in the picnic basket of food. His mind must be going. After coming like one of Earth's freight trains though, that wouldn't surprise him. He smiled at the memory.

Alexa squirmed on the bed, pinching her nipples. He needed fortification before the next round with her.

No glasses in sight. He took a large swig straight from the bottle. Oh, that tasted bad. Her wine selection definitely needed improvement.

A quick glance around the room showed that Erik was gone. Probably in the bathroom. He checked the time left before they needed to leave orbit. It would be close.

He needed a shower. So did Alexa. He smiled. Sex in the shower held appeal. They could come together, wash each other, then come again.

She rolled over onto her stomach and shoved a pillow between her legs. Her hips rose and fell, trying to get some relief.

Braden growled deep in his throat as he watched her ass move up and down. He wanted to make slow, tender love to her. But for now, she needed sex hard and fast to help appease the appetite inside her. "Let me help you." He was more than ready. Without even trying, she made him crazy with lust and longing. He crawled onto the bed, pulled her up on her knees, tossed the pillow aside, and positioned himself behind her.

They would shower later.

With a strong grip on her hips, he pushed into her, only halfway at first, then all the way, when she whimpered in need.

Alexa spread her knees wide and dropped her face to the mattress, leaving her body completely at his mercy, her backside raised with his cock buried deep in her pussy.

He swallowed hard. Damn. His fingers curled around her hips. He pulled his cock almost completely out of her, then pushed back inside to the hilt. Faster and faster, he repeated the in and out movement.

She gripped the sheet and moaned deep in her throat.

The sound of his body smacking against hers filled his ears. In this position, she was so tight, that he didn't know how long he could hold out, even though he'd already come twice.

"That feels so good, Braden. Harder."

Too bad that she probably wouldn't remember most of this. He moved against her with more force.

"That's...ah, perfect. Yes...need...more. Like that," she encouraged in her soft, sexy voice.

Yeah. She loved this, and so did he.

Her hair fell to one side, exposing the back of her neck. It didn't get any better for Branding. Where was Erik? His additional strength was needed to hold her down, or she could end up hurt. A Branding during the high sexual cravings of an Initiation was potentially dangerous if not handled right. A mental bond formed as the mark took hold, and a person in the appetite sometimes fought the connection, because they didn't understand what was happening.

He slowed his movements so he wouldn't climax and lose the opportunity. They both needed to come together at the exact moment when he placed the Brand.

"No...faster."

"Easy, Alexa." He caressed her hips and ass. "I'll give you everything you want. In a minute." Come on, Erik. Get in here.

Alexa rose up and pushed back against him, impaling herself completely. "Now!"

"Shit."

\* \* \* \* \*

Leila stared up at Torque, hardly believing Kam's words. Braden's brother? She saw the resemblance now. Both had that same tall, dark, and dangerous thing going. Torque was a bit broader and more muscular, but he had the same black hair and deep eyes as Braden. Deeper actually. His eyes held a wealth of secrets behind them. Banishment did that to a person, or so she'd heard. The four lesser moons held secret, violent societies that few were familiar with—that few *wanted* to be familiar with.

"Kam said you'd been banished?"

"To the Sand Moon."

His eyes twinkled, almost as if he considered banishment a joke. And the Sand Moon was the most remote. She wondered what he'd done to receive the punishment.

"You never answered my questions." Kam's face held a wary look. "How'd you get off-moon and all the way out here?"

"I wasn't completely unproductive while I was gone. I invented a few gadgets that come in handy from time to time."

"Including a way to circumvent your banishment?"

Torque shrugged. "I gave it a shot. It worked, getting me aboard the ship before it left Xylon's orbit. I hid in the weapons locker, then moved to engineering later once we reached Earth. From there, I monitored what was going on down here. Pretty simple, actually."

* * * * *

Erik re-zipped his pants and tossed the wet towel into the laundry basket. He was under control now. He'd be able to help with the Branding.

He walked into the bedroom. Braden looked to be out of it again. Alexa must have worn him down once more. With three people initiating, that rarely happened. He couldn't imagine trying to initiate a woman alone.

"Hey!" Erik slapped Braden's foot. "Get up. Let's get on with the Branding while we have the chance."

Alexa rubbed against Braden and whimpered.

"Braden," Erik called. "Let's go." He leaned closer. Something was wrong. He slapped Braden's face. "Braden." Nothing. "Geez." He rushed over to the door and yanked it open. "Leila! Get in here. Braden's in trouble!"

She must have been close by, because seconds later, she ran in, almost colliding with him. If he hadn't stepped back, she'd have smashed into his chest.

"What happened?"

"I don't know. He's not moving. On the bed."

Kam came next. "Is Alexa okay?" He glanced toward the bed, then made a quick turn back toward the door. "I'll stand guard. Keep me informed."

Another man strolled in. "What trouble is my little brother in now?"

Erik spared only a glance at the man. Damn. Where had *he* come from? If it wasn't one pain in the ass, it was another. Instead of finding out the details, he spun on his heel. He had a crisis to deal with. "What's wrong with him?" he asked Leila, who was fluttering over Braden with her ever-present medical monitor, that small gadget he'd never been able to make sense of.

"He's been drugged."

"What? Impossible."

A frown crossed her face. She lifted a bottle of wine from the night table. "Where'd this come from?"

"The picnic basket, I guess. You should know."

"I didn't put any wine in the basket." She sniffed the contents, then took a small sip. "I don't taste a specific substance. It's extra bitter though. This has to be it. Did you or Alexa have any of it?"

"I didn't. I don't know about Alexa. I was in the bathroom. I didn't even see Braden drink any of it. Damn. Those Egesa must have planted it, hoping Braden and Alexa would drink it. Then they could materialize in and take her, without a fight, before anyone even knew what was happening. Can you revive him?"

"I can give him a counter-agent and a stimulant, but there's no guarantee it'll work."

Alexa raised Braden's hand and sucked on his fingers one at a time.

"Do it," Erik ordered.

Torque stood at the foot of the bed. His gaze raked Alexa's naked body. "I'll take his place. Erik, Kam, and I will finish her off. How much time left in her sexual appetite?"

"A couple of hours." Leila looked over at Erik, her brow wrinkled in worry.

"You're not touching her," Erik said. "Kam! Get in here. Help me with Alexa."

"I can't!"

Torque turned toward the door and laughed. "What's with him? He scared of girls now?" His gaze returned to Alexa.

Erik covered her with the sheet. He didn't like the way Torque kept ogling her. "Check on him, Leila."

She nodded and hurried from the room.

Torque rubbed his hands together, then slid his jacket off. "That's all right. I think we can handle her. If we need a third, Leila can help out. That'd be hot! I'd love to see some girl on girl action. It's been too long between fucks for me. And there's nothing like a group fucking-frenzy to get back in shape." He reached for the sheet.

Erik drew back and smashed his fist into Torque's chin.

Taken off guard, the man fell and hit his head on the wall. He slumped to the ground. "I don't think so, Torque. Not this time." He checked the man's injury. Not severe, but he would be out of it for a while.

\* \* \* \* \*

Leila put her hand on Kam's arm. "What's wrong?"

He leaned against the wall outside Alexa's bedroom. "Nothing. I just can't help with her." He turned pleading eyes on her. "Don't let Torque touch her either. Braden would kill him...and us, too."

"Braden doesn't want anyone touching her." She scratched her head. "Well, I guess he changed his mind about Erik. I'm very confused about that. Why did The Council banish Torque? What's his fight with Braden? There sure seems to be one. And why can't you at least help a little with Alexa? You don't have to penetrate her if you don't want to. In fact, Braden specifically told me no penetration if something happened to him and someone else had to step in."

"I can't, Leila."

"Why not?" she pushed.

"She's...my sister."

"What?" Nothing could have surprised her more. It was impossible. Kam's brain must be scrambled. "That doesn't make sense."

"It's true. We don't have time for me to go into all the details right now. But it's a fact. Now get back inside and do what you can to help."

The last thing she wanted to do was leave without the shipload of answers she craved, but she knew she had to. She'd find out everything later. Did Alexa know about their connection? Did Braden? She rushed back into the bedroom, closing the door behind her. Her gaze fell on Torque. "What happened?" She knelt beside him and checked him over.

"He hit his head. He's okay. What's with Kam? Where is he?"

"He's going to stand guard outside. And don't ask me anymore about it, because I can't explain." She stood up and went to Braden's side.

"Well, shit, Leila. What about Braden? He still hasn't moved."

"The stimulant isn't working. I can't give him anymore. Not for at least another thirty minutes, until his body starts to self-heal. It would be too dangerous."

Erik pulled the sheet off Alexa. Her soft cries of distress filled the room.

"What are you going to do?" Leila asked. She chewed on her thumbnail.

"As little as possible. Just enough to keep her brain waves stabilized, until you can get Braden revived. In the meantime, get on Braden's vid-cell and get us some help down here."

\* \* \* \* \*

Kam paced in front of the bedroom door. It was too quiet in there. Why hadn't Leila sent Torque out? If they had a problem, he'd hear. So all must be okay.

But if Torque touched Alexa, all hell would break loose later. Especially if anything went wrong. For Braden to lose another woman because of his brother...

A noise drew his attention. He turned toward the living room, and pain exploded in his stomach. He fell to the floor.

"I'd hoped for a better fight from you, Warrior."

Holding his stomach, which felt on fire from the punch he'd received, Kam stared up at Dare. How had he gotten loose? Shear stood behind him.

A woman he didn't recognize was with them. She must have found and freed the two.

Dare reached inside his jacket and pulled out the shield control. Shear confiscated all of his equipment. Damn! What else could go wrong?

\* \* \* \* \*

Leila snapped the vid-cell off. "Laszlo says no Warriors can transport down right now, Erik. And we can't come up."

No way! Certainly, he hadn't heard her right. "Are you shittin' me?"

"Unfortunately, no."

"Why the hell not?"

"The Marid ship is attacking, and they can't lower the shield. But the main problem is far worse."

He didn't want to hear *worse*, but he knew he had no choice. "What?"

"Right before the attack began, Warriors started defecting in mass over to the Marid ship. There's trouble back home, another uprising from the banishment zones, reportedly organized by Daegal. They think The Lair is going to fall this time, and are apparently afraid of Daegal's wrath if they don't switch sides now — willingly."

"I don't believe this is happening. Who do we have left on Earth?"

"I don't know. The long-range tracking computer is unmanned right now. We're on our own."

"Braden has a locator. See if anyone is in the city."

Leila found and searched Braden's coat. "Here it is." She flipped it on. "I'm picking up a few signals in some cities south of here. No one in Black Marble, except for us. I'll try to make contact with a general emergency code. I'll leave the signal on auto-transmit. With luck, someone will come to our aid."

# Chapter Twelve

Erik refused to concentrate on the big problem and decided to take care of the immediate one. His gaze traveled down Alexa's nude body and back up again. He massaged her breasts, brushing his thumbs across her nipples. She had beautifully full tits, perfect for sucking. He licked his lips, tasting her in his imagination. His gaze again drifted down her body, this time settling between her thighs. The dewy curls there looked soft and inviting. Another tasty spot.

Out of the corner of his eye, he noticed Leila was doing everything to avoid watching. "You can watch. It's all right."

"I don't want to."

He chuckled. "Right…" Maybe parrying with her would keep his mind off what felt like an impossible situation.

Her head jerked around, and her gaze locked with his. "Just because you like to watch, doesn't mean everyone else does, too."

"How do you know I like to watch?" His smile widened. Without taking his eyes off Leila, he tugged on Alexa's nipples. He knew she liked that.

"Yes," she whispered and squirmed on the mattress.

Leila glanced down, then quickly snapped her eyes back up. "I've seen you at a Lair party or two."

She did want to watch, Erik realized. She just didn't want to admit it. It took all his resolve not to laugh aloud. "That means you were there also, sweetheart." He had her there. He pinched Alexa's nipples until she whimpered.

Leila's gaze again dipped down, then back up. She shifted, pressing her thighs together. "Don't act so pleased with yourself. I only attend when business calls. A lot of men over-indulge at those things and end up having a heart attack."

"Not me. I'm a rock. Hard as…" Literally. He chuckled, thinking back on a party or two. Maybe that's why Leila had refused him, and all others, at the last joining. She hadn't been there to fuck. He squeezed Alexa's breasts.

She tugged at his wrist, drawing his attention. Her eyes looked desperate. Her hips rose and fell. "Please…"

Leila took out her monitor and scanned. "Her vitals are dangerously high, Erik."

He glanced over at Braden and sighed. He was running out of options. "I'm sorry, Braden." His voice came out scratchy, hoarse. "I won't let you lose this woman. I'll protect her with my life. With my very soul, if I have to."

A small sound escaped Leila, and Erik shifted his gaze to her. Were those tears in her eyes? He cocked his head, trying to figure her out. She'd always intrigued him. And frustrated the heck out of him, at the same time.

A flutter of emotions crossed her face as she stared at him. Tenderness, understanding, compassion, and…regret?

He mentally shook the thoughts away. He was imagining things. Still, he felt the need to say something; for *she* was the woman he truly wanted beneath his hands, his body. The thought struck him hard. He cleared his throat. "I have no choice, Leila."

"I know. Braden said no penetration, unless—unless you've already…"

He shook his head. "I didn't. He wouldn't want that, I know. Neither would she, if she were in her right mind."

"Would you, if you could?"

"I can."

At her frown, he puffed out a gust of air. He'd intended that as a joke to lighten the situation. Bad idea. "Sorry. I just meant that I'm capable. Would I? Honestly, at one point, yeah, I would have. Now? No, I don't think so."

She'd stiffened when he first answered, but seemed to relax at the rest of his words. Interesting. He'd have to explore that in more detail later.

"Why?"

"I saw them together." The words came out before he could stop them. He looked away, not wanting her to question him further. He didn't want to deal with any mushy feelings that he didn't fully understand himself.

He leaned over and kissed Alexa between her breasts, then flicked his tongue over each nipple until they were wet.

"Suck, suck," Alexa begged.

Erik groaned. He sucked one deep, then the other, pulling hard on the distended nipple, until even Leila moaned.

He reached for Leila's hands. "Pinch her nipples."

"What? I—"

"You have to. I can't do this alone."

"You're lying. You just want to watch."

"Would I lie about something like this?" One side of his mouth quirked up. He trailed his tongue downward, across Alexa's skin. Over her ribs, down her stomach. Her legs fell open, and the scent of her sex stirred his senses and his cock.

He watched Leila gently squeeze Alexa's nipples. Her eyes remained fastened on the mattress as if not looking at Alexa made what she was doing a duty instead of a pleasure. He pushed Alexa's knees wide and licked at the sticky moisture on her inner thigh. The taste of her filled his mouth. Delicious, just as he'd imagined.

Alexa reached for his head. "Yes…"

His tongue flicked closer to the source of that moisture. He glanced up. Leila was watching him. She tugged harder on Alexa's nipples when their eyes locked. He wondered if she even realized it. "Use your mouth," he whispered. "Suck on those beautiful tits of hers, Leila."

She gasped, clearly in shock, then glanced at the breasts she was fondling. "I don't think—"

"Like this." He lowered his head between Alexa's legs, eyeing her clit. Leila wouldn't look away this time. He'd bet his damn blue balls on it.

The bedroom door flew open and three people stalked in. Leila jumped up. Her heart clenched hard.

The three monsters from her past.

Her stomach churned and bile rose in her throat, making her nauseous. Dare, Shear, and…Rave. Daegal couldn't have sent a more effective trio.

Erik jerked upright and moved forward, standing between her and the three. He raised his disruptor and fired.

Dare dove and fired his weapon, missing his target. A lamp exploded, barely missing Leila, who'd shifted to Erik's side. He didn't have his shield jacket on, and Dare had ripped the control out of hers. They were doomed.

A disruptor beam flew past her head. She screamed and jumped onto the bed and over to the other side.

"Stay back there!" Erik ordered and moved to block her body from them. "Get down!"

Without the light of the lamp, darkness surrounded them, except for the lightning outside, which sent streaks across the room. The eerie play of light and shadow made Leila shudder.

A sound of barely-contained anger rumbled from Erik's throat, and he fired his disruptor again.

Rave fired back, grazing his shoulder.

Erik stumbled backward.

"Erik!"

"I'm okay."

Rave's laugh of triumph filled the room. "You need to find some more powerful friends, Leila, dear," she taunted. "Your current group is mildly entertaining, but that's all."

Erik sent a shot flying toward her face, and another toward Dare. In the dark, his aim was off, and he missed hitting anything vital on his targets, which would have incapacitated or disintegrated them.

Shear returned the shot, drawing blood on Erik's arm. Another beam flew past.

Leila shrieked, rubbing her leg where the disruptor shot grazed her.

"Dammit. Stay down!" Erik never took his eyes from where he thought his targets were, as he continued to fire their way.

Leila ducked, barely evading a shot that flew past her. It exploded a small television nearby.

"Fight *me!*" Erik demanded. "Leave the others alone. They're helpless."

Leila tugged on Braden. No response. She rushed to Torque, trying to revive him. Wait! He had a disruptor. She felt along his belt.

Nothing. Shit. It must be in his jacket, which was not within reach. She looked toward the door. No way could they get out of there. She couldn't get to any of the transport-connectors. They were on the other side of the room. Where was Kam?

"You're outnumbered," Shear shouted, followed by an echoing laugh. "Surrender, or you all die!"

\* \* \* \* \*

Gabriella clapped her hands as she watched the screen. "I wish the sound was working. It was so nasty of you to send those three, considering their history with Leila."

Daegal chuckled. "I thought so. Wickedly nasty. I'm glad they were on-ship in Earth's orbit." He clicked a button and the computer video of Leila's Initiation played on the center screen.

A frown crossed Gabriella's face.

"What's wrong, my dear?" His cock hardened as he watched Dare mount Leila.

"You play that thing too often. Just like—"

"Jealous?"

She sashayed over to him and dropped to her knees. "Seems pointless, that's all." She pulled open his pants and ducked her head. "I give the real thing."

"Ahh…"

Gabriella's slurping and licking, along with Dare's frantic fucking of Leila, while Rave fondled herself on screen as she and Shear watched, made him come hard and fast. "Yeah. Get all of it." He held the back of Gabriella's head, not letting her go, until she'd sucked him dry and his dick fell limp. There was a lot to be said for the real thing.

\* \* \* \* \*

139

Torque rubbed his chin and struggled to a sitting position. What had happened? The wall behind him scratched his back, and bright lights from above hurt his eyes.

A musty odor hung in the air. Bars and gray walls surrounded him. Hollow, metal clanks and distant screams floated down the corridor.

A cell. He'd been in so many of them during his lifetime that the realization didn't elicit anything more than a frustrated moan.

Braden sat on the floor to the left, rubbing his head. The woman, Alexa he thought her name was, lay on the bunk behind his brother. She seemed to have made it through her appetite, because she was sleeping quietly. Sane or not, they wouldn't know until she woke.

Kam had curled up in the corner opposite him, on the floor, and wasn't moving.

Erik and Leila lay jumbled together in the far corner, just beginning to stir.

The last thing he remembered was Erik's fist hurling toward him. He rubbed his jaw. That's what he got for trying to help. He should have stayed put on the Sand Moon.

The click of a camera up in the far corner of the cell drew his attention. Its red light flashed. Obviously, they were somewhere on the Marid ship. And closely monitored. The Egesa would probably split them up soon, depending on what Daegal intended.

Braden must have finally gained his senses, for he turned quickly toward Alexa. He grabbed the thin blanket on the cot and covered her naked body.

"What happened?" he shouted.

"Take a good guess." Torque pushed to his feet. He almost laughed at the shocked look on Braden's face. "Yeah, it's me, little brother." He examined the bars. Reinforced steel. Primitive, but effective.

"What are you doing here, Torque?"

"I thought I was rescuing you."

Erik pulled Leila into his lap and held her close. "Are you okay?" He swiped the hair from her eyes.

She nodded, then gasped and pushed his hands away. "Are you okay? You were hit."

"I'm fine. They just grazed me."

His hand caressed her thigh. "They got you, too."

She brushed at his fingers. "It's nothing."

"You haven't started to heal yet." His brow furrowed.

That caught Torque's attention.

"Leave it," she snapped.

A frown crossed Erik's face, and his eyes narrowed.

"You'd better check on Kam," Torque suggested, before Erik could question her further. He could tell the interference wasn't appreciated, but the man kept his mouth shut.

Leila glanced up at him briefly, a look of relief in her eyes, then scrambled off Erik's lap. "Kam, wake up." Her hands fluttered over him, trying to bring him around.

"These aren't my pants," Braden said, tugging at the band around his waist.

"Maybe they didn't like looking at your naked ass as much as hers," Torque replied, nodding toward Alexa.

"Funny."

"Is she okay, Braden?" Erik asked, staring at Alexa with a worried look on his face.

"I hope so. Physically, she seems uninjured."

"Are *you* okay?"

"Yeah. I've got a hell of a headache though."

"The wine was drugged."

He rubbed his temple and looked over at Torque, their eyes locking. "That would explain it, I guess."

Torque broke contact and examined each corner and wall of the cell. "There's no way out." He crouched down next to Kam. "What's wrong with him?" he asked Leila.

"I don't know yet."

He touched her thigh. "You should see to that."

She nodded, but that's all the acknowledgment she gave him. Obviously, at least to him, she hadn't gone through the third step of the Initiation. She couldn't self-heal. Generally, he didn't come across that with the younger women. Most weren't opposed to sucking cock, especially if the initiating Warriors were halfway skilled lovers.

"You have to Brand her, Braden. It's the only way to save Alexa now," Erik said, his eyes and voice intent. "You'll know where she is at all times. They'll have to let her go. There will be nowhere for them to hide her. The Egesa won't kill her, like a normal Branded Breeder, not once they discover her secret. They'll want to break her genetic code to learn how to defeat us biologically. And even at that, they can't come after her until they find a way around your mark. It's what you have to do."

"I can't. Not here. Not like this. I won't."

"What's with them and the woman?" Torque asked Leila, his voice lowering so only she could hear.

"She's a super breeder. Newly discovered."

He turned to stare at Alexa. No wonder they were protecting her like a rare find of jewels. He stood and walked over to the cot, staring down at her. "Erik's right, Braden. You have to Brand her. If you don't, I will. Her safety has to be preserved."

Braden surged to his feet. "You lay one hand on her, Torque, and I'll kill you with my bare hands. I swear it."

Standing nose to nose, Torque studied his younger brother with interest. Something more was going on with him and this woman. He could see it in Braden's eyes. Possession, vulnerability. Love?

No. That couldn't be. His brother had sworn off love long ago. Except for Frost. Pain pierced him at the memory of the nickname he'd given the woman. She'd been one cold bitch, no matter how loving she acted with Braden. His brother had refused to listen to anything negative about the whore. Then she'd maneuvered *him* into a compromising position. Braden had walked in on them. He'd blamed Torque for the entire affair. Torque suspected deep down that Braden really did know the truth though, because he'd shied away from serious relationships since. Regardless, Frost had disappeared from their lives after that, which was for the best.

He raised his hands in mock surrender. "Fine. You do it then. I don't want some strange woman shackled to me for life anyhow. I have enough problems already. Actually, my Brand might not even take, given my banishment status."

Erik touched Braden's arm. "There's no other way."

"Even if I were to agree, we're being monitored." He indicated the camera. "They'll see and stop me before I can complete the procedure."

"Disable it."

"That'll bring them down here just as fast. And if Alexa can't climax, it won't work. I could end up doing more harm to her than good, if I push too hard."

Torque rubbed his chin. His gaze fell on Leila, still trying to revive Kam. Maybe there was a way. "We need a distraction, that's all. It's do-able, unless she wore your dick out. You've never had problems making a woman come. Or at least you never mentioned it."

"Like I would." Braden snorted. "Any trouble will bring guards down here. I don't think it's a good idea." A look of worry crossed his face. "How's Kam, Leila?"

"He seems all right. I can't find any visible wounds, other than a lump on the head from where they knocked him out. I think he'll be okay. He just needs some time. He's more susceptible to head trauma than the rest of us, and he's had more than his share lately."

Torque tried again. "Do you want to hear my idea or not?" Someone had to take control of this situation. They were wasting time.

"Not particularly. I already said—"

"Braden," Erik responded. "Let's hear him out. What did you have in mind, Torque?"

"A little *show* for the camera with Leila. Enough to keep whoever is watching occupied, but not bring them down here."

Leila rose and stepped over to them. "Excuse me? What kind of *show*?"

Torque smiled. "A little flash and tickle."

"Yeah, right." She shook her head. "Like they won't know I'm performing for the camera and realize we're doing something in the background. Forget it."

"Unless you have a partner...or two. Consoling you. Making you feel better. Helping you deal with your captivity. While Braden's putting his mark on the woman, Erik and I could—"

"No."

Torque took a step back. The response had come like a trap snapping from the other three all at the same time. "All right. Fine. Come up with another idea then. Just make it fast."

Ruth D. Kerce

Voices filtered into Alexa's brain. Voices from outside. Worried voices. Something was wrong. She had to wake up.

Pushing up from the depths of her mind, she fought her way to consciousness. Light pulsed against her eyelids, and her mouth felt uncommonly dry.

Fragments of memories flashed through her mind. Braden, Erik, Leila. And Kam. So much deceit. So much still to learn.

Her eyes fluttered open. "Braden?" Certainly, he was near. She struggled to sit up. Then she saw him, kneeling next to her, concern in his eyes.

"You're awake. I hadn't expected you to come around so soon. Are you all right?"

She held the blanket against her skin. Scratchy. She glanced beneath it. "I'm naked." She was actually surprised at how calm her voice sounded. But, somehow, she didn't feel panicked. Yet.

Braden turned to a man she didn't recognize. "Torque, give her your shirt."

That's when she noticed that Braden and Erik were shirtless. Erik looked wounded, but healing. Braden looked uninjured.

The memory of Braden's naked body flashed through her mind. And how he'd transferred the healing ability to her. She had to shake her head to rid herself of the erotic image.

Her gaze flickered over their surroundings. A cell. Not good.

She saw Leila crouched on the ground, a wound on her thigh. Was she hovering over Kam? Concern rose to near fear. "Is Kam okay?"

"He'll be fine, Alexa," Braden answered.

She relaxed, her muscles releasing, but her heart still pounded. She took the offered shirt and tugged it on beneath the blanket. "Where are we?"

"On the Marid ship," the man whom Braden had called Torque said. "I imagine they'll be coming for you soon."

Braden rubbed his chin. "We have to keep you away from them. They can't sterilize you, but they'll keep you imprisoned. They'll come for Leila, too."

She shivered at the thought. And at what Braden probably *wasn't* saying. "Anyone have any ideas?" She tossed the blanket aside and slowly got to her feet. Dang, she was sore. Everywhere.

Torque backed off, mumbling to himself. Braden sat down on the cot. Erik crowded into the corner and refused to look at her. More memories—sexual memories—flashed through her mind. She pushed them aside for now.

"When they come for us, maybe we can overpower them."

"They'll send assassins," Braden replied. "It's the most effective, given the situation. We'll be essentially helpless without any weapons. We won't stand a chance."

She sat down on the cot next to him and took his hand in hers. She trusted Braden. He would keep them safe somehow. She had to believe that. She wanted some sort of permanent relationship after this was over and done. She needed it. Never had she experienced closeness as she felt with him. A closeness beyond the mere connection of their bodies. "What do you think?"

He squeezed her fingers. "Element of surprise, maybe. Come up with something they won't anticipate."

"How many will they send?"

"I don't know. They won't expect much of a fight out of you or Leila. I imagine they'll send two or three assassins to deal with the rest of us. Maybe some Egesa to drag you and Leila out of the cell. That's how I'd handle it."

"But they'll be armed. So what can we do?"

\* \* \* \* \*

"We can't sterilize her," Dare transmitted a second time, impatience in his voice. He watched the prisoners on the cell monitor, switching the view to a close-up of Alexa.

Shear leaned over the transmitter. "Daegal, are you there?"

Silent moments passed before a hesitant reply finally came. "The sterilization doesn't matter. We have her. That's enough. As long as she hasn't been Branded, she's ours. Get her separated from the men. Don't let any of them place their mark on her."

Rave ran her fingers up and down the front of Dare's shirt. "We're watching them. Don't worry. We want Leila, too."

"Oh, yeah." Shear salivated, drool wetting his chin. "I've got some payback to take out on that bitch."

"Fine," Daegal said. "She's all yours, as long as you record whatever you do to her. I want to see."

Rave laughed. "We'll give you hours of entertainment before disposing of her."

"Disposing? You're not going to sell her as a sex slave?"

Dare grabbed his crotch. "Maybe. If she survives, and begs us nicely."

Shear laughed. "She'll beg all right." He rubbed his hands together. "But it'll do no good. Both those whores are breeders we can't sterilize. They have to die. Alexa will be the perfect appetizer, before we devour luscious Leila. I'm gonna teach that little cunt to show me some respect."

"I don't want any of them killed, until we question them," Daegal ordered. "They're too important. Do you hear me? I've already issued that order to all Egesa and highbred assassins, and I expect it to be followed."

The cell monitor buzzed, then went to fuzz.

Shear's head snapped around. "What the fuck?"

"My monitor just went blank." Daegal's voice rose across the open channel. "What's going on?"

"I don't know," Dare transmitted.

Rave checked her weapons. "Nothing to worry about, I'm sure. They can't get out of there. And they won't have time to do a Branding." She ran a hand down Dare's chest, then massaged his cock through his pants. "Come on, boys. Let's go get them. Time for the party to begin."

# Chapter Thirteen

Alexa lay on the cot on her stomach. She tried to control her breathing as much as possible. Her heart pounded so hard she wouldn't be surprised if it lifted her right off the stained, wafer-thin mattress.

The black shirt she wore smelled vaguely of Torque. The back of the soft material rested above her bare ass. Braden lay on top of her, the front of his pants open. He nuzzled the back of her ear.

Despite the seriousness of their situation, she felt itchy and needy from his weight and touch. He stroked her sides softly with his fingertips, trying to ease her tension. It didn't help. The warmth of each tender stroke simply made her more aware of the growing need to touch him, too.

He'd brushed the hair away from the back of her neck, exposing the skin there. Vulnerable for branding, he'd said in a husky tone, though he hadn't explained what that meant. Certainly, he didn't mean it literally. There was still so much she didn't know about him and these people, so much she needed to learn. She'd accepted a lot at face value. Mostly because of Kam, her mother's journal…and her own disturbing dreams. Not to mention her attraction to the man on top of her.

Braden's warm breath tickled her ear. "Stay sharp."

She nodded and shifted her head on the hard pillow to get a better view of the cell. Her gaze traveled up to the camera. Its red light no longer flashed. They'd be here soon to investigate. Torque had disabled it, so they would have no choice but to send someone down to find out what had happened.

Her gaze moved to her brother. Kam lay in the corner, eyes closed, still as a corpse. A brother. She wasn't quite used to the idea of having a sibling yet. They had a lot to discuss. A lot to reveal to the others when the time was right.

If it hadn't been for the unusual star-shaped birthmark he'd shown her under his left arm, common to the family line on their father's side, he'd said, she never would have believed his words. She had the identical mark. And she remembered her father had one, too.

She might have been better off not believing. Thinking it all a weird coincidence. Then she'd be toasty warm in a real bed right now, watching television and munching on potato chips, instead of fighting for her life. Maybe…or maybe she'd be in an even worse situation than she was now.

Murmurs drew her attention to the far end of the cell. Erik and Leila. And Torque—she wondered who that man was. He seemed somehow familiar. It was an odd feeling. She hadn't the time to question Braden about him yet.

The two men sandwiched Leila between them. Her jacket lay discarded in the corner. Their hands roamed her body. She looked very uncomfortable. Erik looked irritated as hell. Torque was the only one who seemed to be enjoying himself. His palms cupped Leila's breasts, and his rapt gaze locked on her nipples, as if he could see the actual flesh instead of just the hard buds poking against her shirt.

Erik was whispering in her ear, probably trying to reassure her, as Braden had. She whispered something back, and he immediately pushed Torque's hands away from her breasts. Torque scowled, but said nothing. The man just curled his fingers around Leila's hips instead.

A scraping noise drew closer from somewhere down the corridor. A moment later, an elongated shadow inched forward from outside the cell.

Alexa stiffened.

"Easy." Braden moved against her in the age-old rhythm of lovers. He licked the back of her neck, and a powerful shudder rolled through her. The force with which he affected her, even though this was simply part of a plan, was almost scary.

Leila's pretend moans filled the cell as the two men fondled her. The sounds seemed so real that her own nipples hardened and her thighs clenched.

Erik kissed and licked the side of Leila's neck, while Torque rubbed his groin against her. She arched her body forward into his, but reached out for Erik.

"Looks like they've started without us," a man's voice whispered from outside the cell. His words rang somewhere between amusement and annoyance.

"Look, Rave. The Warrior is going to Brand her," another man said in a clear panic.

"Shh. Calm down, Dare. I'll stop him. It takes time. He won't have enough. And they're all so hot to get it, they haven't even realized we're here yet. We can use that to our advantage. Remember not to kill them...yet. Move light." It was a woman who spoke this time.

And she was wrong. All their voices were low, but Alexa was able to make out the words. She hoped Xylon hearing was as good.

"You two take Erik and the other man," the woman ordered. "They must have disabled the camera for privacy. Idiots. We don't give prisoners privacy."

*She* was the idiot if she really believed their carnal appetites took precedence over their reasoning abilities. Maybe that was the way of The Dome people, but not the more highly evolved Warriors.

Two creature-people accompanied the assassins. Alexa shuddered. Braden had called it right. Three assassins, along with two Egesa, entered the cell.

The female assassin came right at them, less cautiously than she probably should have. When she leaned forward with some sort of device in her hand, Braden's elbow shot back, catching her on the chin. She stumbled backward with a scream, and the device clattered to the floor.

Chaos erupted in a flurry of punches, raised voices, and struggling for drawn disruptors.

Kam was on his feet in a flash. He'd woken up right after they had killed the camera, so they'd modified their plan immediately. She couldn't help but wonder if his unconscious state all that time had been a ploy, while he waited for the perfect window of opportunity. Either way, it had worked out brilliantly because the Marid crew hadn't deemed him a threat. Kam grabbed the woman around the neck and applied pressure. She slumped and went down.

Alexa wanted to help, but she could barely catch her breath with Braden still on top of her. He refused to move, even when she pushed up against him. Shouts and angry words filled the air. She fought the rising panic building inside her. She needed to stay calm or she'd be of no use, but she wasn't accustomed to being involved in physical confrontations. And she'd been in the middle of more than her share lately.

Only when the female assassin lay immobile, and Erik and Torque had physically engaged the other two Pain Masters, did Braden shoot up and pull her off the cot. He snapped the neck of one of the unarmed

Egesa who got too close, then practically tossed her at Kam, who dragged her from the cell.

"Come on!" Kam yelled, tightening his hold on her arm.

They ran down the corridor, looking for a way out. She heard continued yelling and fighting from the cell. If Kam hadn't been dragging her forward, she'd have returned to the fray to help, despite her urgency to get free. Please let Braden and the others be all right, she prayed.

A moment later a blaring alarm went off.

"Shit!" Kam skidded to a halt, and she stumbled into him. He steadied her as he scanned the area.

"What do we do?" She'd been so calm earlier, when she had first woken up. Now that they were in the thick of things, she felt sick to her stomach and ready to hurl.

His gaze fell on a ventilation shaft. "In here. There won't be any cameras to follow us." He opened the grate, shoved her inside, then followed close behind.

* * * * *

Braden hadn't been in an old-fashioned fistfight in years. But they had no choice. The disruptors, quickly lifted from the assassins after their entry, wouldn't work for his group. The weapons were modified and useless to the Warriors. He ducked a left from Dare.

Torque and Erik pounded Shear. Leila was nowhere to be seen, nor was the second Egesa. Concern hit him full-force.

"Where's Leila?" he shouted. He knew Kam and Alexa had gotten away. That part of the plan had worked beautifully. Pain Masters were powerful enemies, but most often careless, and relied on brute force rather than intelligence, or even common sense, as was proven by their casual entry into the cell.

Erik stopped in mid-punch. "Did she get away?"

"I don't know!" Braden landed a blow to Dare's jaw.

Shear punched Erik in the gut.

He grunted and doubled over. "Damn."

Torque returned the favor, sending Shear to his knees. "Come on! Suck it up, Erik. Get back in here. Braden!" he shouted over his shoulder.

"What?" Braden kicked out, missing his target. "I'm kinda busy here." He took a light blow to the arm, as he sidestepped Dare's charge.

"The woman. Kam didn't kill her. She's coming to. And either reinforcements are on the way, or they're getting ready to hold a convention down here."

A moment later, Braden felt it. The ground. Strong vibrations. And a foul odor reached his nostrils. Egesa headed their way. Lots of them.

✶ ✶ ✶ ✶ ✶

Leila fell to her knees, rubbing her aching thigh. A yellow-eyed creature pranced around her, chattering something she couldn't understand.

"Good job. Now leave us."

Her gaze followed the deep voice, but she only saw shadows. The Egesa backed off and disappeared through the door. She wanted to follow. She needed to find her way back to the others.

When she turned, a wall of monitors captured her attention, and she froze. One screen was only white noise. Their cell probably. Another screen showed... She couldn't believe it. The spy who'd been at Alexa's house. The woman was naked, chained to a wall, with some sort of collar around her neck. She looked pale and drained. She'd obviously made it back to the Marid ship, but didn't look well. Why would they chain their own assassin?

Another monitor showed Erik. He wasn't in the cell. He'd fisted his massive cock and was slowly stroking himself. She swallowed hard at the sight. Alexa's bedroom. She recognized the background now. The Marid ship must have had the inside of the house under surveillance the entire time. But how? Xylon would have known. *Should* have known, considering their outside surveillance, and the one inside sweep they'd made, before deciding against invading the home's privacy to that extent.

The large center screen flipped on. She blinked a couple of times, not believing what she was seeing. No! Her own humiliation was on video. Her Initiation, attended by Dare, Shear, and Rave. How had they gotten that? They'd performed the rite in The Lair. Someone had to be a double agent, filtering information to The Dome. It was the only explanation. And the realization made her sick.

She shuddered at the pictures moving across the screen. Her ceremony had been typical, nothing special. But the sexual appetite that had followed… While in a state where she couldn't defend herself, those three monsters had totally victimized her.

"Quite a show," the voice in the shadows said. "We watch it often in The Dome. It's an Egesa favorite."

Leila chewed on her thumbnail, and her whole body shook. She felt violated all over again.

On the monitor, Dare was holding her wrists, while Shear sucked too hard on one of her nipples, twisting the other one painfully. Rave's tongue slashed her clit, demanding a reaction. When she got none, the woman's teeth sank into the bud of flesh, and Leila arched in agony on the screen.

As she sat before the screen, a small sound of distress escaped her. All the memories and feelings returned in a wave of torment. Still on her knees, she turned toward the darkness. "You bastard! Who are you?" Was it Daegal himself aboard this ship and hiding in the shadows? "Show yourself!"

\* \* \* \* \*

Alexa took a shaky breath. She wiped the sweat from her brow. The shaft walls were closing in on her. She could have sworn the tunnel was getting narrower with each breath she took.

"It's all right," Kam said, apparently sensing her discomfort of small places. "This will lead us to their transport bay. We can steal an orbiter to get to the Xylon ship—as long as it's still nearby."

"How do you know? You crawl through ventilation shafts often?" She knew she sounded snippy, but couldn't help it.

"Turn left."

She followed his directions. "How do you know which way to go?" This was crazy. Any minute a whole pack of lizard-people would probably descend upon them. How had she gotten herself into this situation? She ducked under a defect in the shaft.

"The Egesa use old Xylon freighters, slightly updated. I'm familiar with the layout."

He tugged on the back of her shirt.

"What?"

"You're giving me more of a view than I think you want your brother to see."

Lovely. "Sorry." She lowered her butt a fraction and crawled faster. She'd never realized how claustrophobic she was. Her knees hurt, she was cold, and she had to use the bathroom. She'd never again complain about having a boring life. "How long have you known about me?"

"Forever, it seems."

She hesitated at that. It wasn't the answer she'd expected. "Did you know I was a super breeder? Did Braden?" Visions of Braden and Erik leaning over her naked body filled her head. She squirmed at the memories. Never in her life had she ever imagined engaging in a threesome. Well, maybe she'd *imagined* it…

"Braden didn't know until Leila did the test and told him. You were there. You know that. Keep going."

She noticed he bypassed answering her first question. She moved forward, a thousand questions still clouding her brain. "What happened to you, Kam? Were you taken away from Mom and Dad? Or were you sent away?" When he didn't answer, she glanced over her shoulder at him. "Kam?" He looked almost pale. "What is it? Am I flashing you again? Maybe you should go ahead of me."

"Your parents were never officially mated, Alexa," he blurted, avoiding her eyes by turning his head to peer through a side grate.

She simply stared at him. Her muddled brain wasn't processing well today. Too much had happened. "What are you talking about? Sure they were. And they're your parents, too. But you were taken or sent away to grow up on Xylon, while I remained here to grow up on Earth. Isn't that the way it all happened?" An uneasy feeling fluttered through her. She wondered if this had been a set-up all along, just to convince her to help them. But she and Kam had the birthmarks… "We do have the same parents. You didn't lie about that, did you?"

He finally looked back at her. "Just our father is the same. We have different mothers. Our father is mated to my mother, always has been. During a Breeder Release, he had an affair with your mother. You were the result. He initiated her and couldn't get her out of his system, I guess. And he went back for more. Repeatedly, from what I understand."

What? Breeder Release? What was that? Never officially mated? She remembered her mother writing in the journal that she had suspected another mate. When she'd read the journal, there had also been a brief mention of another child — lost. She'd assumed that to be Kam, but apparently not. A miscarriage perhaps?

"Do you know where our father is?" That was the foremost question burning through her mind, right now, the question that had been burning through her mind for years. "No one else seems to. Leila said so."

"He's still with my mother. He's doing some sensitive, secret work for Xylon. They're living on another planet right now. But you didn't hear that from me. It's classified. Go on. Move."

Her father was alive. Tears burned her eyes. She could see him if she wanted. Kam would allow it. She knew he would. But her father had lied to her. Lived a double life. No wonder her mother had been so bitter. Knowing there was another woman had to have broken her heart.

"Here." Kam tugged on her shirt as she passed a grate. "Move aside. We'll go through here."

She scooted out of his way. They definitely weren't at the transport bay. It looked like a storage room on the other side. At least there shouldn't be any cameras in there.

Kam kicked out the grate. It clattered to the floor, and they both froze. When no one came to investigate, he crawled out, then helped her out. "Are you holding up all right?"

"I'm fine. Let's just go."

He listened at the door. Carefully, he slid it open and peered out. "All clear. I don't see a camera in this section. We'll be able to move undetected for a while longer. Let's make the most of it."

"Wait! I found something."

\* \* \* \* \*

Leila scrambled to her feet and backed toward the door, trying her hardest not to look at the monitor that displayed her Initiation. Especially now that Shear was landing a strap against her back and butt. She shuddered. Never again would she let anyone treat her that way!

At the time, in the sexual appetite, she hadn't been in control. Since then, she always made it a point to be in control of all sexual situations where she was involved…or not get involved.

"Too bad there's no sound," the voice in the darkness said. "But then, I have a good imagination. You haven't been fucked properly since then, have you, my dear?"

Her back hit the door. She reached behind her and felt for the control, but couldn't find it. She'd been with two men since her Initiation—both completely unsatisfying encounters. She doubted she'd ever enjoy sex again, after what those three monsters had done to her.

"There's no escape, Leila."

She had to figure something out. Stall until she did. "What do you want?"

"You," the voice rumbled, growing husky. "I can't get the image out of my head."

"Forget it." She'd rather die than let anyone violate her again. "I asked who you are. Daegal?" She shuddered at the possibility.

"I am someone who can give you a life of leisure, if I choose…or a life of pain. Those are your only choices. Forgetting it isn't an option. Don't be a fool. Take what I'm offering. I have a lot of power. Not only on this ship, but on Marid as well."

She knew he'd never agree to let her go, no matter what. So she had to sound reasonable here, at least from his point of view. "And if I refuse to choose?"

"I intend to have you, dear Leila, whether you cooperate or not. Whether you choose or not. If you don't choose, I'll assume you prefer pain." He chuckled.

A shiver of ice ran through her. "If I cooperate, will you let me live?" She had *no* intention of cooperating, but men who thought with their dicks weren't always at their sharpest. She might be able to fool him.

"You'll live either way. And I'll have you any way I choose. Cooperation is up to you. You know the consequences of the choice you make...or don't make."

"Yes." Her mind raced, trying to piece together a plan. "You've been quite clear. But maybe you'd like me to do some things that would be more pleasant with my cooperation." She hated what she was about to suggest, but it might work. "Like maybe...that." Casually, or so she hoped it appeared, she pointed to a different monitor that showed Alexa licking and sucking Braden's engorged shaft, while Erik fondled her breasts from behind. She wished...she shook her head. Now was not the time to entertain silly thoughts. "I'm very good and have been known to bring a man to his knees. Maybe we could strike a different type of a deal besides simply a life of leisure."

She knew exactly how he'd react. He'd pretend to agree, then try to double-cross her. Typical male behavior, no matter the species. And that's what she was counting on.

A moment later, he responded. "What kind of a deal?"

* * * * *

"What did you find?" Kam asked.

Alexa handed him a device. Certainly, it was important. "A cell-thingy. Isn't that what it's called?"

"Vid-cell. It's one of theirs. We can't use it. Their hand-helds won't connect to the Xylon ship." He banged the backside of it. "It doesn't even look like it's working."

Disappointment filled her. "Can't you hot-wire it or something?"

"It's not a car, Alexa. Besides, as I said, we can't use it. Even if it was working." He peered out the door again. "I see a ladder. Good. We head down. I know a shortcut."

He returned the cell. She stuck it in the pocket of Torque's shirt. Just in case. The natural packrat in her wouldn't let something go that might prove handy. When Kam cocked an eyebrow at the move, she simply shrugged. She peeked out the crack in the door. "Won't there be cameras in the shaft?"

"I don't know. Could be. We'll find out soon enough. It's our only viable option at the moment, so let's not worry about it until we have to."

"Okay," she drawled the word, not sure this was the best plan of action, but unable to come up with an alternative.

# Chapter Fourteen

Braden looked up at his chained wrists shackled to the wall. He tried to shift, pull himself loose, but it was impossible. With each unsuccessful tug, his anger and frustration grew. Locked in tight. Even his ankles.

This had not turned out as planned. Erik and Torque stood imprisoned next to him—Erik directly beside him and Torque third in line—both also shackled immobile to the gray wall.

One dim light hung from the center of the cell, casting eerie shadows. Some sort of straw-like material covered the floor, and large brown bugs crawled through the mess. The smell was overpowering. Like something had died within these walls. A camera and monitor hung from one corner as in their previous cell.

Rave stood in front of them, her arms crossed under her breasts. She looked every bit the dominatrix, as he'd seen in one of Erik's sex videos, picked up during a previous Earth mission. All in black, from head to toe. Hair and fingernails included. She just needed a whip to make the image complete.

Dare and Shear weren't with her. They were probably off somewhere licking their wounds. The Warriors had beaten them up pretty good. That one bit of knowledge made him feel some sense of satisfaction. Victory had been so close, until reinforcements arrived. Then he and the others had been outnumbered.

The entire ship must now be searching for Alexa and Kam. He'd heard the alarm go off. He just hoped they had gotten to the transport bay and were able to secure an orbiter.

"This is fun."

"Shut up, Torque," Braden replied. "You all right, Erik?" His friend had a nasty bruise on his temple, and a long, red scratch across his chest.

"Yeah. I'm fine."

Rave stepped closer. "You were stupid to fight. There's no escape."

"Really?" Braden cocked an eyebrow. "Could have fooled me, since at least two of us got away. Maybe *stupid* is a word better reserved for Marid assassins."

Her hand lashed out across the face. "Mind your mouth, Warrior."

Braden pressed his tongue into his cheek. Damn, she had a vicious whack.

"Where's Leila?" Erik asked.

Rave's eyes burned into Braden's; pure evil shone in those depths. Finally, she moved away to stand in front of Erik. She studied him closely. "You care for the Healer."

He glanced away, refusing to meet her eyes. "I care for all Warriors."

"Yes...of course." She caressed his cheek, smiling when he jerked, just before she touched him. Her fingers trailed down to the wound on his chest. She curled her nails into the scratch until he winced.

"What are you going to do with us?" Torque demanded, drawing her attention.

Rave relaxed her claw hold and shifted over to her third prisoner. "Whatever we want." She eyed him up and down. "You're a big one."

"More than you know, honey." He flashed a wolfish smile.

"Oh, really?"

Braden recognized the calculating gleam in Torque's eyes. What was he up to now? Trying to distract her from inflicting pain on Erik was part of it, but not all. Flirting with the woman wasn't going to work to their advantage. She wasn't that stupid. Though it would be nice if she were. Maybe Torque would somehow muddle her thinking enough to release one of them. He'd worshiped his brother once, long ago. His own, personal hero, he'd thought, as younger brothers tended to do. But circumstances, which he'd rather not relive even in his memories, had changed that perception forever. He felt closer to Erik now than Torque. It shouldn't be that way, but it was.

Rave rubbed Torque's cock through his pants. Her eyes widened, and she looked down. Slowly, her gaze rose back to his. She casually shrugged, but even Braden could see her interest.

"So?" she asked.

"My brother's equally...talented."

Braden coughed, the air catching in his throat. Talented. He supposed that was one word for it. He didn't like the direction this was headed. If he didn't put a stop to it, the situation could end up getting out of hand. "Torque…"

Torque's smile widened.

Whatever his brother was planning, it couldn't be good. Torque's plans never were.

Rave looked over at him, then dropped her gaze to his crotch. Braden shifted uncomfortably at her intense scrutiny. He doubted he could even get his cock up for someone like her.

She looked back at Torque. "I guess I should have paid closer attention when he was naked. But like I said…so?"

"How about a double-fuck for our freedom? Both of us in you at the same time."

Braden held his tongue, but it was difficult. He glanced at Erik, who stood there with his mouth hanging open.

"There's a whole Dome filled with people I can choose to fuck me whenever I want, however I want. Why should I—"

"Not like we can do you, babe. Believe me. We're specially trained to work together."

'Specially trained'. Braden almost laughed, and he could have sworn he heard a snort from Erik. He knew his brother was just trying to get her to unshackle at least one of them.

If chains weren't securing his ankles, he would have kicked out at the first opportunity. But then, incapacitating her without one of them being free to unlock the chains was useless. Still, he'd love to put her out of commission, simply for the satisfaction of doing so.

No matter what, with the camera monitoring them, freedom would be hard won. They needed a break of some sort—a mistake from her or one of their captors.

Rave chewed at her bottom lip as she looked between the two of them. She tugged open Torque's pants. "I'll have to see it first."

"Of course." Torque smiled. "Help yourself."

"As if you could stop me…" Eagerness shone in her eyes. She yanked down his pants and his cock sprang forth. "Oh, goodness!"

Braden saw her visibly swallow. Torque had an impressive package. Too impressive for some women. And the man always seemed ready for action.

Her fingers curled around him.

He visibly stiffened, then a smile eased across his face. "You like? I'll fill you up like you've never been filled," he bragged. "You'll come so hard, they'll hear you scream on Xylon. What do you say?"

* * * * *

Kam pushed open a panel and peered inside.

Alexa shifted uncomfortably. It didn't look promising. All she saw was darkness.

He twisted back toward her. "Through here."

"There? Are you sure?" She peered around him again. "It looks like...nothing." And she didn't like the look of nothing. Badness and creepies hid in the depths of nothing.

"It's a small throughway. It connects to the transport bay, the security bay, some other places. I think."

"You don't know?"

"This is a modification. It's the old water shaft line. Pipes used to run through here."

A musty odor reached her nose, and she sneezed. "Sorry. Allergies."

He urged her into the darkness. "Come on. I think we lucked out finding this. It should be safer than the ladder shaft."

The panel shut behind them and a blanket of darkness descended. She didn't feel lucky. Just the opposite. She rubbed her arms. "Cold." And claustrophobic. She couldn't see three feet in front of her.

Kam moved ahead of her, keeping her close. "Grab onto my belt and don't let go. It's slippery in here. I don't want to slide away from you, especially as we keep going down."

She worked her fingers between the leather and his pants. "Okay. Do you think the others are all right?"

"We'll come back for them, if they don't get out. We'll bring a whole army of Warriors if we have to. Laszlo won't stand for Marid taking so many high-ranking prisoners, nor will The Council."

Alexa had her doubts. It seemed to her if Xylon could have stopped Marid's evil with an army of Warriors, they would have done so long ago. But then, a lot of evil existed even on Earth that powerful nations couldn't stop. Politics and war. Some things just weren't intended to be understood.

\* \* \* \* \*

He stepped out of the shadows, and Leila's breath caught in her throat. Deformed?

No. A mask. He had on a full facemask with only eyes, nose, and mouth holes. He also wore gloves, she noticed. Strange. Maybe he'd suffered an injury, or he was sensitive to light. Not that much light existed in here. He wasn't Egesa. His eyes weren't yellow. So it definitely was Daegal himself, a highbred assassin, or maybe the Marid ship's commander.

His voice had started to sound familiar. She'd really wanted to see his face. She swallowed hard as he approached. "So, do we have a deal then?" she asked in as steady a voice as she could muster.

He took off one glove, and she stared in fascination. Expecting what, she wasn't sure. But it was a perfectly normal hand. That same hand rose to her face, and he grazed a finger across her lips. "Suck it," he demanded, his voice hoarse with need. "Give me a demonstration."

She took his finger into her mouth and sucked, keeping eye contact the entire time. He had penetrating eyes. Familiar eyes. The thought struck panic inside her. She knew him! Yes! Definitely. But from where?

He cocked his head, and his eyes narrowed.

Her heart thudded against her ribs. Did he suspect her thoughts? She swirled her tongue around his flesh to distract him.

A smile stretched the hole in the mask around his mouth. "Very…arousing." He pulled out his finger. "On your knees. I'll fill your mouth with something bigger now."

She raised her chin. "You didn't answer me."

"About?"

"The deal?" Now she was getting nervous. She'd been certain he'd agree, or at least pretend to agree. She couldn't appear too cooperative. He'd get suspicious if she complied easily. They couldn't sterilize her, so death probably was in her near future, no matter what he said. She had to be ready for anything.

"Ah, the deal. Let me get this straight…" He opened his pants and pulled out his cock. His gaze shifted to one of the screens, which now showed the Warriors in chains, and Rave playing with Torque's hunk of flesh. "You'll suck me and fuck me, whenever I want. Willingly, as my slave. I destroy the file of your Initiation and allow your friends to go free. That's it. That's all you want."

She avoided looking at the hard shaft he was slowly stroking. "That's all."

* * * * *

Kam stopped short, and Alexa's nose poked him in the butt. She backed up. Her knees ached from all this crawling. "What is it?" she asked, as she felt him stiffen. She followed suit. If he was tense, she figured she should be, too.

"We're not alone. Something's with us."

Her pulse kicked up a notch. "Some *thing*?" She didn't like the sound of that. "What? Where?"

"Behind us. An Egesa. I can smell him. We're going to move forward. Then when I say, you crawl like crazy." He pulled her in front of him.

"Kam, no. We'll be separated. And it's too dark. I can't see." Fear struck her hard. She reached out in front of her like a blind person seeking obstacles to avoid.

"Crawl straight until you get to the end. Don't go out any side panels. Wait until you find a grate. Don't panic. Keep your focus. I'll be right behind you."

A low growl reached her ears. The sound vibrated ominously against the walls. Hair stood up on the back of her neck and on her arms. This was not good. Standing hair meant bad stuff was about to happen. "Kam?"

"Shh. Get ready."

* * * * *

A group of Egesa threw Braden, Torque, and Erik into another cell. Braden tugged at the collar around his neck. "What are these things?"

"Remote-controlled torture devices. Effective, so don't underestimate them. They also transmit our location and vital signs," Torque explained.

Braden turned sharply toward his brother. "How do you know?"

"I've been in enough trouble and cells in my life. I picked up a few things."

Probably more than a few, Braden thought.

"Well, your planning skills leave something to be desired, Torque," Erik complained.

"Hey, how was I supposed to know the bitch preferred women? She practically salivated at the sight of my cock."

Braden had seen her interest, too. She'd stroked him like a woman ready for a good, hard ride. Something more was going on here. There was another reason Rave had turned cold so quickly.

* * * * *

Rave turned off the vibrator on her belt. The signal to report immediately. Braden and company could wait until later. She planned to have lots of fun with those three, or at least the two brothers. She wasn't so sure of the other one. She didn't like his eyes. She'd seen the look before—the eyes of a man who felt like he had nothing to lose. Except when she had mentioned Leila. There was something there. Something that might prove useful or at least interesting.

Quietly, she slipped into the ship's main chamber. Leila stood not far from the monitors. She had wondered what had happened to the woman. Interesting. She listened, knowing *he* had seen her, but Leila hadn't. She tinkered with the controls on the monitor panel. A little emotional torture for her three collared boys.

"There's one adjustment to the deal, my dear. Then I'll give you what you want."

"What's the adjustment?"

Rave heard the shakiness in Leila's voice. The sound excited her. Fear was a powerful emotion, and she loved to exploit it to her advantage.

He spun her around and held her arms behind her. "First you're going to make Rave come a couple of times for my entertainment, then you'll do me."

Rave laughed at the panicked look on Leila's face. He sure knew how to have a fucking good time. She stepped forward. "Sounds like a deal to me."

* * * * *

"Go!"

Alexa crawled as if her life depended on it. She couldn't see and hoped she wouldn't smash into a wall. She heard Kam breathing hard as he crawled behind her. And she heard something else.

A growl. Close. And a foul smell. Moving closer. Fast.

"Go, go, go!" Kam urged.

The panic in his voice spurred her to move faster. Her lungs burned. Her side hurt. Her legs were starting to cramp. He could have easily out-distanced her. But he stayed behind, protecting her back. Her heart swelled with emotion. She heard a disruptor shot.

Kam screamed out in pain.

Alexa skidded to a stop and turned around. He was no longer directly behind her. She reached out. "Kam! Kam!"

"Keep going." His voice carried to her. "Save yourself."

Another sound, electrical, reached her ears in the darkness.

"Kam!"

Nothing.

She whimpered. Indecision held her frozen for longer than was prudent. Then finally, she turned and crawled for her life. Tears streamed down her face. Please, please, please…

She saw something. Light. Yes. The open grate. She could make it. Almost there.

Without hesitation, she pushed open the grate and tumbled out, unable to move another inch. She was breathing hard — half from fear, half from lack of oxygen.

The transport bay. She saw ships. And thankfully, that's all. No Egesa, or other humanoids, were wandering around. At least, not in this section.

She shifted back toward the opening. Nothing came out after her. No creature. But also, no Kam. She wiped her eyes and took in a lungful of breath. "Kam," she whispered.

The only response was a vacuum of silence.

* * * * *

"Can you pick the lock?" Braden asked Torque.

"Not while the camera's on. It's a shitty lock, too. One of those Earth-like models."

Braden felt his brother's frustration. "We have to figure out a way to get free fast. Before they can get to us, even if they see us on the camera."

"Good luck." Erik paced the cell. "With these collars on, they have complete control." He peered through the bars. "Hey, look!"

Braden and Torque turned at the same time. "What?" they asked in unison, then frowned at each other.

"It's the woman, the assassin who came to the house. In the other cell. Diagonal to us."

"Who?" Torque stared out the side of the cell, looking over Erik's shoulder.

"The assassin who hurt Kam. That damn female caused us a lot of trouble."

"Looks like she's the one hurting now. I guess she didn't accomplish whatever it was she was supposed to do. They've got her chained and collared, and it looks like she's been beaten."

"Forget her." Braden couldn't afford to worry about every prisoner on the ship. A cold attitude perhaps, but his team had to come first. He sat down on the cot. "We need a plan."

Erik turned and went visibly rigid. "Son of a bitch!"

Braden's gaze snapped up to the camera, where Erik was looking. The monitor beside it, which had been reflecting images of their cell, now showed something else. Leila, Rave, and a masked man.

It took a moment to register with him what was happening. Then it clicked that this was their chance. He jumped up. "Hurry, Torque. Pick the lock while they're transmitting instead of watching."

"On it."

Braden's gaze focused on the monitor, and his anger grew. He slanted a look at Erik, who had turned fire red. "Don't watch it."

"Like hell. I'm memorizing every second."

Erik's response was too low, too deadly. And too intense. He gave his friend a wide berth. Braden walked over to somewhat shield the view of his brother in case the camera switched back to record mode.

* * * * *

Leila held herself as still as she could. She was afraid if she moved, they'd view it as an escape attempt and do who knows what. She would have been able to handle her captor once his pants were down. She'd planned to damage him beyond repair, destroy the file of her Initiation, then get to the transport bay. Rave's presence changed everything.

"I thought you'd enjoy her serving you, Rave. While I watch."

"Yes. Always. But did we get the other breeder and Warrior?"

"We lost track of them when they entered the ventilation shaft. We'll get them eventually."

He sounded quite sure of himself. Leila glanced at the monitors. She didn't see Alexa or Kam anywhere. Maybe they *had* gotten to the transport bay undetected. She could no longer see Erik, Braden, or Torque. The monitor where their images had been was currently projecting what was happening in this room.

Rave laughed. "Yes, I suppose we will. They can't hide forever. In the meantime, I think the Healer, here, needs to take a submissive position for us. Don't you?" She turned halfway and smiled toward the monitors, then turned back.

"Right...now!" Rave slapped Leila, and she fell to her knees. The woman's laughter filled the room. "Ah, that's so much better."

# Chapter Fifteen

"I'm gonna kill that bitch!" Erik shouted at the monitor. "Tear her hair out, baby. Do something! Don't let them hurt you like that. Inflict some damage yourself. I know you can do it. You've busted my balls enough times."

"Do you have it?" Braden asked Torque, glancing back at Erik.

"In a minute. In a minute."

Erik paced, hit his palm with his fist, paced again — never taking his eyes off the monitor. He muttered, cursed, then fell deadly silent, which worried Braden more than the man's raving.

When Erik got quiet, he got dangerous, conserving his strength for whatever fight he thought lay ahead. Braden had seen it before. He didn't want to be around if Erik blew.

"Hurry up, Torque."

"Don't get your dick in a knot. I'm almost there."

Erik growled low in his throat, and Braden's gaze shifted back to him. No matter what his friend said, or how he often acted, Braden knew that he cared about Leila a great deal. He could only imagine Erik's pain and feelings of helplessness.

His gaze rose to the monitor, and he cringed. If that were Alexa... He disregarded the thought. Better not let his energies move in that direction. One thing at a time. He needed to concentrate on escape. That was the most important thing, right now.

He didn't know how, but he'd make sure his people got out of there safely and back to Xylon where they belonged.

All of them.

* * * * *

Pain exploded through Leila's body. She would not let this happen! She couldn't. Not again. She'd never survive it.

Her head jerked back when the masked man grabbed her hair. The back of her neck cracked, and more pain speared through her.

Rave slowly peeled off her clothes, letting each piece fall one by one at Leila's feet. "I do so love a good come." Her black, g-string panty topped the pile.

The man chuckled. "Yes. I know. Move closer and spread your legs." His grip tightened in Leila's hair as Rave positioned herself. "Put your tongue to good use, dear Leila. Make Rave, here, purr."

They couldn't make her do this. She'd simply keep her mouth shut tight. She tried to pull her head away, but the man's hold was too strong.

Rave laughed and fingered herself, spreading her moist folds wide. "Quick flicks, then long licks, Leila. I'm sure you remember how I like it."

She'd spent years trying to forget. Bile rose in her throat, and her chest hurt so much she thought she might pass out. Until her three initiators were cold in their graves, her nightmare would never be over.

"I don't think she's going to comply, Rave."

"Sure she will. If you don't do this, Leila, we won't fulfill our end of the bargain. I know some sort of deal took place. I heard that much."

The masked man laughed.

"Oh, and Warrior Erik will be slowly tortured over and over again. Not enough to kill him, but enough to eventually drive him insane."

"No! You can't do that. You can't hurt him." Her gut churned at the thought of Erik in such pain. She knew what Rave was capable of. "Please. I'll…I'll do it. Whatever you want." She barely got the words out without choking.

Something skidded across the floor and stopped beside her hand. She stared at it in shock.

"What the crap is that?" the masked man bellowed.

"Grab it!" Rave shouted.

Leila snatched the object, a Pain Inducer, off the floor and shocked Rave on the hip before she could move far enough back.

Rave's screech filled the room, and she collapsed.

"Rave!" the man shouted. He grabbed his disruptor.

Leila immediately jerked backwards to put him off balance and shocked him in the thigh.

"Argh!"

He went down with a grunt and a thud. The Inducer hummed, set to almost full force. Rave and the masked man lay unconscious, their bodies twitching from the shock.

"Hello?" she called out into the darkness. Someone must be there. The Inducer didn't just slide across to her on its own. Her muscles clenched in anticipation, not knowing what or who to expect.

"Here."

She relaxed and cocked her head back toward the shadows where the masked man had come from. That voice… "Kam?" It couldn't be. Still on her knees, she scrambled toward the sound.

"Over here."

It *was* Kam. She bumped into his side, and he groaned. Blood. She could smell it. "You're hurt. Come into the light. Let me see." She helped him to his feet and dragged him over to the chair in front of the monitors. "Your leg. What happened?"

"An Egesa. Are you okay?" He touched her face.

"I'm fine." She jerked back from his touch, then fell to her knees and ripped his pants leg open to the hip. Ragged skin and blood came into view on his upper leg. The wounds were bad. He must be in agony. "How did you get this?"

"I found a throughway to the transport bay. Unfortunately, one of the Egesa must have seen Alexa and me enter. He came up behind us."

"How'd you get in here?" She probed the wound for tenderness.

"Hey, easy! There's a back entrance. I couldn't get in the front. I was trying to locate the main monitors, so I could find the rest of you."

"Where'd you get the Inducer?" Not that it was important, but she needed him to stay conscious, so she'd try to keep him talking if she could. She picked fabric out of the wound, cleaning it the best she could. An infection in a wound this size would be deadly for most. At least a Warrior, with self-healing ability, stood a chance. He was lucky the Egesa hadn't disintegrated him.

"Rave dropped it in the cell. Only thing that saved me. I was able to zap the Egesa with it when he got too close. I couldn't get past the smelly thing though. We struggled and ended up turned around somehow. After the current hit him, he bloated up like a giant sea puff. I had to come back." He winced.

"Sorry. Did Alexa get to the transport bay?"

"I think so. But she can't get out on her own. You need to get to her. You can pilot an orbiter."

"I have to take care of you, right now. I don't have anything to help the pain or to prevent infection. They took my equipment. I can stop the flow of blood for now." She yanked at his belt. "But that's all."

"I'll heal. Don't worry about patching me up. Just get to the transport bay. Take the Inducer with you."

"What about their disruptors?" she asked indicating the two sprawled on the floor.

"The weapons are modified. They won't work for us. Don't use the throughway. Go down the main ventilation shaft. It won't take you all the way. You'll have to transfer to the ladder tube when you reach security, so be careful. Go down one deck, then re-enter ventilation and go the rest of the way, if you can. I don't know from there if it reaches the transport bay, but it's your only option."

"I'm not leaving you here."

"Yes. You are. Right now, I'm expendable. Alexa isn't. Xylon needs her super breeder genes."

"I know what's at stake. Let's not argue about it. I have to put this on you." She needed to stabilize Kam. She'd use his belt as a tourniquet and hope it held.

The door to the control room popped and scraped open, squealing in protest.

"Kam!" Leila moved to shield him.

Erik, Torque, and Braden rushed in.

She breathed a sigh of relief. "Over here."

Erik's concerned gaze immediately focused on her. He rushed across the room and grabbed her by the shoulders. "Are you all right?" He pulled her against his chest, wrapping his arms around her.

"I'm fine. Kam is hurt," she said, her voice muffled against his chest. Her arms circled his waist. He felt warm and safe, and oh so strong. She never wanted him to let go.

"Where's Alexa?" Braden demanded.

"Hopefully in the transport bay," Kam answered, his voice weak.

"We have to get these collars off," Torque said. "I'll see if I can find the controls."

Leila heard him punch some buttons and flip a few switches. This would all be over soon.

Everyone went still and quiet. Erik's arms eased away from her.

She glanced up at his narrowing eyes, then stepped back and turned to see what had happened. She followed their gazes to the monitors. Every screen reflected the video of her Initiation. Dare was pumping his cock roughly into her from behind, while Rave smacked her face, and Shear bit down on one of her nipples. No... "Turn it off. Turn it off!" Physical and emotional pain burned through her as she experienced the horror all over again.

Torque hit a button, and the screens went black. No one said anything. No one moved.

Nothing could be worse than this never-ending torment from her past. She wanted to sink into the ground and hide from them all. She felt Erik behind her. She wished he'd touch her, hold her again, make it all go away. Or say it didn't matter. He made no move to do any of that. What must they think of her now? Tears slid down her cheeks, and she swiped them away.

Braden was the first to break the silence. "All right, everyone. We have business. We won't stay undiscovered for long. Not with these collars on."

Leila turned when she felt Erik move. He walked across the room to stand over Rave and the masked man. A look she couldn't discern crossed his face as he stared down at the naked woman. His intense gaze rose to meet hers, then he turned away, dismissing her completely.

She'd never seen such a cold look in anyone's eyes. Her heart thudded hard in her chest, and she swallowed the lump in her throat. She didn't know if he blamed her or not. She never could read him. But she knew his feelings had somehow changed. And she ached for what might have been.

Braden turned to his brother. "After we get these collars off, we're going down the throughway."

"No," Kam murmured.

"You know about the throughway?" Leila asked.

"I used to navigate one of these freighters and submitted plans for their conversion right before The Council decided to junk them all and invest in new ships instead."

"Egesa," Kam mumbled.

"What?" Erik asked, crouching down over the masked man.

"He was attacked by an Egesa in the throughway," Leila explained. "The body is blocking the way. Even if we manage to move it, they'll probably be watching that passage for the rest of us."

Braden clamped a hand on Kam's shoulder. "We'll get you back to The Lair, somehow. Don't worry. Leila will fix you up good as new."

Leila watched Erik pull at the mask.

"Damn."

"What?" she asked, moving closer.

"I can't get it off. It's adhered somehow."

Torque's head snapped up. "Found it. These collars are history."

\* \* \* \* \*

Laszlo flipped some switches, trying to get the information he needed. Monitors snapped on and off. If he thought whacking them on the side would help him find what he needed, he'd try it. He hated technology. All the Monitor Assistants had left to parts unknown, and he didn't know how the tracking equipment worked.

So many Warriors had defected or gone into hiding, not only from the ship, but on Xylon too, that The Lair was weak. He should never have left the planet.

Another uprising from the banishment zones. He feared what he'd find once they got back home.

He couldn't find the team he was looking for. They hadn't defected. They'd never turn their backs on Xylon. He knew they were still in the thick of things…somewhere.

But were they dead or alive? He really doubted they were dead. Though most others would consider it a distinct possibility, he knew better. He'd learned long ago not to underestimate anyone in that group. They wouldn't give up easily.

He checked the time. The entry point back to their star system was almost upon them. If the team didn't show up soon, he'd have to leave without them. He had no choice. If he had enough crew left to navigate the damn ship.

* * * * *

They all exited the engineering shaft. Ventilation was under guard on the deck below security, and they couldn't re-enter. Using the engineers' shaft wasn't safe, but their last chance. And luck had been with them. Only one Egesa had stumbled upon the group, and Torque had taken care of him with speed and efficiency.

Braden came out first, his eyes immediately searching for Alexa in the transport bay. He spotted her crouched behind some barrel-like structures. She was safe. Relief flooded through him.

He saw two Egesa enter on the far side of the bay. Other than that, the area seemed deserted. Probably some sort of shift change. Their window of opportunity wouldn't last. They needed to hurry.

Leila tumbled out of the shaft. She looked drained. He'd have to look into her Initiation. He hadn't known that she was one of the females abused by Dare, Shear, and Rave before they were banished from The Lair. From Erik's reaction, he suspected his friend hadn't known either.

Erik emerged and dragged Kam out after him. He hefted Kam over his shoulder. The man had fallen unconscious from blood loss and pain shortly after they entered the shaft.

Torque brought up the rear, still trying to wipe the Egesa's black, sticky blood from his hands.

They quickly made their way over to Alexa.

At their approach, her eyes widened in fear, then she visibly relaxed. She rushed forward and fell into his arms. Braden covered her lips with his in a tender kiss. She felt so good against his body. She'd been crying. He could taste the salty tears. He held her tighter, wanting to take away all her pain.

"Do the kissy-face stuff later, you two," Erik interrupted.

Alexa pulled back and looked his way. "Kam!" She rushed over to him, new tears rolling down her cheeks. "Is he alive? An Egesa came up behind us in the ventilation shaft. He saved my life." Her hands fluttered over him.

Braden owed Kam a lot. He wouldn't forget what he'd done for Alexa.

"He'll be all right, Alexa," Leila assured her. "As long as we get him back home."

"There's our ride." Torque pointed to a nearby orbiter. "It's open, with a clear launch path."

"Let's go." Braden grabbed Alexa's hand, and they all ran up the orbiter's ramp.

An alarm blared.

"We've been spotted! Strap in, everyone." Torque took the pilot's seat.

Braden sat at navigation.

Erik pulled out a sleeper and lay Kam on it. Leila strapped him in, then helped secure Alexa.

Braden turned in his seat. "Leila, get on communication. Tell the Xylon ship we're coming. Erik, man the weapons. The Egesa will fire their lasers as soon as we clear the bay. Their hand disruptors can't do much damage, so don't worry about any minor hits we sustain while still docked."

Alexa couldn't stop shaking. She pulled at the strap across her chest. She wanted to help Kam, help the others, but knew there wasn't anything she could do.

"Hold on!" Torque shouted.

The orbiter's engines charged to full, the ship vibrated and shot forward, out of the bay, and into space.

An on-ship alarm pierced the air.

"What's that?" she shouted.

"They've locked onto us!" Braden yell back. "Stay strapped in."

The orbiter lurched. Something hit them hard from outside.

"Shot starboard," Erik reported. "Minimal damage. Returning fire."

Leila flipped switches and pushed control squares. "Xylon 306108, this is Q-Team 03. We're heading your way in a Marid orbiter. We are being fired upon. Request assistance."

Another jolt hit them. Then two more, from a different side.

"Shit!" Braden hit some controls. "The Xylon ship is firing at us. Leila! They think we're Marid, probably on a suicide mission to ram the orbiter into their engines."

"I can't get through to them. They're not responding."

Kam groaned and moved his head. He said something, but all the noise drowned out his words. Alexa unstrapped herself and staggered to his side, barely able to keep to her feet with the ship jerking back and forth. "What is it?" She lowered her ear to his mouth.

"Kam says to use Channel 108," she relayed.

"The channels don't go that high," Leila responded.

"It's a control-only channel," Braden shouted back. "Damn! I thought The Lair ships discontinued those years ago. It's worth a shot."

The ship jolted as three more shots hit them.

"It's supposed to be an over-ride," he explained. "If it's still active, that particular one will open the Xylon transport bay. They'll know it's us."

"I've never heard of it," Erik replied.

"It's classified. Leila, try it!"

"I can't. The Marid system won't connect that high. I'd need some of their communication circuits to add to the board."

"Someone better come up with an idea," Torque responded. "Two more major hits, and we're gone."

"Wait!" Alexa pulled the vid-cell from her pocket. "Will this help? It's one of their communication devices. Kam said their hand-helds couldn't connect to the Xylon ship. And it's not working—"

"Doesn't matter." Leila snatched the cell. "The circuits will charge. And a transmitter board can lock into any system."

# Chapter Sixteen

Alexa's eyes fluttered open. She yawned and stretched her sore limbs. As she turned over onto her back, a brown and gold ceiling came into her line of vision. Where was she now?

It was disconcerting to keep waking up in strange or unexpected surroundings. This was the third time it had happened to her lately.

Once they'd finally docked on the Xylon ship, she'd fallen asleep immediately in the quarters Braden had ushered her into. And this was not the same room. She had no clue how long she'd slept. She didn't even know if she was still onboard the ship. It didn't feel like it.

Memories of Braden holding her tenderly made her smile, and she felt all warm inside. He'd told her that she'd done well, and that he'd protect her forever. Not a declaration of love, and *forever* was a scary thought, but at the same time, a measure of comfort and security lay in his words.

Now what? She didn't know what choices she'd make about her future. She figured whatever choice she did make would be permanent, so she had to be absolutely certain that she did the right thing.

Oh, this bed felt good. The soft mattress cushioned her body like a cloud. Draped across her was a deep blue, silk sheet. She peeked underneath. Naked. Figured.

Her eyes scanned the room. Deep greens, blues, and browns. Masculine, but safe. That's how it felt.

Only one room, it looked like. A combination bedroom and living space, with a small kitchenette, and what she assumed was a bathroom behind one of the three closed doors she saw. The other two probably being a closet and the entryway.

A brown couch and a couple of green, over-stuffed chairs sat in the center of the room. It looked sort of like an old-fashioned, fancy hotel room on Earth. She'd expected alien furnishings, strange colors, and textures.

"Braden," she called.

No one seemed to be around. She eased off the bed. "Oh…" Every muscle hurt. She needed a hot shower and a good massage. The image of Braden washing her, then kneading her limbs and sore back came to mind. A tantalizing thought.

She needed to find something to put on. She could hardly remember the last time she'd been clothed properly. A tall dresser stood next to the bed. She began rifling through the drawers. Underwear, handkerchiefs, a box marked *Toys*. Toys? Oh, no. Please.

Did Braden have a family? Children? She was so stupid. She'd asked Leila about other women, but not about children. The thought made her chest ache.

The box wasn't very big to contain playthings. She gently lifted the lid, as if expecting a monster to jump out, and peeked inside. She almost laughed, and her worries melted away. She should have known. Sex toys—a cock ring, vibrator, anal beads, plus some items she couldn't identify.

A deep chuckle reached her ears.

She spun around at the sound. A gasp stuck in her throat. She grabbed for the sheet, tugging and pulling until she was able to cover herself.

"I've already seen you naked."

Her heart pounded. "When?" Probably while they were on the Marid ship, before he'd given her his shirt.

"In your bedroom." A wolfish smile crossed his face. "I got so close to helping with your Initiation. That would have been…satisfying."

*No!* "Who are you, Torque?"

He pushed away from one of the doors. "Braden didn't tell you about me?"

"We haven't had time to talk."

He stepped in front of her. "My brother never was much of a talker."

Brother? Yes. She saw the resemblance now. No wonder he seemed familiar. "Where is Braden? For that matter, where are we?"

"We're in Braden's quarters in The Lair."

"We're on Xylon? Already?"

"Once the ship entered the system, we were close. You actually slept for almost two days."

"I did?"

"Braden's at a Council meeting or what's substituting as a Council meeting. Not many of the original members are still here. He asked me to watch you while he was gone. Make sure you were all right."

"And Kam?" This place had an odd feel to it. The room had no windows. She felt air circulating though, and large pictures of alien-looking landscapes and seascapes kept her from feeling closed in. The pictures seemed familiar. Similar to visions she'd had in her dreams.

"Your brother will be fine."

Their secret was out. "You know?"

"He told us. Braden pitched a fit about it, but that was to be expected. My brother doesn't like it when he's uninformed. Seems Kam and Laszlo manipulated quite a few people to go against The Council's recommendation of who would initiate you. It was all supposed to be very hush-hush. I don't know the details. Why'd you keep it a secret about Kam? You could have said something at any time."

"I guess I was trying to get used to the idea myself. Besides, the time never seemed right to say anything. Things got crazy fast."

"Doesn't matter now, I suppose. Laszlo's disappeared, and Braden is ranking Warrior, so he has access to all the files and information at this point. At least, everything that was recorded."

A measure of pride filled her. Braden would make a great leader. "Not you? You're older, aren't you?"

"Yeah, I'm older." A grin stretched Torque's mouth.

When that's all he said, she fidgeted and clutched the sheet tighter. "What happens next?"

He shrugged. His gaze dipped down the front of the sheet, then back up again. "What do you want to happen?"

She felt uncomfortable being alone with this man and wished Braden would hurry back. "Do I really have a choice?"

He closed the space between them. "You always have a choice." He reached out and plucked at the sheet. "You could even come with me."

Alexa couldn't suppress the nervous laughter that bubbled out of her. She backed up and bumped into the dresser. "Why would I do that? Why would you want me to?"

"You're a super breeder, right?"

"So I've been told."

"Super breeders are rare. And have certain sexual needs. What's yours? Your cunt looked like a real tasty morsel. Do you like being eaten? Or do you prefer getting fucked up the ass, maybe?"

Alexa inhaled sharply and felt her face heat. "How dare you be so crude!"

"Life here is restrictive. I could show you adventure, Alexa."

"I think I've had enough adventure for a while."

"I'll teach you to love it. Crave it. Crave me." His hand rose to touch her cheek.

"Don't." She crowded against the dresser. Why would Braden leave her alone with him? He had to know what his brother was like. If he did touch her, she'd scratch his eyes out. She only wanted Braden touching her. A brief memory of Erik flickered through her mind, but she pushed the sexual images aside.

"Move away from her, Torque."

Alexa jumped. Braden. Thank goodness. She hadn't heard him enter. His hands clenched, and the muscle in his jaw ticked. He looked wound tight and ready to explode.

Torque raised both hands in supplication. "Just trying to find out her loyalties. For your own good, brother."

"Don't do me any favors. I'm not going through this with you twice. I told you to stand *outside* the door."

Twice? Alexa's gaze shifted from one man to the other. The tension was palpable.

"I thought I heard her call out."

Had she? Right before she woke up maybe. She'd been dreaming of Braden. So it was possible, she supposed.

"The new Council has decided to lift your banishment due to your help in getting us back home. They're getting you a room and rank assignment now. You should see to it or they're liable to give you a closet and trash duty. You're not on their top ten of favorite people."

"Why? Just because I refused to train as a Dispenser and burned down the facility? They can kiss my ass. See you around, bro." He glanced back at Alexa before stepping out the door. "Enjoy her...while you can. Unless you replace the rest of The Council, they'll turn on you, as they did Dad. They'll take her from you and put her away for the good of Xylon, no matter what you do or say. Just as they tried to do with Mother. On this one thing, at least, listen to your older brother."

Alexa saw Braden stiffen. After Torque closed the door, she asked, "What did he mean by all that? Put away? What's a Dispenser?"

"Nothing for you to worry about."

She practically growled at his response. Frustration and impatience built up inside her. "Don't put me off."

He let out a heavy breath. "A Dispenser is Xylon's version of a Pain Master, like those three who came after us on the Marid ship. The other subjects are not open for discussion at this time." Braden walked toward her, a scowl on his face.

His attitude left something to be desired. She'd leave it alone, for the moment, but only because the intense look on his face as he approached gave her pause. She'd have backed up, but there was nowhere to go. She knew he'd never hurt her. Still, that Alpha male thing was unpredictable.

Maybe he intended to grab her, kiss her, and toss her onto the bed. That would be okay. Instead, he squeezed past her and opened one of the dresser drawers.

He pulled out a silky, black shirt with short sleeves. "Here. Wear this. I'll have more appropriate clothes sent up."

Their fingers brushed as she took the garment from him. A little shiver of excitement traveled all the way up her arm. She studied the material. "More than a tad small for you, isn't it?"

A smile tugged at his lips, and he shrugged.

Probably some female's. She turned her back, dropped the sheet, and slipped on the shirt. The material felt soft against her skin and molded to her body, but barely covered her butt. When she turned back around, Braden was grinning. "What?"

"Nothing. You've just got the sexiest ass I've ever seen."

He reached for her, but she sidestepped him and strolled over to one of the seascapes on the wall. "What are these controls?" A red button and a green button were on the side of the frame. The whole thing was huge for a picture, probably five feet by five feet.

"Push the green one."

She pressed the green button, and the blue-green waves in the picture moved back and forth. Some sort of bird cried out in the distance. She even smelled the sea's salty spray. "Nice." She turned back toward him. "Why aren't there any windows, Braden?"

"Not practical."

"Because?"

"We're underground."

Alexa's stomach clenched. Underground. "Why?"

"It's where The Lair is located. Warrior Headquarters. We have an uprising on the surface. We're safer down here until we can get it under control. And we *will* get it under control."

"So, what do we do now?" She couldn't seem to settle her thoughts. She still didn't completely understand who these people were. Not really. Who her parents were. Who she was.

"What do we do now?" A grin quirked his lips. "I have a few ideas."

"I'm serious, Braden." Torque had said The Council would take her away. She shuddered at the thought. She'd have to trust Braden to protect her from that possibility.

"So am I."

Falling into his arms now, like this, didn't feel right. She tugged at the bottom of the shirt. "I'm not here simply for your sexual pleasure, you know."

"Did I say you were? Though that role would work for me." He chuckled.

"I'd hoped to explore Xylon."

"We will once it's safe. I'll show you around. It's beautiful, especially at night."

"Even with the Egesa?"

"We have protected zones."

She looked at the five multi-colored moons in one of the landscapes. The sky was an eerie dark red. "These are pictures of the planet and moons."

"That's right."

"What's the weather like up there?"

"Right now, we're having a blizzard. Our weather patterns and seasons are similar to Earth's. Perhaps a bit more extreme, but nothing you won't be able to handle."

She nodded, surprised by how warm she felt. They had good temperature control. "Where will I live?"

"With me, of course."

She turned toward him. "I'm still my own person, Braden. And you're not my only lifeline here. I have Kam."

Braden's eyes darkened. He stalked her, until he had her trapped in a corner. "You belong to me, Alexa. Kam is my friend, but you are my woman." He immediately stepped back and ran a hand through his hair. "Shit. Sorry. That sounded…"

"Jerk-ish."

He grinned. "Yeah." He held out his hand. "Come sit with me. Please."

She hesitated a moment, then slid her hand into his. His fingers closed protectively around hers, and he tugged her to the couch. They sat side by side, and angled toward each other, hands still clasped.

"I'd like you to stay with me, Alexa. By my side."

Her pulse jumped. His fingers tightened around hers, and she suspected the calmness in his voice belied what he was actually feeling. Or maybe that was just her own feelings. "Are you asking me to marry you?"

"I…no. Not exactly."

She couldn't help the disappointment that flowed through her. She'd thought for a minute… "What did Torque mean by enjoy me while you can? And please don't say that it's nothing." She had a bad feeling about all this.

He rubbed his chin. "It's…complicated."

"Everything I've experienced with you so far has been complicated. I need to know."

"The old Council originally selected Laszlo to initiate you."

"The former leader who's disappeared?" When he arched an eyebrow in query, she replied, "Torque told me that much."

"Yes. To initiate and to mate. To produce Warrior children. Normally, a woman has a choice in these matters."

"Normally?"

"Super breeders don't."

She stiffened. "You lied to me! You said I wouldn't be forced."

"I said you wouldn't be forced to go through the Initiation. And you weren't. I, personally, would never force you to do anything you didn't want."

Alexa withdrew her hand. She rose to her feet. "You people are crazy." She waved her arms in the air. "Everything is so out there. So over the top."

"Our numbers have been weakening. We need a strong Breeder Program to strengthen our power with the best matches. Kam and Laszlo found out about your super breeder status from genetic material provided by your father. They decided you and I would make a better match. I also think Laszlo has someone else picked out for himself, though he never said that specifically. The Council disagreed, because there's some instability in my family line. They didn't want to take a chance. Especially after Torque went rogue. Even now, my lead position in The Council is shaky."

"What do you mean?"

"My mother was a super breeder. Because of our planet's needs, they wanted her to multi-mate breed. She refused, and they tried to take her away. To force her compliance."

"What happened?"

"She killed herself."

Alexa choked back the sob that leapt to her throat. "I'm so sorry, Braden."

He barely nodded, but a grim look filled his eyes. "I don't really remember that much about her."

"You must have other siblings, besides Torque. Since he's obviously older, and super breeders have more than one child each time."

"Two sisters. One twin to me, and one twin to Torque. They're on Xylon ships right now, patrolling in another star system. They've been called back home because of the uprising. They'll be here in a couple of weeks."

"Torque said I'd be taken away. Will I be forced to multi-mate?" Alexa shook her head. "Geez! I don't know who to direct my anger at first. This is all so ridiculous! I'm not a piece of property for Xylon to breed at will. I want to talk to this Council. I want to talk to Kam." She stalked across the room and punched a button, hoping it would open the door. Closet. She punched another button, and the other door slid open. Corridor. Good.

"Where are you going? You're not dressed."

She stormed out.

He quickly followed. "Come back into the room with me, Alexa."

"I said I want to talk to Kam."

Two men rounded the corner. One sent a wolf whistle her way. "Nice ass, baby."

The other laughed. "Need a hand, Braden?"

Alexa tugged at the bottom of the shirt.

"Shut up, Pitch, or I'll fry *your* ass."

"As long as you stay away from my balls." He laughed and clapped his friend on the back.

Alexa rounded the corner.

"Alexa, stop!" Braden rushed to catch up with her. He moved in front of her, blocking her path. "You need to calm down before you speak to anyone."

She stepped around him. Rounding another corner, she stopped. Elevators. A woman exited, eyeing her strangely. Alexa quickly moved inside.

Braden squeezed in right before the doors closed. "You're upset."

"What gave you the first clue?" She studied the control panel and arbitrarily picked a button and punched it.

They began to move upwards.

Braden punched another button, and they came to a halt. He crossed his arms over his chest and leaned back against the wall.

Alexa glared at him. "Start us up, Braden."

"Not until you calm down. You don't even know where to go."

She punched several buttons, but nothing happened. Frustration built until she felt ready to blow. "What else haven't you told me?"

"You want to know everything? Fine. As lead initiator, I have the right to take you as mistress. As decreed by the old Council, Laszlo is still supposed to take you as mate. I don't know yet whom else they selected, if anyone, given your super breeder genes. But I won't allow it to happen. I intend to Brand you as mine. Mine alone."

It took a moment before she could respond. "Brand? That's the second time you've mentioned that to me, and I don't think I like the sound of it. What does that mean? You should have told me about all this before. Mistress? What happened to my rights? Maybe I *will* leave with Torque." Alexa regretted the words as soon as they left her mouth. A deep hurt filled Braden's gaze, and he didn't attempt to hide it from her. Her heart ached at his obvious pain. She hadn't meant to hurt him. She hung her head. "I'm sorry. I didn't mean that. I'm just—"

"You're scared."

She nodded. "What if you can't get The Council's decision overturned? Will they take me away from you, like Torque said? I couldn't live imprisoned somewhere, letting whoever they decreed fuck me until I ended up pregnant."

"Don't worry about it, Alexa. It's not going to happen."

After a moment of silence, she felt his arms slip around her. She didn't pull back. Despite their confrontation, she didn't want to be apart from him. She needed his strength, his touch. He was her anchor in all this craziness. His lips brushed her cheek, her ear, the side of her neck.

"You don't have to be afraid." He cupped her cheeks in his palms and raised her head until their gazes met. "Do you trust me?"

"Yes."

"Completely."

She sank her teeth into her bottom lip. Complete trust was a lot to ask. After her father had left, she'd never completely trusted anyone again. She looked into his eyes and drowned in his violet gaze.

He lowered his head, and his mouth covered hers in a tender kiss. Their tongues touched, and he slipped his arms around her back. One hand glided down her side and hip, then pushed up the shirt to cup her bare bottom.

She gasped into his mouth. Her fingers burrowed under his shirt, seeking his hard, warm flesh. When her nails grazed his skin, he groaned. She loved the sounds he made when excited.

He broke the kiss, yanked the shirt over her head, and tossed it to the floor. He pulled his own off and let it fall next to hers.

She wanted his pants off, too. She needed him naked and vulnerable like she was. She reached for his belt and tugged.

He brushed her hands aside and lifted her up. "Wrap your legs around me."

She automatically did so, but she really wanted him naked. She was about to say so when his lips latched onto her breast, and he sucked her nipple deep into his mouth. Okay. This was good, too. "Oh." Really good. Her head fell back. "Yes."

Shifting to her other breast, he stroked his tongue over and around the nipple, until she thought she'd explode from need. "I need a quickie, Braden, not this drawn out seduction."

"Mmm," was all he answered. His tongue continued to softly lick her nipples—first one, then the other.

She burrowed her fingers in his hair. Her hips pressed against him as the pressure built inside her. She had to have him inside her. Soon.

His fingers caressed her butt, driving her need even higher. He pressed her back against the wall and licked at the skin between her breasts. His tongue was everywhere, driving her crazy. She tugged on his hair, and he moved to cover her mouth in a searing kiss. Their lips locked. Their tongues tangled. She couldn't get enough of him. Trembling with desire, her legs eased from around his waist, until her feet touched the floor.

Braden stepped back and simply looked at her—a slow perusal from head to toe and back again.

The passion and need in his eyes intrigued her. She didn't even feel an urge to cover her nakedness. She liked the way he looked at her. Suddenly, she glanced up into the corners.

"No cameras. Don't worry." He pulled off his boots and socks. Then reached for his belt.

Alexa's heart pounded triple time. She chewed at her bottom lip and clasped her hands. He was moving too slow. She wanted to tackle him, strip him naked, and impale herself on his hard cock, until she screamed out her pleasure and satisfaction.

He unlatched the leather and pulled it from the loops. "Turn around."

"What?"

He doubled the belt in his hands.

Her breath caught. He wanted...spanking her with his hand to stimulate her sexually was one thing, but this was entirely different. "Oh, no. You are *not* going to—"

"Turn around and put your palms flat against the wall, your arms all the way up. Now."

# Chapter Seventeen

Alexa hesitated, then turned, as he instructed. She kept her eyes locked on his, wondering what wicked thoughts were filling his mind, until the last moment when her head wouldn't turn any further. Then she closed her eyes and swiveled her face toward the wall.

She wasn't sure why she followed his near-order to expose herself like this, but she did. She didn't want to examine her motives too closely. She just knew that giving him total control over her body was something she needed to do. She needed to know if she could trust him. And needed *him* to know that she was willing to trust him, in all things, as long as he didn't abuse that trust. She only hoped that she hadn't misjudged him and really could trust Braden. If she couldn't, more than her physical well-being was at stake.

Once in position, her backside vulnerable to him, her arms raised against the wall, she felt the heat of his body inch closer. Her heart kicked up, and sweat formed on her brow. She could actually hear her own breathing.

"Good decision," he whispered in her ear. "So beautiful and so very…submissive."

"Hmph." She didn't like the sound of that. She wondered how it would feel to turn the tables on him, and have Braden up against the wall.

His fingers grazed her ass.

Pleasure rippled through her, causing her skin to heat and contract. One simple touch from him was all it took for her to react.

The belt brushed her backside, then her upper thighs. At the light touch, she tensed and bit into her bottom lip to stop any mewling sounds from escaping her lips.

Braden's low chuckle vibrated against her senses. "Spread your legs." When she hesitated, he nudged her feet farther apart with his foot.

She swallowed hard, not knowing what to expect from him. Her imagination ran wild with possibilities. Some delightful, some just the opposite.

He popped the belt, and she gasped, then pressed herself flush against the wall. The cold steel felt good against her hard nipples, the plane of her stomach, her quivering thighs. She pressed her forehead to the steel and waited.

A heartbeat passed. Another.

He was waiting for something too, apparently, but she wasn't sure what. She arched her back, thrusting her ass back toward him. An offering. Complete and total. She couldn't do any more than that to show her willingness.

"Ultimate trust. In me," he said, his voice gruff with emotion.

She heard the belt drop to the floor. At the clank of the buckle against the tile, all the energy drained out of her. She'd have collapsed if his hands hadn't spanned her waist to hold her up. "You did that on purpose, Braden. As a test."

"Yes. And you were testing me, too." He kissed the side of her neck, reached up, and slid her hands down her sides.

"Yes. I was." She turned in his arms and rested her cheek against his chest.

His sharp intake of breath touched her heart. He felt their connection, just like she did. She knew that now.

His arms tightened around her.

She turned her head and grazed her lips against his skin, then licked his nipple. One, delicate swipe.

A growl vibrated his chest. One of his hands tangled in her hair, holding her close, urging her to lick that hard bud again. The other hand reached down and popped the snap on his pants. The sound seemed incredibly loud in the small space.

Her fingers immediately found the zipper and tugged it down as she repeatedly flicked his nipple with her tongue. Her teeth nibbled the fleshy nub, then she sucked it into her mouth.

"Ah, good."

She needed him—needed to get as close as she could, as close as two people could get. Her fingers pushed inside his pants and curled around him.

He pulled away from her mouth and hand, stepping back a couple of feet. Before she could protest, he shoved his pants and underwear to the floor and kicked them into the corner. Her gaze dropped to his cock. Long, thick, and oh so hard. He didn't move, allowing her to look her fill. She vaguely registered his hands fisting, opening, then fisting again. A bead of moisture formed on the tip of his shaft, drawing her attention. The memory of his cock—the taste of him—in her mouth came back in a flash, and she licked her lips.

"Shit, Alexa." He groaned, and his knuckles turned white as he clenched his hands tightly. "Don't do that when you're staring at my cock, or I'll lose it right here."

A smile tugged at her lips. His confession of her effect on him gave her a sense of power she found intoxicating.

Before she realized his intention, he moved forward, and his hands were everywhere. Her hands followed, needing him just as badly. They touched and greedily explored each other's body, as if for the first time. He squeezed her breasts, brushed her nipples, massaged her ass. She grazed her nails across his chest, over the hard nubs of flesh, down his abdomen.

His strong, toned flesh pressed against her soft curves. The contrast of male to female caused a primitive reaction in her, a sense of possession and belonging.

Braden lifted her leg and draped it over his hip. His fingers touched her curls, then delved deep to stroke her intimately. "Wet and hot. Hot for me. Say it!"

"Yes. For you." She pulled at his hips. "Now, Braden. Now."

In the next instant, he was inside her, buried deep. Neither of them moved. Their gazes locked.

*Anything for you.* At that moment, she realized, indeed, she'd do anything he asked.

Braden turned her, so her back was against the wall. He rested his palms just above her shoulders and slowly pushed his cock deeper.

She moaned at the feel of him, completely filling her. His smell filled her senses. His taste was on her mouth. She grasped his ass, pulling him closer, pressing her hips against him. "More."

Even against her tight hold, he managed to pull back, then again pushed deep. Slow strokes. Back and forth. Over and over. "It's never felt as good as it does with you, Alexa," he ground out in a voice strangled by emotion.

She was in trouble here, because she felt the same. "Yes. Oh, yes." Whether she liked it or not, agreed with his lifestyle or not, she couldn't deny her feelings. But she also couldn't fully admit them, at least not aloud, not yet. Instead, she confessed her physical need. "Faster, Braden."

"Not this time." He pulled almost all the way out of her pussy, then slowly pushed back in.

Alexa couldn't take this. Her body needed to come. Now. This on-the-edge pleasure had her muscles and limbs shaking with a need so strong that she thought she'd go mad. Her nails dug into his hips. She undulated against him.

"Yeah. That's right. Move against me." He matched his rhythm to hers. Then he slowed the motion way down, again drawing out the pleasure.

Alexa whimpered.

"Soon, baby. Soon." Braden plucked at her nipples and drew his tongue slowly down the length of her neck. "It's going to be so good."

She shivered. "Braden..." She teetered right on the edge of what felt like a massive orgasm, just beyond her reach.

At the sound of her voice, he slowed the movement of his hips even more. "Say my name again," he whispered.

"Braden, please." He was trying to kill her—kill her from want and need.

"Please what?" He licked at the delicate skin along her ear and circled his finger around her nipple. "Tell me."

"Ah, oh. I need to...I need to come."

"Me, too." He nibbled at her earlobe. A growl, from deep in his chest, vibrated both their bodies. "So much that it hurts."

"Then why are you torturing me? Us?"

Braden stilled his movements completely. His body protested. He wanted to fuck Alexa hard and fast, until his cock exploded inside her, and she shattered in his arms. But he wanted something else even more. "Stay with me. Promise. And I'll finish this."

Her hips moved against him, her body seeking fulfillment. "That's sexual blackmail, Braden. I can't think clearly right now." Her teeth sank into his shoulder, then she licked the bite to soothe whatever mark she'd left.

He grabbed her wrists and pushed her more firmly against the wall. Studying her flushed features, he pumped her hard with each word. "Promise…me! Promise…me…or…I'll…pull…out…now."

She whimpered. Her head moved from side to side, and she cried out from the intensity of her need. "Yes, yes! All right. I promise."

Braden didn't care that he'd coerced the promise. He intended to hold her to it and make her never regret those words. He tightened his hold on her wrists and moved against her, quickly building his rhythm until he was fucking her like this was his last time.

"Yes, Braden. Yes!" Her leg tightened around his hip. Her fingers curled around his hands.

He continued thrusting, not letting up on her. He couldn't. His control was gone. Nothing was going to stop him now.

"Yes. Oh, yes! Move, like…yes, like that. Don't stop. Don't—oh, that's perfect." She matched his motion, moving with him, against him, begging him for more with each hard thrust he delivered.

He was never letting this woman go. Never! Alexa was everything he'd ever wanted. Everything he needed. His grunts and groans filled his ears, as well as her mewls and squeaks of pleasure. The feel of their bodies merging, his cock moving deep and hard, then shallow and easy inside her tight pussy, took him to the heights of ecstasy. A low moan, that he wasn't sure which of them uttered, wafted around him.

"Faster, Braden. Yes. Perfect…right there. Yes. A little harder now. A little…oh, oh, oh."

He was about to come. He couldn't hold out any longer. He released her wrists and pinched her nipples, tugging on the buds of flesh. "Come, Alexa," he demanded. "Now!"

"Ah! Yes. I'm coming!" She screamed and dug her nails into his shoulders.

"Yeah. Oh, yeah!" He felt her pussy contract hard around him. His cock erupted, spilling his seed deep inside her. He roared out his pleasure, certain the whole compound must have heard him and not caring if they had.

He collapsed against her, surprised he was even able to remain upright, he felt so shaky.

Alexa breathed heavily against his shoulder. "That was...beyond great."

"I give it an eight."

Braden shoved Alexa behind him as he spun around. "What the" He relaxed. Erik was leaning back against the closed door.

Alexa scrambled for her shirt.

"You took too long, and the auto-override opened the door. Good thing the place is mostly deserted, and it was just me on the other side."

Braden reached for his pants. "Why didn't you say anything?"

"You're kidding, right?"

"It would have been gentlemanly to do so," Alexa said, pulling on the shirt. She stuck close to Braden's side as he dressed.

"Yes. It would have been. Were you two headed somewhere or just looking for a little excitement?" He peered around Braden, and his gaze traveled down Alexa's body. "Nice outfit." He reached into his back pocket and extended a handkerchief to her. "You might want to, uh..."

As he zipped up, Braden glanced at her legs, following Erik's gaze. His come was trailing down her thighs. "Shit."

Alexa gasped and grabbed the handkerchief. She turned her back and cleaned herself up.

"We're going to see Kam," Braden answered, moving in front of Alexa to give her some privacy. "You want to tag along?"

Erik shrugged. "Sure." He punched a button on the control panel. "Why not?"

\* \* \* \* \*

Kam held Leila's hand. "Get that thought out of your head. It's impossible."

"I know what I know. It took me a while to figure it out, but I'm right."

He studied her features and sensed that she wasn't going to change her opinion. She was too smart for her own good. But she was also off the mark. Not by much, but enough. Probably. He couldn't stop the doubts that suddenly flooded through him. He had to get out of here and find the answers only he had access to.

"I need to tell Braden." She took his pulse. A frown crossed her face. "It's fast. Too fast." Her eyes connected with his. "Wait. You...you knew. All along."

He reached out for her wrist. "Leila, you don't understand."

She tugged against him, trying to get loose.

He saw her gaze shift to the security alarm and sensed her rising fear. "Calm down. It's all right. It's not what you think."

* * * * *

Braden, Erik, and Alexa exited the elevator. She lagged behind looking around the sterile surroundings. This was the medical floor, Braden had said. It looked deserted. All white, silver, and clean smelling. Many rooms. Lots of glass.

"Only an eight, huh?" Braden asked Erik.

"Maybe an eight-five. Not bad, considering the location."

"That macho rating shit is stupid, you know." Though she'd have been much more upset if he'd rated her like a four. It was hard to get up a good head of steam with someone who thought she had ten potential.

"I don't think I could handle a ten."

"She's got it in her, you know. But you need to spank her for a ten."

"How do you know I didn't, before you got there?"

"When she reached for her shirt, I saw her ass. It wasn't red or even pink. You should have turned her around and let me smack her butt a few times while you were fucking her. She'd have gone wild."

"I didn't know you were there."

"My mistake."

"Hey!" Alexa called out.

Braden grinned over his shoulder, but addressed his words to Erik. "Maybe we can arrange something."

"Works for me."

"Please stop talking about me like I'm not here. And if you're thinking of another three-way, forget it."

Both men stopped and turned. She walked to stand between them, glaring from one to the other as best she could, daring them to contradict her.

"So, you remember?" Braden asked.

"Yes, I remember. Most everything." She felt her face flush.

"You're really beautiful when you come, Alexa." Erik leaned close and sniffed. "You smell like sex. If that could be bottled, we'd make a fortune."

"Get your mind on something else, will you?" Though, the memory of these two pleasuring her, during the Initiation, made it hard for her to follow her own advice. And the thought of Erik spanking her, while Braden pumped his cock inside her, about made her come again right there.

Braden grinned, then did one of those weird hand signals like during the Initiation. While she was trying to figure out the gesture, he and Erik leaned in and gave her a loud, smacking kiss on each temple. Braden patted her butt, and Erik tickled her ribs.

She squealed, squirmed, and laughed so hard her stomach hurt. "Stop! Just because I'm not screaming about everything that happened doesn't mean you two are free and clear of a well-deserved lecture." Twisting away from them, she took off down the corridor.

Their laughter floated behind her, as she heard them take off after her.

"Left at the corner," Braden called out. "And cover your ass!"

"You're the one who gave me this to wear!" She flipped the back of the shirt up, mooning them, then turned the corner and ran smack into Leila. "Oof." Both of them fell to the floor.

The men rounded the corner and stopped beside the tangle.

"Babe collision."

Braden chuckled.

Alexa looked up at Erik. "Very funny. Help us up. I'm sorry, Leila. Are you all right?"

"I'm fine. Sorry. I should have been paying closer attention." She glanced at Alexa's outfit as she sat up. "You need clothes."

Braden pulled Alexa to her feet.

"Thank you." When Erik just stood there with his arms crossed, Alexa reached out for Leila. "What's your problem?" she asked him.

He simply grunted.

Braden grasped Leila's other arm, and they helped her to stand.

"Thanks." Leila turned to Braden. "I need to talk to you in private. It's important. Business."

Alexa wondered what was up now. The serious look on Leila's face worried her.

"All right," Braden answered, with only a slight narrowing of his eyes. "Why don't you two go visit with Kam," he told her and Erik.

"Good idea." Erik's fingers curled around her arm. "You know where to find us."

Alexa's gaze shifted from Erik to Leila. They were avoiding each other, their own gazes set purposely elsewhere, as if afraid even to acknowledge the other's presence. Something strange was going on between those two. Erik's fingers tightened around her arm, and he practically dragged her down the corridor. "What's with the attitude?"

"Leave it alone, Alexa."

His lips pressed into a thin line. He was hurting. She saw it in his eyes. She covered his fingers with her other hand and squeezed. "I'm sorry."

He stopped, and his surprised gaze met hers. "For what?"

"For whatever's causing you pain."

His cheeks reddened, and he started to pull away, but then his eyes softened. "Thank you." He gently raised her hand and kissed the middle of her upturned palm. "That means a lot to me."

\* \* \* \* \*

Braden rubbed his chin. "That doesn't make sense, Leila. Even if I wanted to believe it, which I don't. If that were the case, he could have taken Alexa at any time. And I never would have been in the position I was." Fear speared through him. This couldn't be happening.

"I haven't figured that part out yet. But Kam knows something. I swear he does. I saw it in his eyes when I mentioned it. He might even be in on it."

"I *won't* believe that." Everything he'd ever believed would be a lie, if Leila's suspicions were true.

"I don't want to either. But can you afford to take the chance?"

No. He couldn't afford to take the chance. Not when it involved Alexa, and maybe even the future of their world. Anything was possible, he supposed. But how could he find out the truth for sure? Worry took hold as he wondered how deep the deception might be. If there even was a deception...

"You have any ideas on how to handle this?" he asked, wanting her input.

"A trap."

"What kind?"

"The ultimate kind."

\* \* \* \* \*

Erik's vid-cell beeped. He grabbed it off his belt. "Talk to me."

"Don't let on that it's me," the voice on the other end replied. "Tell them that you're wanted by The Council, then materialize into my quarters."

Erik hesitated. "Um..." Too weird. What the hell was going on now? "All right." He snapped the cell closed. "Council duty calls. I'll see you two later."

Kam and Alexa waved him off, barely acknowledging his words; they were so engrossed in conversation. He had hoped everything would calm down now that they had Alexa safe and sound. But something was definitely off.

Leila stepped into the room just before he materialized out. Their eyes met briefly. He felt all tangled up inside and didn't know what to do about it. He wasn't used to dealing with these sorts of feelings, and it irritated him. The best way he knew to handle it was *not* to handle it. Not yet.

Erik materialized out of medical and into Braden's quarters. "What's with all the secrecy?" He watched Braden pace back and forth.

"We might have a traitor in our fold, according to Leila."

What else was new? Warriors were defecting in record numbers. They were all traitors as far as he was concerned. But the look on Braden's face made him take the news more seriously. His stomach clenched. "Who?"

\* \* \* \* \*

Alexa's eyes narrowed. "What are you doing?" Kam kept glancing over her shoulder, a worried look on his face.

"Looking for Leila."

"You heard her. She went to get some clothes for me. Do you need me to find someone? Are you in pain?"

"No." Kam struggled to sit up on the side of the bed.

"Wait. What's going on?"

"I need you to help me get out of here."

"Why?" No one had detained him against his will. Why was he acting like a prisoner who needed to escape? Something strange was going on. He looked so agitated—desperate almost. "Kam?"

"Help me." He stood up, but wobbled precariously.

Alexa steadied him. "You shouldn't be walking. It's too soon. Leila said you need at least another twenty-four hours to self-heal since the wound was so severe."

"No choice. I need clothes and a transport-connector."

"Kam, please tell me what's going on!" She felt the need to run to Braden for help. This wasn't normal.

"There's no time to explain, Alexa. Leila could be back any minute." He draped his arm around her shoulders. "Help me. In there." He pointed to a door. "I can wear one of the medical uniforms. Anything is better than this healing-wrap garb I'm in now."

She walked him into the supply room and watched the door as instructed while he dressed. She felt like an accomplice in a crime. "You have to tell me what's going on. You're scaring me." She wanted to help him, but…

He grabbed a transport-connector from a cabinet. He cupped her cheek. "Don't worry. And do what Braden says, Alexa. He's a good man. Always remember, you're dear to my heart."

Then he was gone.

# Chapter Eighteen

"Are you going to tell Alexa?" Erik asked. Worry spread through him. This was not good. He could picture Alexa's explosive reaction.

Braden shook his head. "I don't think so. Not the whole of our suspicions anyhow. This is a touchy subject. The less conflict, the better. We need to know now, without a lot of arguing back and forth. And Leila's right. If he is a traitor, and is monitoring us, this will work. It'll be his last chance at Alexa. He's powerful though, Erik. He doesn't flaunt it, but he is. We'll need to be prepared."

"What if Alexa refuses to be Branded?" It was a big step. A lifetime decision. And for someone new to the Warrior way of life, it could be traumatic.

"I don't know. I'll just have to convince her. There's no other way. She's mine, Erik. I'm not letting her go. And if this is the best way to ensure that, then it will happen. No matter what."

Erik's eyes narrowed, and an unexpected surge of protectiveness hit him. "Her own free will, Braden." The intensity in his voice surprised him, but this was something he felt adamant about. Force of any kind, when it came to Alexa, didn't sit well with him. She was special and deserved special treatment.

With a fire burning in his eyes, Braden stealthily approached. "Yes. Of course, Erik." His stare growing hotter in intensity, he added, "I appreciate your concern for her, my friend, as long as that's all it is."

Erik raised his hands in mock surrender and backed off. "That's all it is, Braden." He knew Alexa wasn't for him, so he had no intentions of challenging Braden for her. A strange ache started in the vicinity of his heart as his thoughts switched to another woman. If only…

Braden's eyes softened, and he too backed off. "I love her, Erik."

"I know." He saw it in his friend's face and heard it in his voice. Braden and Alexa would make a good couple. He had no doubt about that. After watching how they were with each other, he knew they'd last a lifetime.

Quiet settled around them. Erik understood the dynamics of their friendship would change with Braden's commitment to Alexa. But it was time. Braden needed someone like Alexa in his life to ground him. Erik doubted they'd be initiating any more women together. Alexa would never allow it, and Braden felt so emotionally attached to her that he probably had no desire to fill his needs elsewhere. Just as he was going to ask Braden about *his* physical involvement with her, the door slid open.

Alexa rushed in. "Oh! You're both here. Good. I didn't know where else to go."

"What's wrong?" Erik asked. He could see more than a slight disturbance in her eyes and concern filled him.

"Kam left. He wouldn't tell me what's going on, but something's definitely wrong. He took a transport-connector from the medical supply room and materialized out."

"Shit!" Braden responded. "He picked a hell of a time to disappear. We should have put security on him."

"Security?" Her eyes widened, and she looked from Braden to Erik and back again. "So something *is* going on. I knew it."

Braden stalked over to the dresser and grabbed a shirt. He tossed the garment at her. "Put this on, Alexa. That one you're wearing is too short. You shouldn't be roaming the corridors alone in it. You're too much of a temptation. Where's Leila?"

"I don't know." Alexa slipped the longer button-down shirt on over the one she had on. "She went to get me some clothes, but never came back. What's going on?"

A bad feeling struck Erik about Kam disappearing without a word. Especially now. This whole situation had a foul smell to it. Leila might be right after all. "I'll find her. You'll have decent clothes available in no time."

"I'm not concerned about my clothes, for crying out loud."

"I know. You don't need to worry about Kam. He can take care of himself." Better than he normally let on.

"He's still hurt."

"He'll be fine, Alexa," Braden replied. "Erik will handle this for the moment. I need to talk to you about something."

"Right now?"

"Yes. Right now."

"Later, guys." Erik headed for the door. Time to find the worm in the hole.

Alexa didn't like the feel of things. Something was definitely going on. And nobody was letting her in on it. Braden, Erik, and Kam were too protective of her. Or too secretive. She wasn't sure which it was.

She fluctuated from fear to anger to frustration to more than extreme wariness, to say the least. "I'm getting scared, Braden." An understatement if there ever was one. "Please tell me what's happening."

Braden pulled her down to the couch with him and settled her on his lap. "You're safe."

"I'm not worried about myself." Well, obviously that wasn't true, since she'd just confessed her fear, but it went deeper than that, and she was tired of him putting her off. "I'm worried about Kam." And that *was* the truth. He'd grabbed a special place in her heart, and she couldn't just dismiss what was happening with him. "Why would he take off?"

"Kam's always been like that. He gets headaches and goes off."

"Headaches?"

"He's half-Tamarian. Tamara is a planet in a nearby star system. His mother is from there. Their genetics don't always work well with Xylon biology. It creates some health problems."

"Is it serious?"

"Not for the most part."

"For the most part?"

He patted her leg. "He's fine. Leila keeps a close watch."

"How can she keep a watch when he's gone, and no one knows where he is?"

"Don't worry about him, Alexa."

"He's my brother."

"I wouldn't lie to you about his health."

Braden looked sincere, but she wasn't so sure about the explanation, and concern filled her. If it were so simple, why wouldn't Kam just have told her? There had to be more to it. Her brother had been too secretive about leaving, as if he didn't want anyone to know...or anyone to stop him. She tried to read between Braden's words, but his hand rubbing her thigh caused her thought processes to go all haywire, and she couldn't concentrate, as she should.

"I want to talk to you about something. Please hear me out on it."

Uh, oh. That didn't sound good either. What had she gotten herself into by coming to this alien planet? "All...right," she replied, drawing out the words, not sure that she really wanted to hear what he had to say.

"I want to Brand you, Alexa. Wait, now," he added quickly when she stiffened. "Let me explain what that means."

His fingers gripped her leg tighter, and his other arm wrapped around her waist, so she couldn't go anywhere. He'd trapped her. She took a deep breath and nodded. She knew he wouldn't actually detain her against her will if she insisted on getting up, so she supposed it wouldn't hurt to just stay put and listen.

"Okay. I'll listen." Maybe Branding wasn't as barbaric as it sounded. And maybe in the telling he'd reveal more about the new life she found herself a part of. She felt very lacking in information at the moment.


Braden relaxed. She hadn't protested...yet. He eased his grip on her, but kept her on his lap. He wanted her close. He felt more centered when she was near. "Branding will completely protect you from the Egesa."

When she shuddered, a heavy weight settled upon him. He wished he could take away all her fear. He only hoped he could convince her to go through with the Branding. It's not the way he would have planned what was supposed to be a private, intimate act. But, once again, her pivotal position held their future in her hands.

"But I'm safe just being here, aren't I? They can't get to me."

"Theoretically. But we have reason to believe that they've found a way to monitor our activity, and might even be able to get a man past our defenses and infiltrate The Lair."

She glanced around the room. Her teeth sank into her bottom lip. She looked so vulnerable and uncertain. He rubbed her thigh—a light caress.

"These quarters are secure. At least of listening devices. Erik and I checked. We'll do a sweep for video later today. We need to be sure you're protected as much as possible. It's not over yet, Alexa. But I'll be right here with you all the way."

She sat silent another moment before speaking. "How does Branding protect me, exactly?"

He let out the breath he'd been holding. Good. She really was willing to listen. "After it's over, no one but a Xylon Warrior, can touch you sexually. If they try, a poison will seep into their system, and they'll die a very agonizing death."

"How does the poison get into them?"

"Through the sweat glands, from yours into theirs. If the body chemistry is not compatible, the poison activates."

"Hmm, okay. But, um…why the heck did I go through the Initiation, if I could have just done this Branding thing?"

"The Initiation protects you from sterilization and poisons being transmitted sexually *and* non-sexually through torture. It also includes the self-healing element and prepares your body for breeding. A person must be initiated first, before they can be Branded."

"I don't know, Braden. It sounds creepy. And how does that protect me more anyhow? The Egesa could still kill me. Or imprison me."

"You're a super breeder. They won't kill you. Your genetics are too valuable. After the Branding, your body locks, is the best way that I can think to describe it, with mine. They won't imprison you, unless they can find a way around the properties of the Brand, because we'll be connected. We'll know, internally, where the other is at all times."

"At all times?" Her eyes widened. "So much for privacy. I'm not sure I like that idea. How long does this Branding last?"

"Forever."

She glanced away, and her fingers tangled. Her gaze slowly returned to his. "There's no way to reverse it? I mean, what if we hate each other in six months? It's possible, you know."

He chuckled. "We'll have to work it out." He pulled her closer, so her thighs were now straddling him. "It's for the best, Alexa." Time for the absolute truth. He couldn't expose his feelings any more than what he was about to do right now. He took a deep breath, then let it out slowly. "I love you, Alexa. I will always love you. And I want you with me forever."

"You love me?" Her voice cracked.

"I love you."

Alexa's heart took off at breakneck speed. No man had ever said those words to her and meant them. And she believed Braden meant them. The look in his eyes revealed his feelings. She chewed at her bottom lip. "I don't know what to say."

"I see." A sad smile tugged at his lips. "Well, that's too bad." His fingers tangled in her hair. "Regardless, let me Brand you. Please. I'll spend the rest of my life making you happy. That's a promise, Alexa. I'll see to it you never regret your decision."

She wanted to say that she loved him too, and she knew that's what he'd wanted to hear, but those words and the permanence of the Branding scared her. She'd seen so many couples break up. Her parents included. In fact, from what Kam had said, their joining was a complete lie. She hated lies, and forever was a jail sentence if a relationship developed problems.

She'd already promised Braden, in the elevator, that she would stay. But that promise had been given in the heat of the moment. Now, she was able to think more clearly. "Would that mean we were married?"

He grazed his fingers down her arms and shrugged. "Basically. We can have an Earth ceremony, too, if you like."

Basically? She wasn't sure she liked the sound of that, or the way he said it. She did believe in his love. And if he was willing to go through a regular ceremony for her, that meant he respected her feelings on the matter. But commitment was hard. She touched her stomach.

"Don't worry. You're not pregnant."

"I know. I'm protected. I was just thinking about it." She wondered why he would say that though, as if he was certain that she wasn't. She cocked her head. "You can't?" That couldn't possibly be true, given all she knew.

He laughed. "Yes. I can get you pregnant. But only during a Breeder Release. All Warriors are sterile, except during those specific times. You are now, too, and don't need any artificial means of protection anymore. It'll all be explained to you in more detail as you learn about life here."

"Seems strange for a society desperate for Warrior children. You fight so hard to stop the Egesa from sterilizing your people, then you make them sterile yourselves."

"Ours is temporary. Theirs is permanent. It's to control the strength of the species, and the timing of births. I know it's a little confusing."

She rubbed her arms. Everything about Xylon society was confusing to her. "I'm still concerned about this Branding, Braden." And not convinced that she should go through with it. "Does it hurt?"

"Not if done correctly. All male breeders have an implant in their mouths, along the inner portion of the lips. A corresponding chip in the brain activates the device at the proper time. I place a round mark on the back of your neck, at the moment that we both orgasm, and this will bind us as mates."

Her thighs clenched. "Orgasm?"

"Yes. The sexual act is the strongest, most intimate, and oldest bond. Our society is based on that, as are most of our rites. Each Brand is unique. Everyone will know you're mine."

*His.* Her mind was spinning. She wasn't sure she was even taking in everything he was saying. She hadn't really thought that she'd be marked like some dang herd animal. "I suppose we need an audience for this Branding?"

He cocked an eyebrow, not having expected that question from her. Had she overheard something? "Why do you ask?"

"We have yet to have sex in private. Not totally, anyhow."

"Oh." He chuckled. "Sorry about that. And, yes, we need an audience for this." It was just a little lie, but necessary for the safety of them both, and to finish the trap.

"Why?"

"Well…" He didn't want to frighten her any further, so he skirted the issue, and decided to tell her something that at least sounded right. "Since this is a permanent thing, it's required to make sure that you're not forced. Especially if you change your mind at the last minute." That actually wouldn't be a bad policy to put into place, now that he thought about it.

"You'd never force me."

"No. Of course not. But it's still required."

"Who would be there? Erik?"

"Yes. I'd like it to be him. Do you mind?"

"He's becoming a permanent fixture in our sex lives."

"It just seems that way, because of the circumstances."

"Well…I'd rather have him there than anyone else, I suppose. I trust him. I think he has a good heart, even though he tries to cover it up."

She was right about Erik, but he didn't really know how he felt about her getting comfortable with his friend's presence during their joinings.

Sex had always just been sex. And group sex was no big deal. It was normal, even expected, though a few Warriors still declined to participate, with the exception of the Initiation.

Their entire way of life revolved around the joining of bodies and souls. But then, he'd never been in love before, not like this. Even his first *love*, destroyed compliments of his brother, hadn't been this powerful.

The intimate act had now become something else to him—something more. Alexa had become more.

\* \* \* \* \*

When he materialized into her quarters, Leila spun around. She dropped the clothes in her arms.

"What the hell are you doing? You scared me to death."

Erik studied her flushed features. So beautiful. Fury exploded inside him, thinking about how she'd been hurt, physically and emotionally. When he'd had the chance, he should have killed Rave and the masked man with her. It would have been easy while they'd been unconscious. It would have also been in cold blood. That didn't set well. Looking into Leila's sad eyes almost convinced him that he should have made an exception. It might have solved more than one problem, given their current situation.

"You know you're not supposed to materialize into someone's quarters without permission. It's a major offense. I could have you thrown out of The Lair."

"Yeah. But you won't. The Council asked me to go through the rooms, so we can account for everyone. Make sure everyone who's still here has reported in." Not really, but he didn't want to agitate her by telling her that he was looking for hidden surveillance equipment. Any of their rooms, even hers, could be bugged.

"Oh."

"Are those for Alexa?" he asked, indicating the clothes on the floor.

"Yes. Did she agree to the Branding?"

"Braden's talking to her now. Kam's disappeared."

She sank down to the couch. "Oh, no."

"It could just be one of his temporary departures."

"Is that what you believe?"

"No. Not really. The timing was too convenient for it to have been one of his headaches. He would have told one of us."

"I want to be there."

"There?" He'd been staring at her mouth—full and lush. He gave himself a mental shake. "Where?"

"At the Branding. I have to know. See for myself."

"I don't think Alexa would be comfortable with you there."

She stared at him in silence a moment. "Alexa? Or you?"

Oh, boy. Better not answer that one. Not directly. Besides, until he checked her room, they needed to be careful what they said. He turned and pretended to study one of her pink and silver snow-capped picturescapes, while checking the monitor he'd brought with him. No indication of any listening devices. He almost wished it were otherwise. It would give him an excuse not to talk about things. He wouldn't be able to check for video until she left.

"You're going to need help. Braden won't be in the best position to do that, not if he wants to concentrate on the act. I'm assuming he's going to do it for real this time, not pretend. Egesa and Pain Masters are more easily fooled than those we're up against now."

He discreetly pocketed the palm-sized monitor. "It'll be real." He turned toward her. "Braden wants her protected and joined to him as quickly as possible."

"Then let me help."

"How?"

"I'm not a totally defenseless female, Erik. I do have training."

He stalked over to her and pulled her off the couch. He dragged her against his chest. "Fine. Show me what you can do, right now."

She pushed against him. "Don't be stupid. Let me go."

"Make me, Leila. Take me down." The feel of her against him was pure ecstasy, and his body immediately hardened.

"You're being an ass."

"And you're being unrealistic." Regretfully, knowing now was not the time, he released her and stepped back. The look of rejection in her eyes, almost permanently in her eyes since the incident on the Marid ship, was too much. "I'll see what I can arrange. If someone gets hurt, we'll need a Healer fast. It might as well be you." It was the most he could do, for now.

\* \* \* \* \*

Kam turned to Laszlo. "Have you told me everything?"

"Of course." Laszlo watched the monitors. Each displayed a different area in The Lair. "What are they planning?"

"What makes you think they're planning anything?"

He turned to face Kam. He'd confided in Kam when he needed someone's help. Now he wasn't so sure about that decision. "Just because I'm losing my power, doesn't mean I'm losing my mind, too. What are they planning?"

Kam turned away from his intense stare. "I don't know. And they won't confide in me now. Leila's, no doubt, revealed her suspicions. She knows I'm involved somehow."

"What about Alexa? Can you find out from her?" She would be the easiest to manipulate. But that also made her vulnerable — too much so.

"I'd have to get her alone. And I don't think that's possible."

"We'll keep a watch. Just in case. If it comes down to it, will she be loyal to you or side with Braden?"

Kam's eyes narrowed. "Why do you ask? Why would she have to make that decision?"

"Just curious."

# Chapter Nineteen

Alexa felt better now that she'd showered, had something hot to eat, and was dressed in comfortable sweats. Black, of course. These people had no fashion sense when it came to colors. Black happened to look good on her though, despite her pale complexion, so she wasn't going to voice any complaints quite yet.

She listened to Braden on his vid-cell. He'd been on the cell most of the evening, talking to various people. She didn't understand the majority of what she heard him say. And he kept sending her into the bathroom, or kitchenette, or closet to get or do something trivial, trying to distract her. He'd even tried to get her to nap. Not very subtle.

She knew something more was going on than just plans for the Branding. The tension was too thick. His words too intense. The silences that followed even more so.

He looked over at her and smiled, which made her feel somewhat better. He had a great smile. She wished he'd do it more often.

Earlier, while she'd showered, Braden had joined her. She'd thought he wanted shower sex. He'd surprised her. No sex, but their time together was more sensual than any she could remember.

He had washed her gently, shampooed and conditioned her hair, then toweled her dry. He'd lotioned her body until her skin felt like silk, paying particular attention to the back of her neck — an erogenous zone she hadn't even realized existed. He'd helped her dress, and only then had he tended to himself.

The feel of his hands gliding over her body, his lips brushing the back of her neck, had almost driven her crazy, and she'd seriously considered seducing him right there in the bathroom. He must have known, because after he'd finished, one of those sexy smiles she loved so much tugged at his lips, and he kissed her lightly on the forehead, as if not at all affected by what was happening. If he hadn't been hard as a rock, a condition he couldn't very well hide, she'd have been thoroughly bummed out. However, if he could hold off until the Branding, so could she.

After their bathroom encounter, when they were both safely dressed and back in the sitting area of his quarters, he had put out a romantic meal for them, prepared with his own two hands. While they'd sat together, he'd held her hand, caressed her cheek, and fed her unfamiliar juice-filled pieces and sweet oblong selections of food. The alien tastes filled her mouth with an explosion of delicious sensations. He'd even shut off his cell, so they wouldn't be disturbed until they had finished.

He'd made her feel so cherished. They'd talked and laughed, shared their hopes and dreams for the future. And she had realized during that special time together just how much she actually loved him.

Braden set down the vid-cell. "How are you feeling? Warm enough?"

"Yes. I'm fine. When are you going to tell me what's going on?"

The smile on his face faded. "I don't—"

"Please, Braden. Don't pretend you don't know what I'm talking about. Give me more credit than that."

After a long moment of silence, a resigned look crossed his face, and he nodded. "All right." He sat beside her on the couch, took her hand, and laced their fingers. He stared down at their joined hands as he spoke. "Keep an open mind and listen carefully. What I'm about to tell you is extremely important." He hesitated while his gaze shifted to lock with hers. "I'll need your full cooperation for this to work. No second-guessing my decisions. Otherwise, tell me before we start. Later it'll be too dangerous to turn back."

She nodded. "All right. Tell me what you need me to do. I'll listen."

"After you hear it all and understand, you'll have to promise me to see it through to the end, Alexa. If you can't do that for me, we have to stop this now before we put it into motion. I mean it."

Her heart thudded, and her throat went dry. Braden needed her to do something that was apparently a one-way street at full-speed ahead. Scary. The story of her life since meeting him. "I understand."

* * * * *

If his leg felt better, he'd pace. Kam studied the monitors. Erik was moving from room to room. Video, but no sound, allowed him to follow his friend's progress.

Something had happened to the sound long ago, and they'd never been able to get it fixed properly, so he couldn't hear anything more than static and muffled noise when he turned up the receiver. Some sort of energy field, he suspected, caused the permanent interference with the audio. But the video still worked and was, so far, undiscovered. It was better than having nothing. And when a monitored person was alone, video was better than audio anyhow, since they tended not to speak much, if at all, when by themselves.

Kam glanced behind him. Laszlo had taken a break to get something to eat. The man was holding something back. He sensed it very strongly.

He hadn't told Laszlo the plans of the others. They hadn't told *him*, but he knew Braden. He knew what his friend would do. Laszlo probably knew, too. Even though he hadn't said so. Braden didn't have many options, if he wanted to find out the truth. Alexa was the wild card in all this. She would have to cooperate for it to work, and he wasn't so sure that was something she'd be willing, or even able, to do.

Regardless, Kam planned to stick close to Laszlo. If it came down to it, he knew which side he was on. He leaned forward when Erik entered Laszlo's quarters.

He didn't know if he wanted Erik to find the hidden video panel or not. When he'd first learned of its existence, he'd been appalled. Laszlo had convinced him of its necessity, but he still recognized the intrusiveness of the set-up if abused. Like with the video of Leila's Initiation, which had been somehow copied and handed over to The Dome. Or so Laszlo had said when Kam questioned him about it. On the other hand, that video also provided proof of her abuse. Nobody could dispute what had happened. The Council's decision to punish those involved would stand as long as it existed.

Still, right about now, he doubted everything he'd been told. And he didn't know whom to trust. It wasn't a comfortable feeling.

He looked down at the transport-connector he'd taken. He could zip in and zip out before Laszlo returned. Show Erik. Tell him what he knew.

But what if Laszlo *was* telling the truth? His first loyalty should be to the man who had organized and led the Society of Warriors for as long as he could remember.

"Dammit!" Laszlo's voice exploded behind him. "Why didn't you call me?" He rushed up to the monitors. "What's he doing in my room?"

Kam shrugged. "Probably nothing."

"Nothing? He's searching the entire place. You never told him about the control panel, did you?"

"I never said anything about the video. *Control* panel? Is there something else hidden down there?"

"We need to get him out before he finds anything. If he discovers the set-up, he'll assume the worst. And we'll be working blind, because he'll no doubt destroy the damn thing."

The fact that Laszlo didn't answer his question wasn't lost on Kam. Wariness filled him. "Why don't we just see what happens? You've hidden the panel well. He may not discover it. If we interfere, he'll know for sure something exists that you don't want found."

"Why don't you get real?"

"Get *real*?" Kam repeated in an effort to distract Laszlo and give Erik more time. If Laszlo was hiding more than just a video set-up… "Where'd you pick that up from? Some alien satellite feed?"

"It doesn't matter where I got it from. It's an expression. And I know what you're doing. Don't try to distract me by changing the subject. We can't just sit here shooting the breeze and discussing word choices, like it's some quiet mid-day lounge time. This is a serious—"

An alarm went off. Kam jumped up, his heart pounding hard against his ribs. He'd made his decision. His finger slid off the button on the security board. "We'll settle this later. We have a breach. We need to get you out of here and into a safe area."

Laszlo looked hesitant to leave. "What about Erik? We have to secure my quarters. I never believed Braden would send someone in to invade my sanctuary. The auto-vision of protection I set up to activate upon entry must have failed. Good thing I set up this secondary control area outside The Lair to monitor things."

An auto-activated vision? He had no idea Laszlo was powerful enough to be able to do something of that magnitude. Or had been?

Laszlo kept complaining that his powers were decreasing rapidly. Powers no one on Xylon even knew he had, except for Kam.

Laszlo had taken him into his confidence when his health started to fail, and he needed help, but didn't want The Council or Warriors to know. That's when Kam had found out about the hidden power. Visions. The ability to project images into another's mind was apparently the result of some long-ago experiment gone awry, but Kam hadn't yet been able to get all the details out of the man.

He pulled at Laszlo's arm. "We'll check back when it's clear and handle it then. Come on." He stared at the monitors as he pushed Laszlo toward the door. *Find the truth, Erik. I'm in too deep to turn back now. I have to see this through to the end.*

\* \* \* \* \*

Alexa stood in front of the large seascape, trying to calm herself. How had her life turned out so upside-down? She felt a lot like the picture's rolling waves — unsettled.

She glanced at the door. Braden had left over an hour ago to prepare things. Even though she'd agreed to the Branding, it was still scary. But she loved Braden and couldn't imagine her life without him now. Not after everything that they'd been through together. She was ready to make that commitment.

A morbid thought crossed her mind. What if Braden died? Would the Brand only bind her to Braden while he lived? Could she be Branded again, by another Warrior?

All the unknowns about this situation caused her head to ache. She wished they had more time. But she knew their options were limited given the circumstances.

Something tapped against her mind. She rubbed her temple and pushed away the feeling. The strange, mental intrusion had to be her imagination. It was like what used to happen in her sleep right before the nightmares had started. And what had happened right before the erotic vision she'd had of her and Braden. She glanced toward the door.

When he'd left, Braden had posted a guard. He'd also given her a hand-held alarm in case she should need to alert him. And she had a transport-connector for emergencies with pre-programmed, safe destinations already entered. Braden had shown her how to use it. She wouldn't be using it. The thing gave her the heebie-jeebies.

Everything he'd told her went through her mind as she tried to keep it straight. The whole thing was frightening to say the least. She truly believed the Xylon Warriors served an important purpose and feared what would happen should they fall out of existence. Who would be strong enough to fight Daegal and his followers then?

If Leila was right about the betrayal and traitor, then Laszlo was onboard the Marid ship, in a full facemask and in command. Leila even believed in the possibility that Laszlo and Daegal could be the same person.

She felt nauseous, thinking about how The Council had wanted her to *mate* with Laszlo. The birth of long-tongued, yellow-eyed Egesa came to mind, though she had no idea how that really worked. She supposed Laszlo/Daegal wasn't really a lizard-type, but still...

She couldn't imagine the thoughts going through the others' minds. All this affected her too, but not as deeply. They'd lived the life since birth. She was a newcomer, with only limited knowledge of their society.

Maybe the two men weren't the same. What were the odds that he could get away with a deception like that?

Even Braden expressed doubts that the two men were one. He'd said, if so, Laszlo would have taken her when The Council had made its decree.

His actions wouldn't even have been questioned. He could have whisked her to The Dome of Marid, and she'd have been under Egesa control. At that point, the Warrior Council would have just assumed they'd gotten to her during a weak and unprotected moment.

Instead, Laszlo had assigned Braden to initiate and protect her.

Braden even doubted Laszlo could be the masked man. Or at least, he'd said he didn't want it to be true. But Leila had insisted the eyes and voice were the same. Erik was searching for proof, something against Laszlo to confirm he was indeed a traitor to the Xylon people.

Whatever the truth, she trusted Braden to protect her. She wanted to build a life with him, have children. A smile eased across her face, imagining a little boy or girl with Braden's intense violet eyes and dark hair. They could have a real future together, here on this strange world.

A lifetime of love. And the Branding, according to Braden, would be the catalyst of all that happening.

* * * * *

Erik joined Braden in the ceremony room. As he looked around, he realized it had been quite a while since he'd last initiated a woman here. Somewhere along the line, he had pulled back from the ceremonies, slowly decreasing the number of rites he participated in, without even knowing why. They just weren't as fulfilling as they used to be. More like a chore in most cases, instead of his right as a high-ranking Warrior. He'd enjoyed helping to initiate Alexa. But that was a special case, with a special woman. A once in a lifetime opportunity he didn't figure would repeat itself anytime soon.

A pang of sadness overtook him. He wished he'd been part of Leila's Initiation. He could have prevented a lot of heartache for her. And maybe their love/hate relationship would have taken a different turn. He shook the thought away. Nothing he could do about it now. The past was over and done. He scanned his surroundings again.

Warm reds, cool blues, and shiny brass decorated the room as usual. A large bed with a thick mattress and lots of pillows sat in the center. Picturescapes of purple and green Xylon mountain ranges, with silver clouds drifting across the sky, filled the walls. Light music, barely audible, wafted through the room. Fresh air, pumped in from the outside, slid over his skin.

"I found proof. There's a hidden control panel in Laszlo's quarters," he said, focusing his attention on Braden, who was fiddling with the music controls, flipping through the selections. "Not only does it contain a Marid transmitter board, but the whole compound is wired for video, though apparently not sound. I left it active. He'll be able to see exactly what we're doing and when. It's the perfect trap. Although, if Laszlo discovers I found it, he may not show tonight."

Braden turned toward him and frowned. But then, he nodded, as if resigned to the findings. "We'll have to take that chance. I think he'll still come. He doesn't have much choice. It's the only way for him to get Alexa before she's Branded. His last chance."

"What if he decides one super breeder isn't worth going up against us? Or what if he sends someone else in. There's no guarantee he'll come himself."

"He's only going to see me in the room with Alexa. He won't think I'd put more Warriors here during the Branding. Since it is his last chance, I think he'll be the one to come. I doubt he'd trust another. I wouldn't."

Erik shook his head. "I don't know, Braden. Seems to me that Laszlo is smarter than that. We're not dealing with Egesa here."

"Well, we'll find out. The Branding will take place regardless." Braden left the control area and walked over to Erik. "Anything suspicious in Kam's quarters?"

"Not that I could find, and I did a thorough search. There's something else. Leila wants to be here for this. Would that be all right with Alexa?"

"Why?"

"She has a large stake in the outcome given her involvement. And she *was* the one who tipped us off. She has a right, I think."

After a moment of hesitation, Braden replied. "I can probably arrange it. Well…" He chuckled. "I'm not really so sure, but Leila might be needed for medical purposes in case someone gets hurt. I'll approach it from that end and see what I can do. Is there a blind spot in here?"

"The corner beside the door." That had gone better than expected. Alexa must be fairly committed to what was going to happen if Braden thought there was a possibility of her agreeing.

"You'll need to materialize into that location, so you're not spotted."

"No problem."

"If nobody shows, you two disappear after the Branding is done. Unless there's trouble, I don't even want to know you're here."

"Understood. We'll leave. And I won't intrude again. Unless invited," he added with a laugh.

Braden laughed, too, and clapped him on the back. "You're a good friend, but don't hold your breath on that one. I intend to be quite possessive of my breeder mate."

* * * * *

Laszlo turned on Kam. "There's no breach."

"What do you mean?" *Busted*. Shit.

"This place goes on auto-shutdown when there's a breach, just like The Lair. You wanted me out of the room and away from the monitors so I couldn't see what was going on. You set that alarm off yourself. You don't trust me."

"It's not that."

"Isn't it? I'm disappointed in you, Kam."

There was a time that would have stung deep. "This is all too strange, Laszlo. You're not telling me everything." His hand covered the disruptor on his belt. Just in case Laszlo hadn't been honest about his waning powers, he had to stay sharp.

Laszlo's gaze shifted to the weapon. "So, it's come to this. You'd actually turn against me."

"Not if you tell me the truth."

"I've told you everything. Daegal and I are not the same person. And I'm not a Marid commander. Leila is wrong. I have been protecting our people as best I can with my weakening powers."

"Why keep everything a secret from The Council? Your actions, your power. All these years." How could The Council not know? Records existed. Even if classified. "This isn't your fight alone."

"It was necessary. The Dome has monitors set up in The Lair compound. I've destroyed as many as I've been able to find. But I'm sure there are more. They know a lot of our secrets."

"You're not making sense, Laszlo. Unless you're more involved than you're saying and fear that discovery would jeopardize your position." From the agitated look Laszlo gave him, Kam figured he'd just discovered at least the partial truth. And if so, he would not rest until he found out the whole of it.

"Daegal has vision powers too, Kam. Like me. But his powers are also weakening. We do have the ability to defeat him. If we're smart."

"Like you, and weakening like you, too? How…coincidental."

Laszlo frowned and mumbled something that sounded suspiciously like *not really*.

"What about the Marid commander from the ship? The masked one? How's he involved in this?"

"With our power decrease, we can't project visions at will anymore—not easily anyhow. For Daegal, he mostly uses other methods now to control and keep power over The Dome. And that's the truth. You have to trust me in this."

"You didn't answer my question. You're twisting something to serve your interests, Laszlo. What is it? If you want my help, you had better tell me now. All of it. Have you been using visions to control us, too? All of us on Xylon?" He grabbed Laszlo around the collar with both hands and jerked him forward. "What is the truth?"

# Chapter Twenty

Braden looked at himself in the full-length mirror. A smile tugged at his lips. Not bad, if he did say so himself.

He'd showered, gotten a quick haircut and shave, and dressed in his best pants and shirt.

He hated that tonight could be marred by violence. He wanted the ceremony to be special for Alexa, and he intended to make it the best he could for her, despite what else might occur or what the outcome might reveal.

The shame of all this was that there was no way around it. As long as Daegal's people wanted Alexa, whenever they chose to do the Branding, they took a chance on an Egesa or Marid assassin popping in. Even if it didn't turn out to be Daegal or Laszlo, the fact that they'd send anyone in for basically a suicide mission—as far as he was concerned, still made things dangerous. Unless they could find a completely secure location, which was doubtful at this point. And if he *didn't* Brand her, the attempts to get her would simply continue to escalate and never stop, until they finally succeeded or until they ran out of volunteers willing to try.

Once she was Branded, they wouldn't come after her again. They wouldn't attempt to kill her. He was confident of that. She was too valuable. They'd wait until they could crack the Brand and deactivate it, something neither side had been able to do yet.

Even if they killed *him*, she'd be safe. He'd arranged for it. Alexa didn't know, nor would she ever, unless it became necessary. It was simply something he had to do to ensure her survival.

After one last glance in the mirror, he turned and began to pace in front of the bed. He was surprised at the level of nerves assaulting him. His palms were actually sweating, thinking about the Branding. He'd studied extensively on how to do it properly, so it would increase Alexa's pleasure rather than detract from it.

He felt better knowing Leila would be nearby if he botched things. It had taken some fast-talking to convince Alexa to allow another observer in the room, but she'd finally relented to the logic of having a Healer on hand.

Actually, he had a feeling that she secretly liked being watched during sex. Because even though she had initially protested, and he'd had to keep explaining his reasons, she'd still relented more easily than he'd thought she would.

She'd probably enjoy attending The Lair Joining Parties, where couples could watch others having sex or participate and be watched. But he wasn't certain how *he* felt about that. As he'd told Erik, he intended to be very possessive about her, from here on out, and he hoped Alexa felt the same way about him.

A noise on the other side of the room drew his attention. He turned as the door slid open. Alexa stepped inside. Damn! She absolutely took his breath away.

The door slid closed behind her, and she stood just inside the room, looking sexy and wary. His heart melted.

Leila must have helped her dress. The outfit had a definite Earth flair. He'd always been fond of that planet, the clothes, the furnishings, and especially the women.

Alexa looked beautiful. The black sweats were gone. She wore a shimmering, black and silver, wrap-like dress that hung down to her calves, and rode high on one hip. The deep vee neckline revealed more than a hint of breast. Her hair hung loose and shiny around her shoulders, just the way he liked it. And she had on a touch of face color. Only enough to enhance her natural beauty.

"Hi," she said in a voice so low that he barely heard her.

"Hi," he said in return and held out his hand. "You look beautiful."

A blush crept up her neck. "Thank you." She stepped forward and placed her palm into his. "I'm nervous." She glanced into the corner.

"Me, too. They're not here yet. Do you like the room?"

"Very much so. It's decadent."

A smile split his features, and he felt better knowing that she was experiencing the same emotions he was. "You bring out the decadent in me." When she laughed at his words, the sound filled him with a joy he wasn't accustomed to feeling. He liked it.

"I think you were probably decadent long before I came along," she responded.

"You might be surprised."

"Somehow I doubt it. You look exceedingly handsome tonight."

"Thank you."

"Braden…"

Uh, oh. She sounded hesitant. Maybe she'd changed her mind. Disappointment hit hard. "What?" He barely got out the word without choking on it. His fingers tightened around hers. His chest felt tight, and his pulse pounded rapidly in his veins.

"I love you."

Braden froze. *Love.* The blood roared in his ears, and he practically sank to his knees. His whole body shook. That was the last thing he had expected her to say. He hadn't realized until this moment how much he'd wanted to hear those words from her. He drew her into his arms and held her tight. He couldn't even speak.

She ran a soothing hand over his back. She apparently knew how her words were affecting him. Then she raised her lips to his ear. "I love you," she whispered. "I want to be with you, Braden. For now and forever."

His entire body heated and hardened. The knowledge that the traitor might be monitoring this moment filled him with rage. It should be private! The urge to whisk Alexa far away was overwhelming.

The air in the corner shimmered. Erik materialized. A moment later, Leila showed up beside him. Their appearance brought back the reality of the situation. He was careful not to acknowledge their presence, and had already instructed Alexa to do the same.

He pulled out of her arms and swallowed the lump in his throat. "Shall we begin?"

She bit her bottom lip and nodded.

Alexa's nerves shot through the roof. She avoided looking into the corner. She knew she'd made the right decision in doing this. The uncomfortable feeling she'd had earlier was gone. Later she'd tell Braden what had happened. She just wished all this could have been under different circumstances.

Braden dimmed the lights in the room. A soft, romantic glow surrounded them. He led her over to the bed and again pulled her into his arms.

"Just you and me," he whispered in her ear.

She caressed his cheek. "Just you and me."

He helped her onto the bed, and she relaxed against the pillows propped along the headboard. Braden slipped off each of her black shoes and set them carefully on the floor.

Despite their 'just you and me' declaration, from her position, she couldn't help but notice Erik and Leila. Leila avoided eye contact and looked a bit uncomfortable, but Erik winked at her and smiled. Typical Erik. She felt like laughing and sticking out her tongue at him, until Braden began massaging her foot, then all coherent thought was lost. Braden knew exactly how to touch her to make her focus completely on him and the pleasure he was giving.

His fingers slowly moved upward, over her calf, her one exposed thigh, which was bare because of the design of the dress. His other hand pulled open the tie closure and eased the silk strand from around her waist.

Alexa's heart sped up as he opened the wrap dress. His sharp intake of air pleased her. Underneath, she wore a black silk thong and demi-bra that cupped her breasts perfectly, leaving her nipples exposed. Her newly shaved legs were smooth and bared for his touch. She thought the entire outfit quite daring, but Leila said it was perfect and would drive any man mad with desire.

When Braden shifted to the side, she thought she heard a strangled sound from where Erik stood, then an *oof*, as if Leila had elbowed him. She didn't dare look.

Braden leaned down and kissed her stomach, just above the belly button. Her muscles quivered when his tongue dipped into the indentation.

His hands splayed across her ribs, warming and caressing the skin. With just his fingertips, he eased one hand higher, barely touching her flesh. Although she felt a bit self-conscious with Erik and Leila in the room, Alexa couldn't stop a sigh of pleasure from escaping.

Across the top of one breast, his fingers brushed with a feather-light touch. Then he moved lower, and his thumb grazed her exposed nipple, raising it to a hard bud.

"Oh!" She arched into his hand.

He lowered his head and touched the nipple with the tip of his tongue.

Pure, wet heat. "Yes…" Pleasure zipped down her body. "Lick it, Braden."

"Yes, ma'am." Laving the hard flesh gently, he licked her nipple until she squirmed beneath him and shoved her fingers into his hair, trying to drag him closer.

Braden took her nipple into his mouth and sucked slowly, taking his time.

"More," she begged. "That feels so good." Moisture gathered inside her thong, and she felt tight and needy.

He rubbed her other nipple with his thumb. When he squeezed the fleshy bud between his thumb and forefinger, she practically came right then.

He sat back and smiled down at her.

Their gazes locked, and she saw the love for her in his eyes. Her chest rose and fell as her emotions for him welled up and overtook her. Love, desire, caring…and so much more.

The wetness around her nipple felt cool. The rest of her felt fire hot. She wanted him naked and inside her, loving her until they both exploded from the passion.

The need must have shown on her face for he slowly unbuttoned his shirt and drew it down his shoulders. Her gaze slid over his body. He was perfect. Toned, exuding sex, and he burned completely for *her*.

He stood up, reached out, and pulled the thong down her legs, stopping here and there to caress her skin. Once the garment was free of her, he tossed it across the room.

Erik caught it in one hand.

She gasped, unable to stop her reaction or avoid looking at the man in the corner.

He held up the thong and turned it just so. Purposely, making a show of it. He brought the material to his mouth, and without taking his eyes off her, tongued the inner crotch.

"Ah…" she moaned, and arched on the bed. Her clit throbbed as if he was tonguing *her*. That man was just too…too…she couldn't think of a word fitting enough to describe him. She quickly averted her gaze. She didn't know what else Erik planned to do with the panties, nor did she want to know. Her entire body clenched hard as various wicked thoughts flickered through her mind.

Braden crawled up on the bed. He pushed her thighs apart. "Relax and let me take control."

Alexa didn't argue. There was no point. Braden was *always* in control. In bed was no different. She didn't really mind, most of the time. But then, she did have future plans to change that. At least, every once in a while. Her gaze shifted to the intent look on his face, and her heart raced in anticipation. Then, she felt him touch her.

His fingers spread the folds of her wet core, and he stared between her legs, his eyes filled with hunger.

Raw need raged through Braden. Alexa was the most desirable woman he'd ever known. And she was all his. He lowered his head and swiped his tongue along her inner folds. Soaked with her juices. Delicious.

She trembled at the contact, arched, and moaned.

He trembled in return, the feeling odd to him. No woman had ever affected him like this. She was so responsive to him. He slid his palms beneath her ass and lifted her pussy to his mouth. He fed slowly, thoroughly, wanting all he could get. And wanting to give her more pleasure than she'd ever known.

A whimper reached his ears—Alexa's, but then a similar sound also came from elsewhere. Leila. He cut his eyes to the corner. Erik was kissing Leila's neck, right below her ear, his arms wrapped around her waist.

Leila's gaze followed him, as he continued to eat Alexa. From the enraptured look on her face, she was enjoying the feeling of being touched. Good. He knew it had been too long for her.

Erik lifted his head and mouthed the word 'careful' to him, before his mouth once again lowered to Leila's neck.

One last tongue-flick against Alexa's clit, then he heeded Erik's caution. Not wanting her to climax yet, he lowered her hips and wiped his mouth. Alexa's flushed features revealed her level of arousal. She was ready. And so was he.

"Turn over."

Alexa slowly turned onto her stomach, keeping eye contact with him as long as possible. He noticed, once she was on her stomach, that she turned her head toward Erik and Leila, instead of away.

He stood beside the bed and stripped. For safety reasons, he'd positioned himself so Erik could protect his back and he'd be able to see what was happening in the rest of the room. He reached down to unhook Alexa's bra, and peeled it off her body.

Her blonde hair covered the back of her neck. He moved the strands aside and placed a soft kiss on the delicate skin there. Every inch of her was like a new taste sensation.

A low moan escaped her lips.

His tongue began a slow descent, starting at the top of her spine. Lower and lower, he trailed the length of her back to the top of her ass. He flicked his tongue a few times, then started back up her body again.

Alexa whimpered and rolled onto her side. He was about to protest, when her hand circled his hard cock and drew him to her mouth. The words he'd thought to speak stuck in his throat.

Her tongue swiped the head of his shaft, licking off a bead of moisture. He growled. Too much sensation. He'd never be able to hold out if she decided to draw him in completely.

He gently disengaged her and pushed her back onto her stomach. His hands grazed her body, moving lower. Then he climbed onto the bed to mount her. "On your knees."

She rose up.

"No, just your knees. Not your hands. Keep your head down. Yeah, like that. Beautiful."

"Beautiful," Erik echoed in a low voice.

"Shh," Leila immediately responded, sounding irritated.

Braden tried his best to ignore the corner. Good thing the room wasn't wired for sound. He'd been kidding himself earlier when he'd spoken to Erik. He should have realized there was no way that he and Alexa could pretend Erik and Leila weren't there.

His position behind Alexa fully exposed them to Erik's and Leila's view again. But there was nothing he could do about that.

It was time to make her his. He couldn't wait any longer. Heart hammering, pulse pounding, he had to have her. With a low groan, he eased into her from behind. Pure, hot sin.

She made that sexy little sound he loved so much—half moan, half purr. And all his.

His fingers curled around her hips.

He pulled his cock almost completely out of her, then slowly buried himself deep. He clenched his teeth, controlling his body, not wanting the ecstasy to end.

"Faster," she begged, her plea followed by a small whimper.

The needy sound in her voice made him crazy. He brushed the blonde hair from the back of her neck. So smooth. So beautiful. Soon she'd wear the mark of a mated breeder—his mark. All would know she belonged to him. He leaned over and licked the back of her neck, letting his tongue linger.

She shuddered and pushed against him. "I need…all of you."

His heart expanded. With this woman, their joining was more than physical. She was his life, his soul. He pushed deep inside her, all the way in.

"Yes. Now. Start thrusting. Hurry."

His cock throbbed painfully, and he groaned. The time had come. She wanted it, and so did he. The urge to fuck her was so strong that he couldn't hold back any longer. Nor did he intend to, for she was right. They needed to hurry.

The air beside them shimmered. "Damn," he muttered. A man in a full facemask materialized, hands on hips, and ready for battle.

"Stop the ceremony."

She stiffened and tried to pull away to cover herself against the intruder.

He held her tightly around the waist and kept them intimately joined. Nothing was stopping him from making her his.

"I've come for the woman."

Panic hit him, though he had expected this. He pushed her down to her stomach, covering her with his body. Protecting her.

The intruder tugged his pants open. "Pull out of her. I'm going to fix it so the bitch won't ever be able to breed."

No way. No one was going to stop him, or take her from him. He held her arms pinned to the mattress, so she couldn't move, then surged into her, over and over, demonstrating his possession.

"This…woman…belongs…to…me!"

She squirmed beneath him, called out his name.

He ignored her. He had no choice. He had to Brand and Breed her, before it was too late.

"She doesn't belong to you, Warrior. Not anymore. She is *my* whore now."

Alexa tried to pull away. What was Braden doing? "Let me up!" They had to stop, delay the Branding, get the intruder out first. She'd been so close. If he'd only waited a moment longer, they could have completed the ceremony.

A disruptor beam shot across the room.

The masked man stumbled backward and hit the wall. He managed to keep to his feet and clamped a hand over the wound to his arm.

Erik stepped out from the corner. "You're out-numbered, Laszlo. We know it's you." He held up a monitor. "Voice analysis confirmed."

"Wait." Alexa pushed back against Braden.

The masked man's eyes widened. He reached for the weapon on his belt.

Erik fired again. The weapon disintegrated. "We don't want to kill you. Give up before it comes to that."

"You can't defeat me."

Alexa struggled beneath Braden's body, trying to get more air into her lungs. He was crushing her. "Listen to me. It's not—"

"Brand her, Braden," Erik interrupted. "Now! In case he's opened the entire security net, and teams of Egesa are on their way in."

Erik fired once more, and the man crumpled to the floor.

The masked intruder quickly recovered and pushed himself to a sitting position, looking dazed.

Alexa gasped when Braden thrust into her. She felt her hair pulled back, away from her neck. If he thought she was going to orgasm while all this was going on, he was nuts! She'd never be able to complete the rite like this. Even though she'd promised earlier not to let anything stop them.

The air shimmered, and two more forms materialized. Kam and…Laszlo.

All movement in the room stopped.

The masked man swore, hit his transport-connector, and disappeared. Kam spared only a moment's glance at the bed, then he too disappeared.

Laszlo's gaze met hers. "I'm sorry it had to be this way, my dear." His eyes narrowed to slits, and he raised his hand. Sweat broke out on his brow, and he seemed to be having trouble breathing. His gaze slid to Braden. "Brand her, while there's time."

Erotic images, to the extreme, flitted through Alexa's mind. Dark fantasies she'd never revealed to anyone, not even Braden. Her body immediately spasmed. Braden tensed as he too climaxed, and his seed spilled into her.

She felt his mouth suction onto the back of her neck. Colors exploded inside her head. She screamed from the combination of pleasure/pain that wracked her body, then she collapsed beneath Braden's weight, completely spent.

# Epilogue

Silence hung heavily in the air. Only the Warriors' breathing filled the awkward stillness of the room.

Laszlo was gone.

Braden shifted his weight off Alexa. His mind was a jumble. He traced the Brand on the back of her neck. The round mark, with his unique personal design, was almost transparent, but present. "Are you all right?" He stroked her back. "Did I hurt you?"

She shook her head, but didn't speak. He wasn't sure if that was a good sign or not. She was probably in shock.

Braden looked toward the corner by the door. "What happened?"

Erik held Leila close to his chest, stroking her hair. "Damned if I know," he answered. "The monitor confirmed the masked man as Laszlo."

"I don't get this. Did you get a fix on the man with Kam? *That* was Laszlo. Or a look-a-like."

"No. Sorry."

"Shit, Erik!"

"Hey! I tried. The sequencer jammed, then he was gone before the reset took hold."

"The man with Kam *was* Laszlo," Alexa said, turning over and covering herself with a blanket.

Leila turned in Erik's arms. "How do you know, Alexa?"

"He told me."

Braden grabbed his underwear and slipped them on. "What do you mean?"

"Earlier today. While you were gone and before Leila came to help me prepare. Laszlo and Kam materialized into your room. They said I didn't need to fear the Branding and told me what was going to happen tonight. They wanted to make sure that I wouldn't back out."

"Dammit! Why didn't you tell me?"

"Kam didn't want me to say anything that might change the outcome. They said the Branding was the only way to keep me safe and to prove that Laszlo wasn't a traitor. You and I are meant for each other, Laszlo said. A perfect match. He took away any last doubts I had."

Braden's heart thumped. The traitor wasn't Laszlo. Otherwise, he would have snatched Alexa while in the room, before she was Branded. The thought of losing her made him ill. Though he'd taken precautions, he never should have left her alone, even for a short time.

Laszlo's visit to Alexa could have been a set-up to fool them, he supposed. But if so, it would be a foolhardy one. And he couldn't believe that Kam would betray them. He had to believe, did believe, that Laszlo was still on their side. Braden returned Alexa's sweet smile, grateful for what Laszlo had done in taking away her lingering doubts.

"How could the monitor confirm the masked man as Laszlo, if it wasn't him?" Leila asked. "And I recognized his eyes and voice when we were on the Marid ship. I swear I did."

Alexa shook her head. "I don't know. He said that he and Kam needed to handle things, and we were to stay out of it."

"Yeah, right." Erik snorted.

"We have to accept the fact that we don't know enough right now to figure this thing out." Braden looked across the room where Kam had been. "I have to believe that the man with Kam was Laszlo, like Alexa says. And I believe he's still on our side. I believe they both are. Somehow, I think Laszlo put erotic images in my head, and I suspect Alexa's too, so we could finish the Branding."

"Yes," Alexa agreed.

"How could he do that?" Erik asked, practically barking out the words.

"I don't know." Braden also realized that the vision he'd had of Alexa, back while in the graveyard, had come true right down to the last detail. Was Laszlo responsible for that, too?

"He does have the ability to project images," Alexa explained, confirming Braden's suspicions. "He told me. I had a vision of me and Braden in this room long before it happened."

Braden's gaze snapped to hers. "Me, too."

"This is all too weird for me," Erik replied, looking around the room as if still expecting an invasion. "Where'd he get powers like that?"

And how much had their own minds been manipulated? Braden couldn't help but wonder. He wasn't comfortable with this new turn of events. Laszlo had used the power for the good of Xylon, to pair him and Alexa as mates. But Laszlo could just as easily use it for evil, if the man decided to turn.

Leila stepped over to the bed, her face a study of concentration. "If the masked man wasn't Laszlo, and was a Marid commander—Daegal or not, why didn't the compound shut down when he breached security? Nothing happened. Nothing changed. That's always been one of our advantages over The Dome. The ability to identify when someone from the other side penetrates our walls."

Braden shook his head. "I don't know. Erik and I think there's a small hole in security somewhere that could allow one person at a time to get through undetected. Or maybe the masked man was a Warrior once. Maybe someone related to Laszlo that we don't know about, who turned, and still has access to The Lair. That would account for the monitor readings and resemblance. Though our equipment is designed to be more sophisticated than that, so—"

"Fine. If all or any of that is true, then where the hell is Kam?" Erik asked. "He's dick-deep in this. There's something more going on here."

"My brother is a good man!" Alexa protested. "I know he is. Don't you dare imply otherwise."

At that moment, Kam materialized inside the room.

Erik grabbed him by the front of the shirt. "What the hell is going on?"

"Let go of me."

"Let go of him," Alexa protested at the same time.

"Enough!" Braden ordered. They needed to stick together right now, not argue. "Kam, what's going on? Let him go, Erik."

Erik released him, and Kam stepped back out of reach. "Laszlo isn't a traitor or double-agent. He hasn't betrayed Xylon. He's gone after the masked man. I need to follow."

"No!" Alexa protested. "If you go, you might never come back."

"What's your role in all this?" Erik asked.

That's exactly what Braden wanted to know, too.

"He needed help and confided in me. I found out that Daegal, like Laszlo, has the ability to project images. Both their powers are fading, so Daegal especially is desperate to find other ways to remain in control.

He's staying hidden from all but his most loyal followers now. And as long as he thinks he might be able to get valuable information out of our Warriors about Xylon, he's hesitating to launch an all-out assault."

"This is fucking unbelievable," Erik mumbled.

"Braden," Leila interrupted.

"What?"

"The masked man, it just registered with me what he said."

"What are you talking about?"

"He said, *I'm going to fix it so the bitch won't ever be able to breed*. He had to know Alexa had already gone through the Initiation. She couldn't be Branded otherwise."

They all looked at each other in stunned silence.

"What's it mean?" Alexa asked.

Another long moment passed before Braden answered. "Marid must have found a way around the first step of the Initiation Rite. A way to sterilize our protected women."

Alexa bit her bottom lip. She slid her hand into his.

He squeezed her fingers, looking deep into her eyes. His love for Alexa, and hers for him, had opened his heart. Not only to her, but also to all the Xylon people. Their safety was his responsibility now. And he didn't take that lightly. He looked over at Xylon's ranking Healer. "What can you do, Leila?"

She paced, obviously gathering her thoughts, then she stopped in front of him. "We can't strengthen what we're already using. The only hope is to neutralize whatever they're using to get around our protection. I'll need a sample of the compound, so I can break it down."

"And how are we supposed to get that?" Erik raked his fingers through his hair.

"There's only one way," Kam answered without hesitation. "We go in. To Marid. And steal it."

"And neutralize Daegal while we're there," Braden added. "I'll take it to the Council for a vote." He turned to gaze into Alexa's eyes. He raised his hand to caress her cheek, then slid his fingers around to the back of her neck, needing to feel his mark on her. "This isn't going to deter us. We're going to build a long and loving life together, Alexa. I give you my promise."

236

Her eyes softened, and she squeezed his hand. "I know. I trust you. And I love you."

"I love you, too, sweetheart." He leaned in to kiss her tenderly.

The others materialized out of the room, leaving them in privacy.

Alexa slid her arms around him and melted into his embrace. Nothing had ever felt as good to him as her soft touch. Braden intended to keep this woman, his one true love, safe and close to his heart forever.

# About the author:

Ruth D. Kerce got hooked on writing in the fifth grade when she won a short story contest—a romance, of course. And she's been writing romance ever since. She writes several subgenres of romance—historical, contemporary, and futuristic. Her books are available online in many internet bookstores. Her short stories and articles are available on several websites. She has won or placed in writing contests and hopes to continue to write exciting tales for years to come.

Ruth welcomes mail from readers. You can write to her c/o Ellora's Cave Publishing at 1337 Commerce Drive, Suite 13, Stow OH 44224.

**If you enjoyed this book you may also enjoy the following books from Ellora's Cave Publishing, Inc.**

Darkeen Dynasty: Raeder's Woman by Angelina Evans

Deep Heat by BJ McCall

Heroes Heart: A Hero Betrayed by Jan Springer

Saurellian Federation: Price of Freedom by Joanna Wylde

Swept Off Her Feet by Camille Anthony

The Sailmaster's Woman: Arda by Annie Windsor

# Why an electronic book?

We live in the Information Age—an exciting time in the history of human civilization in which technology rules supreme and continues to progress in leaps and bounds every minute of every hour of every day. For a multitude of reasons, more and more avid literary fans are opting to purchase e-books instead of paperbacks. The question to those not yet initiated to the world of electronic reading is simply: *why?*

1. *Price.* An electronic title at Ellora's Cave Publishing runs anywhere from 40-75% less than the cover price of the <u>exact same title</u> in paperback format. Why? Cold mathematics. It is less expensive to publish an e-book than it is to publish a paperback, so the savings are passed along to the consumer.

2. *Space.* Running out of room to house your paperback books? That is one worry you will never have with electronic novels. For a low one-time cost, you can purchase a handheld computer designed specifically for e-reading purposes. Many e-readers are larger than the average handheld, giving you plenty of screen room. Better yet, hundreds of titles can be stored within your new library—a single microchip. (Please note that Ellora's Cave does not endorse any specific brands. You can check our website at www.ellorascave.com

for customer recommendations we make available to new consumers.)

3. *Mobility*. Because your new library now consists of only a microchip, your entire cache of books can be taken with you wherever you go.

4. *Personal preferences are accounted for*. Are the words you are currently reading too small? Too large? Too…**ANNOYING**? Paperback books cannot be modified according to personal preferences, but e-books can.

5. *Innovation*. The way you read a book is not the only advancement the Information Age has gifted the literary community with. There is also the factor of what you can read. Ellora's Cave Publishing will be introducing a new line of interactive titles that are available in e-book format only.

6. *Instant gratification.* Is it the middle of the night and all the bookstores are closed? Are you tired of waiting days—sometimes weeks—for online and offline bookstores to ship the novels you bought? Ellora's Cave Publishing sells instantaneous downloads 24 hours a day, 7 days a week, 365 days a year. Our e-book delivery system is 100% automated, meaning your order is filled as soon as you pay for it.

Those are a few of the top reasons why electronic novels are displacing paperbacks for many an avid reader. As always, Ellora's Cave Publishing welcomes your questions and comments. We invite you to email us at service@ellorascave.com or write to us directly at: 1337 Commerce Drive, Suite 13, Stow OH 44224.

Printed in the United States
76628LV00001B/24

9 781419 950018